HELMINTH

HELMINTH

By

S. Alessandro Martinez

Omnium Gatherum
Los Angeles

Helminth
Copyright © 2021 S. Alessandro Martinez

ISBN-13: 978-1-949054-31-6

First Edition

Dedicated to the strong women in my life who always
supported my writing,
My mom, Yvonne
My aunt, Carla
My grandma, Effi
And my wife, the Illumined Lady

CHAPTER ONE

There were no beginnings, as there are no endings. Time is a factor that concerns only mortals, who live out their short, miserable lives constantly fearing their own demise.

"Thank you so much for being here with us, Rei," Mrs. Brennan told me, her voice heavy with worry and sorrow. "I know Abby would really appreciate it. She... God, how the hell could this have happened?" She lifted a thin hand to her lips and began to sob once more.

I wiped away my own tears with the back of my hand. I wished I could comfort her somehow. But what could I possibly say that might help at this moment? I opened my mouth, hoping words would come out on their own, when I heard soft footsteps behind me. I turned around and felt anxiety crash through me when I recognized Dr. Richardson walking toward us.

Please have some good news, I prayed. But worse thoughts forced my plea aside. *Fuck, what if she's dead? Oh, fuck, fuck, fuck!*

"The doctor's coming," Mrs. Brennan choked out, hastily drying her cheeks. "Something's wrong."

"We don't know that," Mr. Brennan said in a hoarse murmur, wrapping an arm around his wife. "Let's not jump to any conclusions yet. Let's hear what the doctor has to say first."

My head swam as I listened to Dr. Richardson's shoes tapping along the white linoleum floor as he approached.

My thoughts swirled, unclear, my emotions a storm. My heart hadn't stopped hammering inside my chest since my drive over here to the hospital.

"Why would someone attack Abby?" Mrs. Brennan started to wail. Her face broke into a mask of anguish. "Those God damned thugs! Why her?"

"She was mugged," Mr. Brennan reminded her quietly. "Those bastards just wanted money. They were probably on drugs or something. If I ever find them, I'll kill them myself."

"Pieces of shit," I muttered in agreement as the doctor stopped before us. I fervently hoped Mr. Brennan would find the culprits to mete out true justice.

"Mr. and Mrs. Brennan." Dr. Richardson said as he stood before them, his expression somber. Briefly meeting my eyes, he gave me a small nod of acknowledgment, then waited for a lull in Mrs. Brennan's noisy lamentations.

"Doctor Richardson," Mr. Brennan began.

I shouldn't have been surprised when I first saw that his eyes were wet with tears. But in the twenty-four years that I had known Abby and her family, I had never once seen her dad cry.

"How is she doing?" His voice audibly cracked as he gripped his wife's hands to calm her.

"Is she okay?" Mrs. Brennan pleaded before the doctor had a chance to respond. She clung to her husband. "Please tell us that she'll make it. Please, you can help her, right?" She withdrew a shaking fist from her husband's hand, clenched around a wad of tissues, and it rose to her mouth to stifle another sob.

I stared at the doctor, my stomach tightening painfully as I braced myself for the bad news that was to come.

"Mr. and Mrs. Brennan," Doctor Richardson said, removing the round glasses from his wearied face as he regarded them. "Abby is in critical condition. Her attackers...There is no easy way to say this." He paused. "They brutalized her. She has numerous lacerations across her body, many broken bones, extensive internal bleeding, and some swelling in the brain. She's being prepped for surgery right now."

Mrs. Brennan whimpered, burying her face in her husband's chest, and he clung to her as if she were a life preserver. They looked utterly lost.

My throat squeezed itself shut, and I felt as if I might pass out from lack of oxygen. Abby had to go into surgery? *It's worse than I thought*, I realized. *Much, much worse. Oh fuck. This can't be happening. No, no, no.*

"Can you help her?" Mr. Brennan asked, his voice faltering again. He pulled Mrs. Brennan even more tightly into his embrace, and at that moment I wished I had someone to hug me. But Abby had always been that person. She had always been there to offer me reassurances and support whenever I had needed it.

I watched Abby's dad comfort her mom as best a husband could when their child lay unconscious in the ER, beaten and battered, clinging to life.

"We will do our best," Dr. Richardson replied, as he replaced the glasses on his face, infusing his voice with as much hope and positivity as he could. "Dr. Moradi is an excellent surgeon. She's one of the best in the country in dealing with these types of brain injuries. And I know she'll do all she can. She and her team have saved numerous lives. Once the surgery is over, we will transfer your daughter from the OR to a room in the ICU. There she will rest and recover. She'll be well taken care of. Just don't lose hope. Okay? That's the best thing you can do for her now."

"We'll try," Mr. Brennan said softly, stroking Mrs. Brennan's hair and leading her away, back to the waiting room seats. "We will."

"Please help her," I whispered to the doctor, finally finding my voice. I hadn't said anything since he had arrived, and my throat felt unnaturally sore and dry.

"Of course. We will do our very best," Dr. Richardson

answered with a kind smile. "Rei, was it? You're Abby's best friend?"

I nodded dumbly, unable to find any other words willing to come out.

"I know this is difficult," the doctor said, putting a comforting hand on my shoulder. "But Abby is in very good hands here. I assure you. I'll let you and the Brennans know the minute Abby's out of surgery. Okay?"

I nodded. And with that, he turned and left.

Lost in an incomprehensible swirl of emotions, I wandered over to a window to stare out into the quiet, calm night. Given the lateness of the hour, the parking lot below, except for a handful of cars, was empty.

Empty.

Just how I felt at that moment. My body felt hollow, though simultaneously my head felt crammed with too many jumbled thoughts, as though it would soon burst with the worrisome storm that raged within.

"Come on, Abbs," I whispered. "You have to pull through."

I lost it then. My legs seemed to betray me as I sank down onto the floor. Tears flowed freely down my cheeks, and my body was wracked with heaving sobs.

I don't know how long I sat crying on the ground. But I felt like that night lasted forever.

⁓⧚⁓

"Rei, honey. Wake up."

My eyes opened to an out-of-focus hospital room, the fleeting images of my dream beginning to decay. Vivid images of a looming gravestone bearing the name of my best friend had been haunting me and dancing through my head, tormenting me these past three nights.

I was glad to be awake. Between the foreboding dreams and the uncomfortable armchair that I was curled up in, I was surprised I had managed to sleep at all.

As my vision cleared, I saw Mrs. Brennan leaning over

me, her gentle hand on my shoulder, shaking me awake. Mr. Brennan stood beside her, a tired smile on his wan face.

"Mrs. Brennan?" I asked, struggling to fight off the grogginess. "What is it? Did something happen?" I felt a knot of panic form inside me as adrenalin rushed through my veins, bringing me in an instant to alert wakefulness.

"Look," she said, one hand at her mouth, the other pointing to the pale, curly-haired girl lying in the hospital bed.

I jumped up, ignoring the sudden head rush that made my vision swim momentarily. Stepping over to the bedside, I peered at my friend where she quietly lay. Her normally freckled face and arms were a tapestry of purple bruises and bandages that covered freshly stitched lacerations. She looked just as bad as she had the first night three days ago.

But despite the tears forming, I felt the twitch of a smile pulling at the corners of my mouth.

Abby was stirring.

On the other side of the bed, Mr. and Mrs. Brennan leaned over their daughter, watching with anticipation. Abby's dried and cracked lips began to move as if trying to form words, her eyes twitching beneath their lids, and her hands gripping spasmodically at the white cotton blanket draped over her body.

"Abby honey, can you hear us?" Mrs. Brennan whispered, weeping but smiling, her face shining with hope.

"It's us," Mr. Brennan said, his voice rough, trying to hold back a sob.

"Abbs?" I whispered, though I was unsure of whether I had actually said it out loud.

"Maa...Daahh?" the girl whispered in an unrecognizable, hoarse voice. She seemed to be having trouble forming the words. Dr. Richardson's mention of possible brain damage ran through my mind.

We'll get through this, I told myself, trying to stay positive.

Abby tried to clear her throat, but a spasm of pained flitted across her face. "Gray...Grayson," she croaked out. "Wha...Where's Grayson?" Her eyes remained closed.

"Abby," I whispered so quietly my words were merely an exhalation. "Abbs, Grayson is—"

Mrs. Brennan reached over Abby and clutched my shoulder. "Not yet, Rei," she told me in a low voice. "We have to tell her, but not yet." She then burst into tears and she gripped her daughter's hand, mindful of the IV and bandages. "Just rest, honey. Don't talk. We're right here with you. It's us. It's mom and dad. You're safe now. Rei is here too. We're all here for you." Her voice took on the familiar soothing tone I was used to hearing from her. "We're all here. Just rest."

I looked away from Abby for a moment. No, we were not all here for her. One person was missing. Grayson wasn't here with us. And I had no idea how any of us could ever break that tragic news to Abby. She had survived, while the most important person in her life hadn't. She would be heartbroken, her entire life devastated.

"Mr. and Mrs. Brennan," a blonde nurse suddenly said, poking her head into the hospital room. "Dr. Richardson is on his way to talk with you." The nurse had a strangely pitying expression on her face for the briefest of moments.

"Please excuse us, Rei," Mr. Brennan said to me as he and Mrs. Brennan went to go speak with the doctor, though it was clear that neither of them wanted to leave their daughter's side.

"I'll wait here with Abbs," I told them as I took her hand in mine. "I won't leave."

I stood outside of Abby's room by the nurses' station with Mr. and Mrs. Brennan. I visited the hospital every day after work, coming to see how my friend was recovering. I didn't care how tired I was when my shift ended, nothing was going to keep me from being by Abby's side as she began the long road to total recovery.

My boss had gotten angry at me this afternoon for refusing to work a double shift. *Screw him*, I thought. My friend was more important than making damn pizzas.

I had learned that, unfortunately, Abby had indeed suffered some significant head trauma. It was the reason she had been in a coma for three days. She would need speech therapy and would probably have difficulty walking for a while. The hospital would provide her with a physical therapist.

You're a tough one, Abbs, I thought to myself every time I saw her.

Approaching voices jostled me out of my thoughts, and I saw two doctors approaching us.

"Dr. Moradi, Dr. Richardson, I know I've said this many times before," Mr. Brennan began as he shook each of the doctors' hands. "But I just can't thank you enough. You saved our daughter's life. We can never repay you for such a gift."

"We're happy to do our jobs," Dr. Moradi said, pushing her graying hair off her forehead, a smile touching her lips. "It's only been a few days, but your daughter is coming along very well. It will take a long while for her to fully recover from this, both physically and mentally. But for now, I say she should be able to go home in a day or two."

I almost couldn't believe it. Abby was going to be able to go home soon? After seeing the state she had been in, I had to admit that I—privately at least—had not been very hopeful of a full recovery the first time I had laid eyes upon her brutalized body. She had looked so...I didn't want to think about it.

"Yes, thank you so much," Mrs. Brennan said, sharing a hug with Dr. Moradi. "We are so blessed that Abby's life was in your capable hands. Even though we lost a part of her..." She sniffed and wiped a tear from her cheek.

Yes, I thought with great sadness, *we lost Grayson.*

Abby's lost a part of her that nothing will be able to ever replace.

For a moment, everyone looked down at their feet, unsure of what to say.

"I can recommend a good counselor for Abby when she is ready to work on that," Dr. Richardson said. "I'm sure it was very difficult for her when you told her about Grayson."

"She..." Mrs. Brennan's voice trailed off.

"She reacted just about as you'd expect," Mr. Brennan finished for his wife. "Seeing my daughter like that...A father shouldn't have to ever comfort his daughter on the loss of her husband. If I could switch places with Grayson, just to see her happy again, I would. They had just gotten married for God's sake. And Grayson was a truly wonderful guy. I couldn't have asked for a better son-in-law."

"Abby is lucky to have all of you supporting her," Dr. Moradi said, looking at all of us. "I can tell she'll have a lot of love and support through this time of grief."

We all nodded wordlessly.

"We would definitely like Abby to meet both of you now that she's more lucid," Mr. Brennan said after the moment of silence.

"Yes, of course," Dr. Richardson replied, taking off his glasses to clean them with his tie. "But for now, let's let her sleep. She still needs a lot of rest to fully recover her strength."

We all looked over at the open doorway that lead to Abby's room. I could see her sleeping peacefully in her bed, dark eyelids closed against her bruised cheeks, her chest rising softly, while machines monitored her vitals and beeped a steady rhythm.

But standing around her...

"Who the hell is that?" Mr. Brennan demanded with a protective growl.

Two unfamiliar female figures, both dressed in flowing, deep red dresses, their faces obscured by red and gold shawls, stood on either side of Abby. They were faintly murmuring something I could not make out while making strange hand gestures in unison over my sleeping friend. What in the world were they doing?

"Hey!" Dr. Moradi shouted, pushing past Mr. Brennan and striding into the room. "Who are you and what do you think you're doing?"

"Call security," Dr. Richardson said to a nurse before he too rushed in to confront the strangers. How had no one seen them enter Abby's room? We had been standing not a dozen feet from the doorway.

"Get away from my daughter!" Mrs. Brennan ordered in a tone that brooked no defiance as she rushed to Abby's side. Mr. Brennan and I were right behind her.

The figure on the far side of Abby's bed looked up. She removed her shawl, and we were greeted by the smiling, flabby, wrinkled face of a squat elderly woman.

"So sorry, dear," the old woman said in a high, breathy voice with a hint of an accent that I couldn't place. Eastern European perhaps? "We were just praying over the girl here. We meant no harm." Her watery blue eyes glittered behind the folds of her fleshy cheeks. Her face reminded me of a toad. The other figure, face still hidden in a shawl, kept bowing as if in apology, never meeting our eyes.

"Oh," Mrs. Brennan said, sounding somewhat mollified, but still eyeing the two strangers suspiciously.

For my part, I felt quite wary. While they didn't look particularly dangerous, there was something...not quite right about them. There was some weird vibe that I couldn't quite shake. Who was this weird little old lady? Had someone's grandma gotten lost in the hospital? Why had the other figure not removed her shawl? And in the confusion, I could have sworn that Abby had been staring up at the strangers, smiling dreamily at them, though a glance at her confirmed that she was now in a deep sleep. Had I just imagined it?

"Well thank you, but we don't need any of that," Mr.

Brennan said, trying to usher the odd couple from the room.

"As you wish, dear," the old woman said without so much as a hint of protest. She gave a rather dramatic bow and turned to leave the room. "We were just finishing our orison anyway," she added over her shoulder. She turned to look directly at Mrs. Brennan. "You have such a beautiful daughter. A true blessing to the entire world. She'll do great things, that one. I promise you." The old woman took hold of Mrs. Brennan's hand, patting it reassuringly.

Mrs. Brennan snatched her hand away instantly, massaging it as if to dispel a cramp. The elderly woman turned and disappeared out the door. Her companion followed, muttering something unintelligible in a soft drone. As she passed by me, I thought I caught the word, "descendant" in a raspy garble.

"Well, that was very weird," Mr. Brennan said, shaking his head after the two figures had disappeared around a corner of the hallway. He then turned back toward the others and shrugged. "They didn't look like Hare Krishnas or anything." Mr. Brennan chuckled weakly at his own comment.

"We'll make sure nothing like that happens again," Dr. Moradi said sharply, still watching the hallway with a wary expression. When the strangers didn't come back, she returned her gaze to the room, her voice softening. "I apologize. That was a new one for me. I haven't seen those two around here before. But maybe they're some other patient's family." She glanced at Dr. Richardson, who nodded in agreement.

"It's okay," Mr. Brennan said, turning his attention back to his daughter. "No harm, no foul."

No matter what, I couldn't get past my uneasy feelings of suspicion. There had definitely been something off about that old woman and her companion. I couldn't quite say what, though. They had left in a polite enough manner, but they just gave me a strange feeling. I usually trusted my instincts, but with all the happenings lately, I wasn't entirely sure I could rely on them at the moment. My brain felt fried, and I suddenly realized how exhausted I was.

"Rei," Mrs. Brennan said, still massaging her hand before holding out her arms to hug me. "Thank you for being here with us."

"Of course," I replied, squeezing her back. "I wouldn't be anywhere else."

"Abby truly is fortunate to have a friend like you," she went on. "Speaking of friends, do you think we should call Lorena and Corinne? Update them on how Abby is doing?"

"Yeah, of course," I replied. "I'll text them both right now."

Out in the hall, I took out my phone to compose a message to the others. Hitting send, I closed my eyes and took a deep breath, exhaling slowly in an attempt to clear my mind. Abby was alive and on her way to wellness. That's what mattered the most at the moment.

My phone buzzed almost immediately with two texts. Lorena said she still had an hour or two of driving before she would arrive. Corinne would head over here as soon as she was off from work. I quickly texted back, then slid the phone into my pocket.

I hoped everything was going to be all right now.

"No!" I heard a screech come from inside Abby's room.

I rushed back inside to see Abby sitting bolt upright, her eyes wild with panic. The Brennans and the doctors were all attempting to restrain her.

My heart froze. What was wrong? Was Abby having some sort of seizure?

"Nurse!" Dr. Moradi shouted.

"Don't go!" Abby screamed. Her wide-open eyes were staring in my direction, but somehow didn't seem to be looking at me. "Don't go! Don't go!"

"We're not going anywhere, Abbs!" Mr. Brennan tried to calm his daughter. She seemed not to notice.

"We're all here, sweetie!" Mrs. Brennan shouted,

putting her hands on Abby's cheeks, trying to get her daughter to look at her.

"No! No!" Abby yelled, thrashing like a wild animal, still staring straight ahead at no one. "Don't go! Oh God, please don't go!"

"I'm here too, Abbs," I said, finally finding my voice. I rushed to her bedside. "I'm here. We're all here." I had to do something. Make her see that she was not alone.

Abby just stared straight ahead, sobbing, rivers of tears running down her face. I feared that if her eyes opened any wider, they'd fall right out of her head. Where did Abby think we were going? I would never leave her side. Neither would her parents. Who was she yelling at? Was she...was she yelling to Grayson?

A nurse came in with what I realized must be a sedative in a syringe. But before she could reach the bed, Abby vomited the foamy acid from her empty stomach and passed out.

CHAPTER TWO

The bond of the covenant requires sacrifice.

Three months later...

Holding open one of the glass doors for Abby, I followed her inside to the cool interior of the building. The California heat was brutal, and we both sighed in relief. We crossed the small lobby to the bank of elevators, our sneakers squeaking on the tiled floor, echoing in the silent space. I had been bringing Abbs here long enough that I no longer needed to look at the directory on the wall to find the floor and room number we were looking for.

Abby pressed the call button, and we rode one of the elevators to the fourth floor, where her therapist had her office. The long, carpeted hallway was silent. When we first started coming here, I had noticed that most of the doors we passed had identifying plaques attached to them, though I noticed that only a few had "Dr." in front of the names. I had no idea who else shared the building with Abby's therapist, and I never saw anyone else in the halls when we were here.

At the end of the hallway, we finally came to the last door that read "Dr. Eileen Chen."

Abby turned to face me before I could reach the doorknob. "I know I say this every time we come here," she said. "But thank you for coming with me, Rei."

"You don't have to keep thanking me," I told her with a smile. "You asked me to come, and I'm happy to do it. I'm sure it's not easy for you to come here and deal with everything. So I will do anything and everything I can to make it easier for you."

"But I know you had to move around your shifts to get off work at this hour every week. I just want you to know that I really appreciate it. I could always ask my parents to come, but...Well, I just prefer my best friend. You being here *does* help make things easier. But I know there are more exciting things you could be doing for an hour other than sitting there twiddling your thumbs while I'm in there talking with her."

"I'm perfectly happy to be here," I said, and gave her a big hug before we went inside.

I sat down on the small, faux-leather couch as Abby checked in with the receptionist. She was called in to an adjacent room with Dr. Chen, and I was left by myself.

Other than the usual greeting, I had never talked to the receptionist. I'm sure she didn't want to be disturbed while she worked. Besides, she didn't look like the friendly, talkative type. I took a book out of my purse, a fantasy novel about a young queen trying to defend her land from an evil sorcerer. It was good so far. I opened it up to the page held by my bookmark.

The receptionist's phone rang, and she answered it in a professional tone. "Hello, mother," the woman said into the phone, sitting up straighter. "Yes, I'm at work."

Perks of the job, I guess.

There was no way I'd be allowed personal calls at my job during working hours.

After a brief exchange on the phone—I didn't hear anything else, as the receptionist's voice had dropped to a low, private tone—she hung up, and excused herself from the room, saying she'd return shortly.

Leaning back into the couch cushions, I made myself more comfortable. I had read almost two chapters when I suddenly heard Abby sobbing from the other room. I would never listen in on her private therapy sessions, but at the moment, she was crying so loudly, I couldn't help but hear. Normally, I couldn't hear a peep from inside that room, and the clarity and volume totally surprised me. Abbs must have really been bawling.

"He's gone!" I heard Abby's muffled voice wail from behind the door. "He never even had a chance! They took him from me!"

Losing Grayson...Abbs is going through an emotional hell.

Returning my book to my purse, I got up and exited the waiting room, heading over to the elevators. I knew there were a couple of vending machines located on the first floor. I'd go down and get a soda, and come back up in a bit. I just didn't want to be in the waiting room at the moment. I didn't feel it was right for me to be hearing Abby's private conversation.

Pressing the button, I called the elevator to my floor and when the doors opened with a ding, I stepped inside. The carriage held one other occupant: a small boy, probably about ten-years-old, wearing a dark sweatshirt with the hood pulled up so that I couldn't see his face.

"Going down?" I asked. My question hung in the air, but I got no response.

Maybe he's deaf?

I pressed the button for the first floor. The doors slid shut, and the elevator began to descend. I heard faint music, thinking the boy might be wearing headphones under his hood, but I soon realized it was coming from a speaker near the carriage's ceiling. Funny, I hadn't heard actual elevator music in years. It was barely audible, though, and I wondered if the speaker was malfunctioning.

The red digital number to the side of the doors changed from four to three to two. Then we came to a stop. I assumed this was the boy's stop. I waited for the doors to slide open, but they remained closed, my own fuzzy reflection staring back at me from the burnished metal.

"Uh, okay," I mumbled, reaching out and pressing the *open* button. Nothing happened. I jammed my finger into the first-floor button as well, but we remained still. "Shit, you're kidding me right now."

Punching the buttons several more times produced no results. I turned to look at the boy and was taken aback to see that he was now facing the other direction. His face was pressed into the right back corner of the elevator, as if he were in timeout.

"Hey, buddy," I said, trying to get his attention. "Are you alright?" There was no response. I didn't know what to do. "Well, I think we just got stuck in here. The doors aren't opening, and we're not moving at all."

I waited for him to say something, but all I got was more silence. What was going on?

Who faces backward in an elevator?

Reaching out, I was about to tap the boy's shoulder when his arm shot up, slapping the wall of the elevator with a gloved hand. The boy's fingers curled into a fist, and then began pounding on the metal, causing loud reverberations to fill the tiny compartment.

If he was a patient of one of the other doctors in the building, then it was possible that he was experiencing some bad mental trauma just like Abby. And I'm sure being stuck in an elevator was not helping. Although I was sympathetic—my best friend was upstairs dealing with her own problems at the very moment—I was ashamed to admit that I felt a sense of dread wriggle in my stomach at the thought of being trapped in a box with someone who might be unstable—even if he was just a child.

"It's okay," I told him in as reassuring a voice as I could muster, deciding not to touch his shoulder. "We'll get out of here. I'm sure someone already knows there's a problem. They're probably working on it right now." I turned and pressed the alarm button but heard nothing.

The boy started weeping; a soft, agonizingly mournful sound that sent a shiver up my back. Before I could say anything, however, the elevator's speaker crackled with a loud burst of static.

"Hello?" a fuzzy, indistinct voice emanated from the speaker.

"Hello?" I replied, a thrill of relief washing over me. *Thank God.*

"I can hear you! We're stuck in the elevator. I think it's on the second floor, but the doors won't open. Can you do something?"

"Hello? Hello?" the voice asked again. "Are you there? Can you hear me, Rei?"

"Yes! We're—" My words died in my throat. The person had called me by name. Who would know I was in here? It certainly did not sound like Abby. How would she have been talking through the speaker anyway? "Who's there?" I asked, my voice cracking. "Who's talking?"

There was no reply or sound beyond the soft hum of electronic crackling.

"You can speak," another voice said from beside me. It had come from the boy who was still facing the corner. "You can speak...to me."

"What?" I croaked out, the word becoming lodged in my throat for a moment. What was this kid talking about? "I'm-I'm speaking to whoever's there." I pointed a trembling finger at the speaker box, though his back was to me.

"Corruption comes," the boy responded. He slowly turned around to face me, his face hidden in the shadows of his hood.

With stiff, jerky movements like a zombie, he shuffled forward and reached his gloved hand out for me. Instinctively, I stumbled backward in the confined space, my back slamming against the elevator's side. The boy then collapsed onto the floor.

"Oh God," I muttered, feeling like an idiot for backing away from this kid. He clearly needed help of some kind.

Bending down, I reached out toward him, but as I did so, his body seemed to...deflate. All his clothing sunk into him, as if nothing were holding it up anymore.

"What the fuck," I breathed out, snatching my hand back. Overwhelming panic coursed through my veins and along my nerves. What the hell was going on?

There was a movement in the empty hoodie that caught my eye. Something was writhing inside the material. I don't know what possessed me in that moment, but I pinched a corner of the sweatshirt and lifted it up.

Something rolled out of it; a tiny, bloody mass of flesh, kicking and squirming in its own fluids.

"Fucking hell!" I screamed, leaping to my feet and flattening myself against the solid door of the elevator.

Lying on the floor was what could only be a human fetus.

In that moment, the overhead lights exploded, raining down shards of glass onto my head and plunging me into terrifying darkness. I felt a hand grip my shoulder in the pitch blackness at the same time I heard a ding. I felt a sliding movement against my back.

Blinding light flooded the inside of the carriage as the doors swished open, and, panicked, I ran through them without a second thought, right into—

An elevator.

"What in the fuck?" The words erupted from my mouth before I even realized I had yelled them. My pulse was racing like I had just run a marathon. I unclenched the fists I didn't realize I had balled up.

I was standing inside an empty, well-lit elevator. I spun around to see a large number four painted on the hallway wall right outside. What the hell had just happened?

Stepping—almost leaping—out of the carriage, I examined the silent corridor. I was still here on the fourth floor. I hadn't gone down. But how? Did I just have the most vivid waking dream of my life?

I looked back at the elevator, waiting, its doors open. The lights were intact, there was no one inside, no child, no clothing on the floor, no...fetus.

"Rei, I'm done." A hand gripped my shoulder.

"No!" I shrieked, jumping away and spinning around with a flail.

"Holy shit!" A very confused-looking Abby stood there, staring at me. "I didn't mean to scare you." She looked me up and down several times. "Are you okay?"

"I..." I looked at her, trying to calm my breathing. "I-I'm fine, Abbs," I managed to say. "I just...I don't know. Had a weird feeling." There was no way I was going to tell her what I had just hallucinated. She had more important things to deal with than my nightmarish daydreams.

"You sure you're okay?" Abby asked, her brow furrowed in concern. "You look a bit pale and sweaty."

"Yeah, I'm fine," I answered, taking in a deep breath. "I don't think I've eaten anything today, that's all. Just felt a little...woozy."

"We can go grab an early dinner, if you want," Abby offered, her worried expression disappearing.

"Sounds good," I said, starting to feel a little better. I don't know what had happened, but I wasn't going to dwell on it. I had been working a lot of hours lately. Maybe it had just been an exhaustion-fueled daydream.

"Off we go then." Abby smiled. "Pick a place."

"Okay." A surge of dread slithered through me as I watched Abby walk into the elevator. I would have suggested the stairs, but Abby was still in physical therapy for her brain damage. I couldn't make her descend four stories, and I wasn't about to let her ride down alone.

I swallowed a lump in my throat as I stepped inside the waiting elevator.

We ended up at Abby's favorite sushi place, where we ate and talked for quite a while. Little by little she was doing better. The therapy must have been working, but there was also an immeasurable sadness deep in her eyes that I always saw now.

"Dr. Chen suggested something that I think we should do," Abby said, stuffing the last piece of a tuna roll into her mouth.

I took a swig of my beer. "What's that?" I asked, intrigued. I was willing to do anything I could if it meant helping Abby on her road to recovery.

Abby sipped at her iced tea before answering. "She suggested I go on a vacation. Go out somewhere and get away from it all for a few days. She said it would really benefit me. Help me relax and recharge. I want you to come. And let's invite Lorena and Corinne."

"Sounds nice," I said. "I could use a vacation." I definitely felt like I needed a vacation after my waking nightmare episode today. "Yeah, I think I have some days off saved up at work. Let's talk with Corinne and Lorena and see what days would work for them. I'm sure they'll be all for it."

"Great," Abby said, raising her iced tea glass and clinking it against my beer. "Thank you, Rei. You really are the best. I'm so glad I have you." She started to tear up as she smiled at me. I could see that ever-present sadness in her brown eyes.

"Where do you think you would want to go?" I asked, hoping to get her mind back on the vacation.

"Hmm." She rubbed at her eyes, then placed a finger on her mouth, looking deep in thought for a moment. "Somewhere away from all the hustle and bustle." She snapped her fingers. "Hey, your parents had that lake house, right?"

"Lake house?" I asked, confused for a minute before I realized what she was talking about. "Oh, the place up in Washington?" The lake house my parents had bought decades ago. I hadn't thought about that place in years. It surprised me that Abby had even remembered it, especially since she had never been there.

A lakeside vacation, could be nice.

"Should be fine. Let's talk to the other two first, see what they suggest. But you'll have the final say."

"Okay," Abby replied, once again, giving me that smile that tried to hide so much sadness.

CHAPTER THREE

Whom do you believe yourself to be? Turn the ichor-covered gears. Hear them whine in agony and grind like metal on bone. Flesh pulses to the beat of the cosmic echo.

The following week...

"Here we are," I said, as I put my blue Jeep Grand Cherokee in park at the end of the gravel driveway. The two-story house seemed to be still slumbering in the quiet of the early morning. The sun hadn't quite poked through the clouds yet, and beads of dew still dotted the lawn and flower beds.

"Last stop, then we're on our way," Lorena replied from the passenger seat, a perky smile on her round face.

Ever since we had finalized plans for this trip, Lorena had been looking forward to it as much as I. A good old-fashioned road trip with my best friends. I had been eagerly anticipating the adventure, sometimes unable to sleep at night, like a child who knew she was going to Disneyland the next morning.

I stepped out into the chilly morning air, softly shutting the car door behind me, trying not to wake Corinne who was asleep in the back seat. Apparently, the early start I had wanted had been a bit too early for Sleeping Beauty. I had forgotten how crabby she could get in the mornings.

I drew in a deep breath as I walked around the car, looking up at the house before me. I held the breath for as long as I could before I felt the twinge of an ache in my lungs. I exhaled loudly as I turned to walk up the stone pathway to the front door.

The second step up to the porch still creaked as it always did. I reached out to knock, but the door cautiously swung open before my knuckles could reach and rap upon it. A tired, yet-smiling, face greeted me. A face that I had always been happy to see.

"Good morning, Rei," Abby's mom said, warmth in her voice, stepping out of the doorway to envelope me in her customary smothering embrace.

"Good morning, Mrs. Brennan," I replied, hugging her back. Mrs. Brennan had always been a great hugger. There was something about the way she held you that always made you feel like her motherly love could protect you from anything. My own mother hadn't been alive for a long time now, not since I had been a teen. But when she had been, her hugs still never matched the level of Mrs. Brennan's.

"Morning, Mrs. Brennan," Lorena said as she stepped forward to claim her hug as well. "Corinne would say hi if she weren't asleep in the car. The little princess." She rolled her eyes and grinned.

"Oh, stop," Mrs. Brennan chuckled. "Some people just need a bit more sleep than others. Abby's father will sleep all day if I let him." She giggled once more. It was wonderful to hear such a happy sound coming out of her again. "But speaking of Abby, she will be right out. She's just finishing getting ready. Can I get you girls some breakfast before you go? Sausages? Waffles? I can whip up some omelets if you'd like."

"No, no," I said, holding onto Mrs. Brennan's arm as she turned toward the kitchen. "We don't want you to go to any trouble. Really."

"Oh, hush now, Rei," Mrs. Brennan replied dismissively, putting a comforting hand on my shoulder. "You know it's never any trouble to feed you girls. But I won't keep you. I'm sure you're as eager as Abby to get going on your little trip. But I did make you all some turkey sandwiches for the road." She disappeared into the kitchen and returned almost immediately to hand Lorena a bulging plastic grocery bag.

"Thank you very much," Lorena and I said simultaneously, glancing at each other and giggling. We should have known Mrs. Brennan would find a way to feed us. Not that I ever minded. Her cooking was damn delicious. She could somehow even make eggplant or Brussels sprouts taste good.

God, I really missed hanging out here. This house held so many memories. But it wasn't the walls and the roof that made this place special. It was the people that lived inside. People who had enriched my life beyond measure.

"Ta-da! Here she is," a voice announced. Mr. Brennan appeared, carrying a bright red suitcase down the staircase that led to the second floor of the house. Abby followed closely behind him, holding tightly onto the railing as she took each step. She was still doing her physical therapy, and was walking fairly normally again, although she did experience balance issues every now and then.

"How are you doing, Abbs?" I said after greeting Mr. Brennan. She looked so much better than that horrible night. Her skin had regained its sun-kissed glow, and her curly, auburn hair looked healthy and shiny. Yet the dark circles under her brown eyes never seemed to want to fade, as if they had been permanently tattooed on her skin. I pulled her into a hug that I held for a little longer than usual.

"I'm good," she answered, as she pulled away, giving me a warm smile. "Just a little tired is all. I didn't sleep much last night. I was probably too excited."

I knew sleep wasn't the only reason she looked tired. Abby's therapy seemed to have been going so well. But now she looked worse, more depressed. I was still taking her to see Dr. Chen. What had happened?

I was counting on this vacation to cheer her up. I promised myself I would make this the best trip ever for her.

"You can sleep in the car, honey," Mrs. Brennan said. Lorena and I echoed our agreement.

Lorena and Abby bid farewell to Mr. and Mrs. Brennan. Abby's mom held her for a long time before telling her to have fun and be careful. As I began to voice my good-bye and get my hug, Mrs. Brennan anxiously grabbed my hand, her eyes boring into mine, both pleading and fierce.

"Have fun on your trip, honey," she said, but there was a quaver in her voice. "Just...please take care of Abby." I felt a surge of emotion rise within me as I held her gaze. "Look after her. I know you girls will. I know it. But it would help me if I could hear you say that you will."

"Of course, we will," I answered solemnly, then gave both of them a reassuring smile. "I promise Abby will be fine, and we'll all have fun up at the lake."

"The name of that place just gives me the willies," Mrs. Brennan said with a weak laugh. "Devil's Eyes Lake? What's with the name?"

"That's all it is," I answered. "Just a name. Don't worry, Mrs. Brennan. I'm sure my parents wouldn't have bought the house there if the area was dangerous. We'll take good care of Abbs. We always do." I smiled.

"We know you do," Mr. Brennan said, putting an arm around his wife's thin shoulders. "You've always been there for her, Rei. You and Corinne and Lorena are all part of this family. Abby's lucky to have you guys."

"And we're lucky to have her," I said, looking over at the car where Abby now sat patiently in the passenger seat.

Once we left the freeway, the green of the trees and the gray of the road speeding past in a monotonous blur was almost hypnotic. I unconsciously counted each time we passed one of the yellow lines that separated our lane from the oncoming traffic, though I had lost count a dozen times already. The lines on the road were hardly necessary, though. We seemed to be completely alone out here.

We hadn't seen another car in quite a while, not since our last stop.

After polishing off the turkey sandwiches, we made a brief stop in the small town of Black Ashes, Washington to pick up some extra snacks for the weekend, gas up the car, and stretch our legs.

As I filled the gas tank, I watched Lorena's stocky frame dash into the diner, desperately hoping to use the restroom inside. She had been holding it for a while now. I had offered to pull over to the side of the road earlier so she could crouch behind some trees and relieve herself, but she refused as I had known she would ever since the camping trip we had all taken the summer before our freshman year of high school. Lorena had almost been bitten by a rattlesnake while trying to find a secluded spot to pee.

Corinne got out of the car, her long, blonde hair sticking out this way and that from sleeping in the back seat. She ambled around the parking lot, attempting to find a better signal for her phone. I shook my head thinking that thing was permanently glued to her palm.

"How are you doing Abbs?" I asked, leaning in through the open driver-side window, the gas pump ticking away behind me, the dollars and gallons numbers steadily rising. She seemed to be staring off into space.

"I'm okay," Abby replied, turning to look at me. "It's been a long drive. But I know the destination will be worth it. I can't wait to see how beautiful the lake is."

"Me too," I said, nodding. A question had been nagging me. I wasn't sure if Abby would even know what I was talking about, but I felt I had to try. "Abbs, I wanted to ask you something about when you were in the hospital."

"Oh?" she said, no hint of hesitancy in her voice. "What about?"

The scene of those two strange women "praying" over Abby in the hospital flashed vividly through my mind.

"Do you remember any strangers coming into your room?" I asked, trying to sound casual. "Two women who were not nurses, doctors, or hospital staff?"

"Hmm, not that I recall," Abby answered, scratching her head in thought. After a moment she went on. "I remember mom and dad being there. And I remember you. It's all fuzzy, Rei. I can't really remember."

"It's okay," I said, trying to sound unconcerned. I could have sworn I had seen Abby looking up to meet the gaze of that old woman. But who knew? I didn't really know why it had been bugging me so much.

The gas pump indicated the tank was full with a metallic *thunk*. Reaching through the window to grab my purse, I asked Abby if she wanted anything to snack on, but she declined. As I neared the diner, I noticed a few dozen missing person flyers plastered on the dirty windows, many faded with age. For some reason, seeing all those black and white faces staring out at me had given me the chills.

"Rei!" Corinne yelled from behind me. "Can you get me jelly beans if they have any?"

I looked away from the flyers and saw that Corinne had walked back to the car and was now fixing her hair and lipstick in the passenger-side mirror of the Jeep, while Lorena loaded a couple of bags of food into the trunk.

"Yeah," I shouted and went inside. Corinne always ate so much candy, yet stayed so infuriatingly thin.

I picked up a bottle of soda and a bag of jelly beans from the little food mart section of the building. The smell of burgers, pancakes, and coffee wafted over from the dining area, causing my stomach to grumble. We couldn't delay any longer, however. No matter what my stomach demanded. I wanted to reach the lake house before sundown. Besides, we had snacks in the car, and Lorena was planning on cooking something as soon as we arrived.

"Just this for you today?" the cashier asked as I put the soda and candy on the counter. He had bushy, rust-colored hair that fell to his shoulders, large glasses, lanky arms covered in freckles, and a spot of acne on his chin. I guessed he was most likely a high-schooler working part-time for the summer, earning some extra cash.

"Yeah, I think that's all," I replied as he rang me up. My gaze drifted toward the missing person notices once more. "Hey, here's a question for you. What's up with all the missing people?" I waved my hand in the direction of the flyers decorating the window.

"Not from around here are you?" The boy half laughed and half sighed. "And that will be $2.25."

"No, I'm not," I said, handing him some cash. "My friends and I drove up from Southern California."

"I see. Well, no one really knows what's happened to them," the boy explained, nodding toward the grayscale faces printed on the flyers. "Some of those are pretty old. Like, dozens of years old. That one," he pointed to one of the oldest looking flyers in the window's bottom right corner, "I remember seeing ever since I was a little kid. Every so often, it seems like someone around here just...disappears. One day you see them walking around town; the next day, their face is plastered everywhere. It really freaks a lot of people out. But if you ask me, I think it's us younger people just wanting to get out of this boring town. I know I definitely don't want to stay here the rest of my life. My parents would love if I did, though." He snorted, rolling his eyes in the time-honored manner of teenagers everywhere. "So, are you and your friends staying in town?"

"Nope, we're not," I answered, noting that he looked a bit disappointed. I actually felt a little flattered. "We're headed over to Devil's Eyes Lake for a nice, relaxing weekend. Not too much farther from here if the GPS is right. And by the way. Devil's Eyes Lake? What's up with that? Kind of a creepy name. Don't you think?" I forced out a laugh, remembering Mrs. Brennan's question. "Do you know where the name comes from?"

"Oh, of course I do," the cashier said, suddenly brightening up. "Everyone around here kind of knows about it. I'm actually really fascinated with local history." As he handed me my change, I couldn't help but think that this kid looked exactly like the kind of person who'd be interested in history. "A long-ass time ago there was some guy who lived over in the Devil's Eyes Lake area. He used to breed birds. Nothing too unusual about that, right? The thing is, nobody knew where he got the more exotic species that weren't native to this area. Anyway, the guy loved this tiny little bird called the Wagtail. He bred the Pied Wagtail with the Japanese Wagtail. The result was this small, completely black bird with white on its face that looks like a teeny-tiny mask." He framed his glasses with his hands.

"When the guy died, the birds went free," the cashier went on. "Whether they escaped on their own, or somebody let them all out, no one knows. What we do know is that now they're everywhere in this area. They especially love nesting around the lake. And it's weird. All the other Wagtail species migrate, but these never leave here. Anyway, the locals nicknamed the birds the Devil's Eyes because the white patches on their faces makes them look like demonic eyes flying around. Despite their name, my grandma always told me those birds were psychopomps; birds that carry the souls of the innocent off to heaven. It's a common belief in these parts. The name and the story's been around for forever. Like a hundred years or so." He shrugged casually. "But you know how stories can get twisted over time. So maybe that's not even the real reason why the birds are called that. Maybe there never really was some weird bird breeder guy." He shrugged again. "But it's what I've always heard around town." He looked eager to continue the local folklore lecture.

"Well, thanks for the history lesson," I said before he could spew out any more information. I stuffed my change into my purse and grabbed the soda and Corinne's candy off the counter. I guess I hadn't expected an actual detailed explanation on the subject. "We'll probably stop by here on Sunday on our way back."

"Oh, okay" he said as he closed the cash drawer. "See you then. I'll be here." We waved at me as I pulled open the door and left.

I walked back outside, the little bell on the door ringing behind me as if saying goodbye. I headed back to the car and slid into the driver's seat. The others sat inside, patiently waiting for me. Corinne sat in the back seat staring at her little compact mirror fixing her already flawless mascara. I would have preferred she stop primping altogether, but I was glad she was doing it now instead of while we were moving. It always made me nervous to see her fixing her makeup while I drove. What if I accidentally hit a bump and she stabbed herself in the eye?

Lorena sat next to her, absorbed in a novel with a Mayan pyramid printed on the cover, thick eyebrows furrowed in concentration. The book had been recommended by her grandma who knew Lorena always loved reading anything she could find that had to do with her heritage.

Abby sat in the passenger seat next to me, staring dreamily out through the windshield. I wanted to ask her what she was thinking about but thought better of it after seeing the wistful expression on her face.

"My jelly beans," Corinne said as she eyed my purchases. "And more soda, Rei? You shouldn't drink so much of that stuff, you know. There are so many chemicals in it. It's so bad for you."

"Everything is made of chemicals, Corinne," I retorted. I opened my soda, a satisfying hiss emanating from the bottle. I took a swig before buckling my seatbelt. "What do you think your candy is made of? Organic love?"

"That sounds gross," Lorena said with a laugh and a sly look at Corinne.

"Well, whatever," Corinne answered, taking her jelly beans and opening the package. "Don't come crying to me when you get all sick when you're old."

I waved a dismissive hand at her. "You still doing good, Abbs?" I asked as I started the engine. Ever since leaving the hospital, Abby had been uncharacteristically subdued and quiet. It was totally understandable, of course, seeing what she had gone through. But, I had been slowly trying to get her to talk to us more. I missed my old friend.

"Yeah, I'm good," Abby said after a few seconds, then turned and gave me a wan smile.

"Good," I replied, patting her leg. I pulled out of the parking lot and headed back out onto the road. I knew Abby wasn't really "good," at least not fully. Who would be after going through such a thing? But her smile told me that she was trying, and I found that encouraging.

~\|/~

We had left the town of Black Ashes about an hour ago. We now drove through the Washington wilderness, along an empty, twisting highway to the lake area. The chatter, mostly coming from the back seats, was little more than an unintelligible drone as my mind wandered off into a silent contemplation of more important thoughts. Thoughts of how this trip might go and how I could best help Abbs.

Grief is the most painful emotion a person could experience, in my opinion. I knew that all too well. I had lost my father in an awful car crash when I was only fifteen. He had been returning from a business trip in another state on a lonely road late at night. He never made it home. His car had been found the next day wrapped around a tree with his lifeless body crushed between the seat and the steering wheel. The authorities never did determine what had caused the crash, but the consensus had been that he must have fallen asleep at the wheel and drifted off the road.

I'm not ashamed to admit that I had been quite the daddy's girl. His death had been...well, I don't think "utterly devastating" is strong enough to describe it.

That tragedy had been nine years ago, however, and I had had plenty of time to come to terms with what happened. I definitely hadn't handled it well at first. Who would? But I knew I had certainly done much better than my mother, who had spiraled into a deep depression. A year and a half after my father's passing, she threw herself off a bridge and plummeted to her death. Two earth-shattering events so close together in my life. Most people who knew what had happened to my family wondered how I was still standing and sane.

Therapy is a wonderful thing. It helped me. It really did. Nothing would ever take away the pain of losing my parents. Perhaps I wouldn't ever really be over it. Would anyone? It would live with me forever. But I was still here. I had made it through the swirling abyss, coming out the other side, not unscathed, but alive and strong.

And I truly believed my best friend could make it through as well. She was a tough woman.

I glanced over at Abby for a moment. She was staring absent-mindedly out of the window again, her hands folded neatly in her lap. I saw that there were some small white scars across the knuckles of her right hand. I hoped she had punched out the teeth of her attacker.

Poor Abbs. Her grief was still all too fresh and poignant.

Abby and her husband, Grayson, had been married for all of three days when they had been the unfortunate victims of a brutal mugging. The happy couple had been out shopping that night, picking up some last-minute things for their honeymoon to Spain, when two nameless thugs had accosted them at gunpoint, demanding all of their valuables. They took cash, credit cards, Grayson's watch, Abby's necklace.

But when one of the thugs had demanded that Abby give him her new wedding ring, she had refused. She had fought back, infuriating the assailant. Grayson had tried to get in between them to protect his wife. There must have been a scuffle, but the two thugs managed to overpower Grayson and knock him to the ground where they began beating him with ferocious brutality. Abby said she remembered trying to stop them, but her memory after that became fuzzy.

Grayson had been pronounced dead at the scene with three bullet holes in his chest, massive head trauma, and internal injuries. As for Abby, she had ended up in the hospital for almost two weeks. The muggers, who the police never did identify, let alone catch, had beaten her so badly that they had left her in a coma after prying the ring off her finger. And why they had shot Grayson but not Abby, the police didn't know. Perhaps they had simply run out of bullets. Whatever had stopped them from killing Abby, I was glad for it.

And thankfully, Abby was well on her way to recovery. She had woken up from her coma three days after she had first been brought into the hospital. I remember that moment well, watching her stir, hope rekindling inside of me. Though she initially had great difficulty speaking and walking, Abby had recovered. She still had a long road ahead of her, but she seemed to be progressing well. At least physically.

I sighed and tuned into the conversation for a while as I watched the empty road speed unendingly toward us as if the car were swallowing it.

"And do you remember when Rei tried to dye her hair blue?" Corinne said, her words almost smothered by her snorting guffaws.

"Oh my God, yes!" Lorena shouted. "Remember how she was all embarrassed to come out of the bathroom and we had to jimmy the lock so we could get in and see?"

We all laughed. I very much remembered that night in high school. Black hair is difficult to dye, so I had tried bleaching my hair before applying the blue. I had ended up looking like a damn scarecrow.

"Hey now," I started to protest, raising a finger and glowering at Lorena in the rearview mirror. "It wasn't my fault. I—"

"Rei, watch out!" Abby suddenly shrieked from right beside me.

I started with a jolt, my eyes snapping back to the road. Gripping the steering wheel tightly, I swerved to avoid the stocky shape that had appeared on the edge of the road, toward which I had apparently been drifting.

Tires screeching, I somehow managed to miss the figure, avoided crashing into a tree, and came to a whiplash-inducing halt.

"Holy shit, Rei," Lorena whispered shakily from the backseat, catching her breath and staring out of the back window. "You almost hit that old lady."

"I'm...sorry," I barely managed to say, my chest heaving from seeing my life briefly flash before my eyes. I forced my quivering hands to relax the death-grip they had on the steering wheel.

"At least there aren't any other cars on this road," Corinne breathed, craning her neck to look out the back window.

I truly hadn't even *seen* the woman I had almost splattered until I was swerving around her. When I looked in my rearview mirror, there was no sign of the dark shape with its tuft of white hair I had careened around.

Unbuckling my seatbelt, and throwing open the door, I leapt from the car and ran back to where the old lady had been walking. There was no one around; no one I could see.

"Where is she?" I heard Corinne ask as she, Lorena, and Abby jogged up behind me.

"I don't know," I said, my voice a breathy whisper. "There's nobody here." I wiped away the beads of sweat that had sprouted on my forehead. "Did I imagine it?"

"But we all saw her," Lorena said to me.

"Maybe she ran off into the trees," Corinne offered, shrugging her shoulders. "Which means she wasn't hurt."

"You think an old lady moved that fast?" Lorena retorted.

"We don't even know if it really was an old lady," Abby chimed in. We all turned to look at her. "I just saw a shape in the road."

We looked around the area for several minutes before giving up. There was no one to be found. We returned to the car to resume our drive. I started the engine and buckled up, putting my hands on the wheel, but not moving us forward.

"You alright, Rei?" Abby asked.

I sat there for a full minute before finally nodding. I put the car in drive and we were on our way, a little shaken, but all safely in one piece.

"Are we there yet?" Corinne whined from the backseat after forty-five minutes of relative silence. This had to be about the hundredth time she had uttered those words since we had left home. I was sure we were all pretty tired of being in the car at that point. We had gotten up fairly early and had been driving for most of the day to get to the lakeside house. The last couple of hours had us looking at nothing but an endless sea of trees on either side of the empty road.

"Are you okay?" Lorena asked me, leaning forward from the back seat. "Are you getting tired of driving? I can take over if you want."

"No, I'm fine," I told her. "We're almost there anyway."

Lorena had always been the mother hen of our group and always the first one to offer to help, no matter what it was. But I had wanted to drive the entire way. Truthfully, I had always been a bit of a control freak, and so I always planned everything, got the four of us everywhere, and made sure everyone was happy. This obsession annoyed even me sometimes. But when it came to traveling, the others were usually content to let me burden myself with all of the logistics.

Besides, this was a special trip and I wanted everything to be perfect. Perfect for Abby.

I'd never forget that awful night, waking up to the sound of my cell phone ringing on the nightstand. It had taken me a few groggy seconds to realize what the noise was and answer. Abby's mom had been on the other end. I could tell by the sound of Mrs. Brennan's strained, raspy voice that she had been crying. That had snapped me awake almost instantaneously. She had then proceeded to explain that Grayson had been killed and that Abby was in the hospital because of some terrible attack. The memory of that call and the surreal ambience as I rushed over to the hospital in the dead of night still gave me horrible chills.

I think all of this had definitely given each one of us a good reminder about the fragility of life and how easily everything could be taken in an instant by an uncaring world.

When I had lost my parents, I had wanted to be alone, away from everyone and everything. I remembered pushing my friends away just so I could wallow in my own grief, loneliness, and pain. But, after giving me some time to mourn, my friends had been right there, supporting me. I knew it had been because of them that I had made it through with my sanity intact.

It's time that I do the same thing for Abby. She was there for me. She has always been there for me.

Abby and I had been best friends since we were about four years old, and she was like a sister to me. I would do anything for her. What she needed now was a lot of support from her best friends. And I was going to give her all the help she needed, no matter what.

Before they passed, my parents had bought a vacation house out here in the woodsy middle-of-nowhere by Devil's Eyes Lake in western Washington state.

After falling in love with the region on their honeymoon, the lakeside house had appeared on the market for a very reasonable price. They snatched it up right away and hired someone to renovate the place, fixing it up nicely, bringing in brand new furniture and appliances, installing a new septic tank, the works. Sadly, their chance to actually vacation there never came. They had both been busy with work and life when their opportunities were tragically cut short because of my father's accident and because my mother...

"So, you've never actually been up here, right?" Lorena asked.

"Nope, I've never even seen the place," I answered, feeling a bit sheepish.

"Really?" Corinne asked, finally looking up from her phone. "That's weird."

After my parents died, I had never really found a reason to come up here. The house had sort of faded from my memory over the years until Abby suggested it.

"Then how do you know it's habitable?" Corinne asked, looking a bit worried.

"Well, it should have furniture and running water," I replied. At least I hoped it did. "Not sure about electricity, though." My parents had set up a sort of trust to pay taxes and hire a seasonal caretaker—whoever that was—to keep everything in good order, ready for a visit. I left the trust alone after they died and presumed everything went on as always.

"You're shitting me." Corinne put a hand to her forehead and said with a dramatic sigh, "No electricity? You mean there's no wi-fi? And how am I supposed to charge my phone?"

"We'll make do, Corinne," Lorena interjected, poking Corinne in the ribs, making her squirm in a way that always made us laugh. "It will be just like that slumber party we had for Abby's thirteenth birthday. Remember the power went out because of that bad storm? You remember, right, Abbs?"

"Yeah, I remember," Abby said, with a little grin. She looked as if the memory were replaying itself inside her head. "We ended up sitting around with flashlights telling scary stories. That was fun. I liked it. Maybe we can tell some scary stories tonight."

We all chuckled fondly at the memory. Except for Corinne. I could tell that she wasn't into the idea. She wasn't a fan of scary things. But if Abby wanted to do it, I knew Corinne would suck it up and join in.

"This place sure is out in no-man's-land," Lorena said, surveying the wilderness beyond the car windows.

"I haven't seen any people or houses. There's probably no one around for miles."

"Of course," I answered. "It was supposed to be a secluded vacation home, far away from all the troubles of the modern world. Don't worry, Lorena."

"I'm not worrying," Lorena said. "I think it will be fun."

I returned to focusing on the road. The radio couldn't locate any stations through the dense mass of trees that surrounded us, but lucky for us, Corinne had been able to hook her phone into the car stereo so that we could all listen and sing along to songs from our high school days. Every now and then, I'd join in on the chorus of one of our favorite songs. I had always been partial to metal, but the nostalgic rock and pop songs from our younger years brought back good memories of good times.

We did get lost several times driving through the wilderness. We had lost the GPS signal a while ago, and Abby was not very proficient at reading maps. Every time we took a wrong turn, she would remind me that part of the fun of a road trip was getting lost and forging our own path to the destination. Lorena agreed, but Corrine huffed and puffed with impatience as she usually did.

It wasn't until we eventually found our way to a seldom used and somewhat overgrown road that led through the trees. We passed a small wooden sign with an arrow pointing to a drawing of water.

The sun had already begun to set by that time. The cloudy late summer sky blazed with celestial fire. I was eager to get to the house before nightfall so that we wouldn't have to unload everything in the dark. I wasn't sure if there would be any outside lighting for us to see by. I didn't want someone breaking an ankle as she carried her bags inside.

I can't wait to see how beautiful the water's going to look below the orange glow of the sky. Despite not being an outdoorsy tree-hugger, I could very much appreciate the beauty of it all.

A few moments later, the lake and the house finally

loomed out from behind the trees, a shadow against a backdrop of serenity. We all emitted gasps of pure awe. The house was amazing and picturesque. Its mostly square body was two stories high and beautifully constructed out of red cedar wood paneling. A covered porch embraced the front door in shady welcome. The entire east side of the first story was comprised of one large picture window so that the occupants could gaze out into the calm waters while sipping their morning coffee. Above that was a balcony with a railing made out of uncut logs. I imagined putting some wicker chairs and a chaise lounge covered in pillows up there for a cozy stargazing spot. A large chimney stack rose out of the slanted, peaked roof like a turret comprised of cement and round stones. I could just imagine the warm, crackling fires we would have. I felt my face warming already.

But there was one feature of the house that I know none of us had been expecting.

"Rei," Lorena said slowly, gently grabbing my arm. "I thought you told us the house was by the lake, not in it."

"I didn't know," I answered, my mouth dropping open in surprise.

The structure rested within the lake itself about a hundred feet from shore. It sat upon a small island of sorts. Whether the landmass was natural or manmade, I couldn't tell. The house was no more than fifty feet from the island's edge on any given side, which all rose a foot or two above the water like miniature cliffs except for the east bank where the land gradually declined into a sandy beach that facilitated wading or swimming. A bridge, comprised of wide planks of wood and held up by a dozen or so support posts that rose out of the lake connected the private little sanctuary to the shore in front of us. The house numbers had been painted on the nearest left post.

Definitely the place.

And I had never seen anything like it.

"Well, that's different." I couldn't think of what else to say.

"That's pretty awesome, though," Lorena replied.

"So, let's take a closer look," Abby said.

I felt a faint smile tug at my lips as I heard the eagerness in her voice.

"That bridge is big enough to drive across," I noted after tearing my eyes away from our remarkable destination. "I don't know if I should try. It doesn't look bad, but I don't know how stable it is."

"Let's take a look," Abby said and got out of the car before I could respond.

I got out and followed her to the bridge.

Abby took a step onto the first wooden plank. When nothing happened, she bounced up and down on top of it.

"Hey, hey," I said. "Be careful."

"It's fine," she replied. "Seems pretty stable to me." She bounced on the second and third planks.

"I suppose," I muttered, looking at the rest of the bridge. None of the planks seemed loose or rotten from what I could see. "You don't exactly weigh the same as a car."

"I'm finally here," I thought I heard from beside me. I turned toward Abby.

"What was that you said?" I asked, unsure if she had actually spoken.

"Hmm?" she said, not looking at me. "Oh, I was just saying that we're here. We made it. I'm excited!"

"Me too," I said, staring out into the lake for a second before turning back to the car. As I turned, I saw marks resembling old tire tracks on the planks. The caretaker's vehicle? I didn't know the person's maintenance schedule.

"What's the verdict?" Lorena asked, sticking her dark shaggy-haired head up front as Abby and I got back into our seats. "Is it safe?"

"I think it looks fine," I answered. "What do you guys say?"

"Well, if it looks fine," Lorena said.

"We don't want to have to carry everything over the bridge by hand," Corinne said, not looking up from her phone. "Ugh, I don't get any reception here."

I glanced at Abby and Lorena, both of whom just shrugged. I decided to drive across. The hell with it.

The car inched along slowly. I kept my foot on the brake pedal, easing off of it ever so slightly when I felt comfortable enough to quicken the pace. The bridge groaned in protest as we drove over it. The steady thump of the tires sounded somehow like the beating of a heart. Or was it just my own heart thumping in my ears? The sun sank below the horizon, so it was too dark to see just how deep the water below us was. Either way, I desperately hoped the bridge would hold.

We got across without incident, parking the car on the side of the house beside the covered porch. We let out a collective sigh of relief and smiled at one another.

"Well, let's go look at the place," I said and climbed out of the car. The house had looked beautiful and inviting from the other side of bridge. But now it looked quite different as I gazed at it. Up close, I could tell the house hadn't seen any visitors for many years. Cobwebs dangled from all over the porch's roof, and dirt and leaves littered the floorboards. A few windows even had cracks in them. I made a mental note to have Mr. Neilson contact the caretaker to get those fixed.

There was something else, though. Something in the air, the wind. Something I couldn't quite put my finger on. But whatever it was had sent chilled fingers down my spine as if some primal instinct told me that I was trespassing somewhere I shouldn't be.

But that was a dumb thought. I owned this place now. It was–

Had I heard something just then? Or was I just imagining things? I thought I had heard a faint voice floating toward me from far off across the lake. There shouldn't be anyone around here for miles, though. It had sounded as if words...words that had been spoken far away from here and had been carried to my ears by the gentle evening breeze. Perhaps someone was camping in the woods miles away and a fraction of the noise had carried all the way here. But as I listened for more, the only sound I could hear was the peaceful lapping of the water that surrounded us.

I must be more tired than I realized.

I reached into my pocket for the house keys and pulled out the jangling keychain. After I had turned eighteen, Mr. Neilson—my dad's best friend and lawyer—had given me the keys. "Happy birthday," he had said in his gravelly voice, and explained that he had been holding onto them for me, waiting until I was old enough. Mr. Neilson was—

I froze. I *knew* I had heard something that time. I was certain. And it had definitely sounded like a voice. Or had it really just been the wind? No, I could have sworn it had said my name.

Re-

"Rei."

I nearly jumped out of my skin. I spun around to see Abby standing there staring at me.

"Whoa, whoa, whoa," she said, hands raised to show that no harm was intended. "I didn't mean to startle you there."

"I'm-I'm fine," I lied, my heaving chest betraying my words. I tried to laugh it off. "I just didn't hear you walk up."

"Okay, if you say so," she said with a chuckle.

My joy at hearing that happiness in her voice pushed any uneasiness from my mind.

"This place is beautiful, Rei. I'm glad you brought me here. It seems like a great place to get away from...from everything and relax. Thanks." She gave me a tight hug.

"What are friends for?" I said with a smile and squeezed her tightly in return. "Now let's unload the car. It's starting to get chilly out here and we're losing the sun fast. Let me just unlock the house first."

I climbed the porch steps, slid the correct key into the dirty lock, and opened the door. All I could see within the house was a blackness so thick, it appeared to be a room of nothingness. A damp, musty odor wafted over me as if the house had let out a breath, waking up after all these years of solitude. I took a step inside, feeling around for a light switch. After sticking my fingers in several spider webs, and frantically shaking them off, I managed to find the switch and flick it on.

Nothing happened. No lights.

"Damn, there's no electricity," I called out to the others.

I heard Corinne whine in irritation, but Lorena simply nodded and went looking around the back of the house, using her phone as a flashlight.

"There's a generator over here!" she shouted after a few moments. "And looks like someone left us some fresh gasoline." She grunted with exertion a few times and then a motor sprang to life with a whir. The entrance light above my head flickered uncertainly for a few seconds, then remained glowing steadily.

Who would have left gas here for us?

Who had known we were coming up here? Abby's parents, of course. But how would they have left the gas here for us? Strange.

As Lorena came back around we all clapped. She took a dramatic bow, and then we all went about unloading the car, carrying in our clothes, coolers, and bags of food. With the four of us working, we finished the job quickly.

The inside of the house was dusty and was almost as chilly as outside. Fortunately for us, Lorena had been a girl scout in her younger years, and she got a fire going for us. Once the hearth was radiating warmth throughout the house, the place became much more comfortable and inviting.

The walls inside were wood-paneled, like you would see in a rustic cabin. A large, wrought-iron chandelier made to look as it were composed of dozens of antlers hung above us casting weird shadows across the walls and ceiling. The living room was quite large and separated into two sections by a half-wall. The left side had a comfy-looking couch and two squashy armchairs around the enormous, stone fireplace. The second half contained a long table and two lounge chairs that faced the enormous window that formed the entire east wall. Once we removed the dust covers, we saw that all the furniture seemed to still be in good condition, despite a moth hole here and there.

A wooden staircase led to the second story landing. It was quite full of shadows up there without any lights on. I could just make out a hallway and several doors that I assumed led to the upstairs bath and two bedrooms. I'd be sharing a room with Abby, of course. A hallway veered off from the living room, past the downstairs bathroom and the stairs leading to the basement entrance. An archway on the far side led to a darkened kitchen. Lorena went to go check out the cooking space and after switching the light on in there, I heard her make an approving noise.

"Are you guys hungry?" she asked us as she came back from her inspection. "All the kitchen appliances look good. I can start making dinner as soon as I clean them off."

"I'm hungry," Corinne said as she rearranged items in one of her bags.

"Great, then come help me wipe down the counters in here," Lorena said. "Chop chop!"

"Ugh, fine," Corinne said. She always acted like a haughty contessa, but deep down, I knew she didn't really mind helping.

"I'm definitely hungry," I called to them, halfway out the door, walking out to get the last few things from the trunk of the car.

Exiting out into the chilly, fresh air, I saw Abby standing close to the shore of our strange little island, looking out over the lake. Plumes of her breath rose above her head steadily like a steam engine. The moon had risen into the sky, a pale crystal orb that reflected silently and beautifully off of the black, glassy surface of the water.

"Abby, what are you doing? Are you okay?" I asked,

putting my hand on her shoulder. I silently berated myself for asking such a stupid question. Of course she wasn't okay. There was a big hole in her heart where Grayson had once been. *Nice going, Rei.*

"What? Oh, yeah. I'm fine," she said, though the tone of her voice confirmed just the opposite. "I was just thinking about things. You know."

"Okay," I said, not wanting to prod further. I was here to help and support Abby, but I couldn't rush things. Maybe she had come out here for some alone time. We had spent the entire day together in the car.

I followed Abby's gaze to the spot in the lake where she had been staring unblinkingly. I saw nothing except obsidian water.

"We should go inside," I said, removing my arm from her shoulder. "It's pretty cold out here."

"Yes, of course, let's do that," was all she said. She walked into the house a moment later without looking at me.

I stood at the edge of the water for a while, taking in the chill, refreshing air, and low buzzing of insects. A hot tear rolled down my cheek and I quickly wiped it away. It was difficult seeing Abby suffer through this awfulness. My lip quivered as I thought about her lying in that hospital bed, barely breathing, her face a bloodied mess.

With a sigh, I turned away from the water, headed over to the car, and grabbed the last few bags out of the back. As I walked up the porch, making sure I had wiped all the tears from my eyes, I glanced back out toward the obsidian waters. A goosebumps-inducing shiver ran through me, but not from the cold air. I felt...weird, out of place. Like I had just experienced a sudden shift in reality, although that made no sense to me. Maybe I just wasn't used to the outdoors. I had lived my entire life in the city. I wasn't accustomed to this complete silence, isolation, and darkness. That would probably unsettle anyone who was used to the constant glare of street lights, the sight of planes flying through the sky, and unending cacophony of honking cars, road work, and yelling people.

As I reached for the door knob, I heard a soft splash not far from the spot at the shore where Abby and I had just stood. I remained motionless for a few seconds, unsure whether I should turn around and look. It was probably just a stupid fish splashing around, but for some reason, it had completely unnerved me.

Turning around, I risked a glance. A few lazy ripples glided out from a point about fifteen feet from shore. A second later they were gone, returning the lake to its completely still and polished-mirror surface. It made me wonder if the water had been moving at all.

I quickly made my way back inside, shutting the door, and locking it behind me once I was safely within the house.

CHAPTER FOUR

You are trapped in your mortal coil, held back by the hand of creation. But you can be free.

It had taken Lorena several tries to light the small gas stove in the kitchen. It probably hadn't been used since my parents had renovated the house all those years ago. But after many attempts, and some colorful swearing that would have earned her a good smacking from her mother, Lorena eventually got the stove working. It wasn't until around 7:30 that Lorena was able to begin preparing dinner. I could hear all of our stomachs moaning and grumbling.

Soon, the delicious, savory aroma of pan-seared skirt steak wafted through the air. That, combined with the wonderful sound of its juices sizzling, made me hungrier by the minute. I was going to tear into that meat like a starved wolf.

Lorena had always loved cooking and sharing her edible creations with us. She had no doubt gotten her culinary passion from her dad, a chef at a five-star restaurant who made the most amazing Yucatecan dishes I had ever tasted. Tonight's fare was a jicama and citrus salad with corn on the cob followed by a very juicy steak that had been soaking since the previous day in a Ziploc full of whatever secret-ingredient marinade Lorena had concocted. Despite how long I'd known her, Lorena always managed to surprise me with her preparations.

Corinne and I had just finished setting out the dishes and silverware on the round dining table next to the kitchen when Lorena announced that dinner was finally ready. It had been a little over three years since the four of us had last gotten together like this for something more than just a quick lunch or drinks. How time flew the older you got! School, work, and family had the four of us slowly drifting away from each other as life inevitably moved onward. It was disheartening. But it made me even happier that we could all spend this time, even if it was just a weekend, together again, just like the good old times. Though, I wished, of course, that this little trip could have been as a result of much different circumstances.

"...and then you had that stupid Chihuahua in sophomore year, Corinne," I was saying. "That little fucker was mean. No wonder your parents got rid of it."

Lorena chuckled. "Oh God, Mr. Muffins."

"Hey, I loved Muffster!" Corinne said, pouting. "He loved me too in his own way."

"Corinne, he bit your hands and feet to shit," I said. "Don't you remember you always had Band-aids all over your fingers and toes because of him?"

"Oh, oh, oh." Corinne flapped her arms. "Fuck Mr. Muffins. Remember at Brittany Matthew's birthday party when Lorena jumped off the swing set and her skirt got caught and tore off?"

I choked on my food as laughter exploded from my mouth. "Yes!" I wheezed, wiping tears from my eyes.

"Laugh it up," Lorena said, giving us both the finger. "Laugh. It. Up. I'm glad my childhood trauma is so absolutely hilarious to the both of you."

"It was kinda funny," Abby added in a soft voice, causing us all to laugh more.

"How about...Oh, was it eighth grade that Donald Richardson wrote that poem for you, Rei?" Lorena asked. A smirk spread across her face.

"Oh no," I said, not wanting to relive that particular memory.

"Yeah! And he read it in front of the whole class as his

English presentation!" Corinne shrieked.

"'Rei, your eyes are brown like the dirt after it rains,'" Lorena started reciting. How could she still remember how that goddamn poem went?

"Stoooop," I begged, covering my face.

"'Your hair is black like a really, really dark night,'" Lorena continued, a huge shit-eating grin on her face.

"Oh my God, it was so bad!" Corinne pounded the table.

"'Your smile lights up the room like a large lamp,'" Lorena finished. Her face turning red from all the hysterical laughter that followed.

"You can all kiss my ass," I stated.

We all talked and ate voraciously, except for Abby, who quietly nibbled away at her food, saying little as the rest of us chatted away. At least she would grin and chuckle as we recounted our stories and inside jokes. But, understandably, she was in a somber mood. None of us could fault her that at all.

When my father died, I had been thrust into a deep depression, in much the same way as my mother had. A bottomless pit of despair had sucked me into its mire and refused to relinquish its hold on my soul. My own depression prevented me from giving my mother the support she so desperately needed. And even then, I felt extremely guilty because of it. When she eventually ended her own life, I blamed myself furiously, wholeheartedly, and punishingly. It took years of working with an excellent therapist to help me understand the truth of the situation. It had not been my responsibility to take care of her, quite the opposite. She was the mother, and I the young child. The truth seemed harsh to me at first, but I came to understand. Her death wasn't my fault. She had definitely needed support, but being in the same boat, I was unable to provide that for her. I had been buried in the same dark misery that she was.

In the end, I had been strong enough to overcome it. But she hadn't.

The one upside, if it could be called that, to my family trauma was that I was definitely no longer a stranger to the kind of grief that I clearly saw in Abby now. She was dealing with the very same type of depression that I had dealt with. Who wouldn't be after what she had gone through?

But, whereas my mother had had no friends—she had never been a terribly friendly person—to support her, I did. Besides the therapy, my friends are what helped me get through those joyless, agonizing times. I never thought I could repay them for the love and support they showed me. But here was Abby in need of the same thing. And that's exactly how Corinne, Lorena, and I planned on helping her. We were going to be there for her and give her all the ears for listening, shoulders to cry on, and open arms she needed.

"How's the food?" Lorena asked through a mouthful of salad. "My dad gave me this recipe to try out."

We all complimented her enthusiastically on the meal. It was freaking delicious. Lorena definitely knew how to whip up an excellent meal. I had always been a little jealous of that.

"Everyone brought their swimsuits, right?" I asked, setting my knife and fork down, and heaving a big sated sigh. "We should go swimming tomorrow. The lake looks really nice."

"I bought a new swimsuit just for this!" Corinne exclaimed. "I definitely want to get a nice tan."

"I hope the water isn't too cold," I mused. "I don't think it gets too hot around here."

"But you're going to come in the water with us, right, Corinne?" Lorena asked her.

"Well, there isn't anything dangerous in the lake, is there?" Corinne asked hesitantly. "Remember that one movie Abby made us watch where everyone was eaten by murderous fish or something dumb like that?"

"Yeah, sharks and piranhas," I told her in as serious a tone I could muster. "They're everywhere in that water. We just have to be really careful because the lake is infested with them."

"No, it isn't," Corinne huffed, her eyes narrowing. "Stop joking." She looked around at us, salad slipping off the fork half-way to her mouth. "Is it?"

I stared at her until I couldn't hold a straight face anymore and started laughing, which in turn caused Lorena and even Abby to laugh. Corinne just gave us one of her famous exaggerated pouts.

"That's not funny at all," she grumbled, which just prompted more laughter. She set her fork down and crossed her arms over her chest. "Yes, yes, laugh at gullible Corinne."

"Oh, come on," I said, wiping tears from my eyes. "There's nothing in that lake except probably small, harmless minnows." My laughs faltered for a moment as the memory of the splashing I had heard outside flashed in my mind, but I dismissed it. Maybe a *big* harmless minnow.

"Hmph," was all Corinne said as she turned away in her chair, theatrically sticking her chin high into the air. We all just laughed some more.

A split second later, however, Corinne jumped up from her seat as if somebody had pinched her.

"What was that?" she demanded, a note of real fear in her voice.

"What was what?" I asked, following her unblinking gaze to the large east window. I couldn't see anything outside because of the interior lights and the fire being reflected in the oversized glass. I could only barely make out the vaguest outlines of shadowed trees and a solid darkness beyond that.

"I-I thought I heard something," Corinne said, her voice shaking a little as she stared intently at the window, her eyes never moving away from it. "It sounded like it came from outside."

"Right," Lorena laughed. "A strange noise suddenly outside in the pitch black." She rolled her eyes. "If you're going to try to get us back, maybe wait a bit. Come on, Corinne."

Thump!

The rest of us all jumped to our feet, our attention riveted on the window. Okay, maybe Corinne wasn't bull-shitting us. It sounded as if something had just smacked against the glass. There wasn't enough light outside to see anything, though. I could tell that the moon was covered by thick clouds, which blocked any illumination from shining down.

"It was probably a tree branch or something," I said. "The wind could have blown it against the window." I hesitated, not sure I believed my own explanation.

"Maybe we should take a look?" Abby suggested. She stared at the window with laser-focused eyes.

"Hell no, we shouldn't," Corinne said, backing away and standing behind Lorena. "If you want to go outside looking for things making weird sounds in the night, be my guest. But I'm staying right here. Just don't lead the psycho killer back inside!"

"I'll look," I told them, pleased at how calm I sounded. Of course, I didn't really want to go out there, but if I didn't, we would spend the rest of the night nervously looking over our shoulders and jumping at every little sound the house made. Besides, there was probably nothing out there... I hoped.

"I'll go with you," Abby said matter-of-factly. She wasn't asking for permission.

I hesitated for a second. I had really been expecting Lorena to be the one to offer to come with me. Finally, after a moment, I nodded at Abby and gazed around the room, looking for something to take with me. I needed some sort of weapon just in case. Stepping over to the fireplace, I reached down and grabbed a metal poker from the stand on the hearth.

Abby took the can of pepper spray from her purse. It was something she now carried with her everywhere she went. It had always been on her person ever since the mugging.

Abby slowly opened the front door, its hinges creaking loudly in the stillness. Cold, fresh air rushed in, causing the fire to gutter and dance wildly like it was trying to get away. The sudden chill caused goosebumps to sprout across my arms and legs. I could actually feel the hair on the back of my neck standing on end. I had always thought that was just an expression.

I really don't want to go out there, but I can't chicken out now.

"Are you ready?" Abby asked, her pepper spray held tightly in her hand. Her brown eyes met mine, and I saw there a determination I had never really seen in her before. It was as if she were actually hoping someone was out there.

"Are you sure you want to go with me?" I asked her tentatively.

Would I still have the courage to go out by myself if she decided to stay inside?

Fortunately, she nodded, raising the pepper spray to signal her willingness.

"If there's a wild animal out there, don't mess with it," Lorena said, standing close to Corinne. "Be careful."

I stepped out onto the wide covered porch, the wooden planks groaning under my feet as if I were disturbing their sleep.

At first, I saw nothing beyond my own shadow standing within a rectangle of light on the ground. Abby pulled the door closed behind us with a soft click, and I waited a few seconds for my eyes to adjust to the almost complete blackness that surrounded us. A total lack of streetlamps really made a difference, I realized. I had always taken city lights for granted. I didn't know it was possible for a place to get so dark. How did people live out in places like this? Wouldn't they be wary to go out at night?

When my eyes finally adjusted and could make out the

details of my surroundings, I saw that everything appeared exactly the same as when we had arrived, albeit in the lightlessness of the night.

"Do you see anything?" Abby whispered from close behind me. I could feel her warm breath on my shoulder.

"Not yet," I said as I descended the porch steps and stepped onto the soft grass that covered most of the island. I shivered as a frigid breeze washed over me like I had just walked through a ghost. I probably should have put my jacket on before coming out here.

I thought I had heard something then coming from the direction of the bridge. I took out my phone and turned on its flashlight, shining the beam over that way. But it turned out to be nothing more than the support posts creaking in the water.

I stared at the bridge. There was a patch of shadow that was somehow thicker than the surrounding darkness. A vaguely person-shaped outline standing as still as a statue.

"Hello?" I called out, taking a few steps onto the bridge and bathing the spot with the cone of light from my phone. There was nothing there except for an overgrown tree trunk off to the side, which I remembered passing earlier.

Really? I berated myself. *You're jumping at shadows and inanimate objects? Don't let Corinne find out. You'll never hear the end of it.*

"Who were you talking to?" Abby asked from behind me. If I hadn't clamped my jaw closed, the squeal bulging in my throat would have been set loose for the world to hear.

"Abby!" I heaved her name out after gaining control of my voice once more. "No one." I let out an awkward cackle. "No one. I wasn't talking to anyone. I thought I saw something across the bridge there, but it was nobody."

"Okay," she said, leaving it at that. "Let's keep looking around."

Abby and I cautiously made our way around the house. Through the large window that covered all the first story,

I could clearly see Lorena and Corinne standing by the kitchen table, talking to each other, both their brows furrowed. By the furious movement of their lips, I guessed they were talking in rapid whispers, probably wondering if Abby and I had been eaten by now.

The cold wind caused the bushes and trees that grew in front of the big window to sway gently. The breeze ruffled my hair, making it tickle my back through my thin T-shirt. I knew it was just my imagination overreacting, but I could have sworn the wind had said something. Creepy campfire stories that Abby had regaled me with years ago popped up in my mind.

At that very moment, the clouds drifted apart, uncovering the bright face of the silvery moon far above us in its cradle of stars. Taking advantage of the extra luminescence, I looked around carefully at the scenery, hesitantly prodding at the bushes with my fireplace poker.

"Well, I don't see anything," I said to Abby, who stared off over the lake. "Whatever it was, it must have left."

She didn't say anything, silently watching whatever had grabbed her attention in the water.

"It was probably a raccoon or something," I muttered, but I don't know if she heard me. She hadn't moved an inch. "Want to head back in?"

"Yes," she finally said in an airy voice. "Of course."

When I turned away from her and headed back toward the house, I heard a soft, yet distinct, *crunch* as I stepped on something. Lifting up my boot, I saw a shapeless lump lying in the grass and smothered a disgusted noise that rose in my throat.

"What is it?" Abby asked, turning around and walking over to me. She shone her phone's bright flashlight onto the patch of ground where I had just stepped.

A small bird lay motionless in the grass. It had a little body covered in deep jet-colored feathers, with some bright white across its face that resembled a tiny mask. It was one of those wagtail birds the cashier had mentioned.

The Devil's Eyes, as they were known locally, that had supposedly given the lake its name.

The poor unfortunate bird must have smashed into the window, as birds were wont to do, and broken its neck. Right next to it lay another dead bird, although this one was smaller, featherless, and ugly. It was a baby, still pink and wrinkly, with big bulging eyes and little patches of fine fluff. It looked lamentably pathetic.

"Oh no, poor guys," I said, staring down at the lifeless creatures at my feet. A twinge of sadness came over me. I never wanted to see animals get hurt. And even though it was already dead, I felt guilty for stepping on it. I had felt those teeny hollow bones break under my foot.

Abby pocketed her phone and looked away from the dead birds. Her hands reaching up to cover her face as if trying to prevent me from seeing her expression.

"Abby, what's wrong?" I asked, confused and concerned. Had the dead birds upset her in some way? Had it brought up memories of the mugging somehow? It must have. Seeing those once-living creatures lying dead on the ground. Stupid. I shouldn't have let her come outside with me.

"It's nothing," she said after a few moments, but there was a quiver in her voice as if she were trying to hold back a multitude of sobs. Before I could respond, she quickly walked away from me and returned to the house without saying another word.

I sprinted inside after her, grateful to be out of the cold and back where the warm fire was blazing.

"What was it?" Lorena asked as Abby and I came inside. "Was there something out there?" Her eyes locked onto mine. From the tense expressions that she and Corinne were wearing, I suspected they had been reinforcing each other's fear with dumb speculations.

Abby ignored the question and sat down on the couch, grabbing one of the pillows and holding it tightly to her chest like a life preserver. She stared into the fire, biting her lip and saying nothing. I gave Corinne and Lorena a worried glance as they looked at me with quizzical expressions.

"Abbs?" I said softly, slowing walking over to the couch where she sat. Whatever this was, we could deal with it. Maybe she was having a traumatic flashback or something? I just had to be delicate. "Are you okay?"

Abby burst into tears, weeping heavily into the pillow clutched to her chest.

The rest of us moved to her side and sat down next to her on the couch. I was sure the others were wondering what exactly had upset her so much.

"What happened, Abbs?" Corinne asked, rubbing Abby's back reassuringly.

"You can tell us," Lorena said. "You know you can always tell us anything you need to." She then turned to face me, "What was it you guys found out there?"

"There was a dead bird and its baby on the ground out there," I explained to her. "I guess the baby must have fallen out of one of the trees by the window. It looks like the mom went after it. But from the sound we heard, I suppose the poor mom bird hit the window and broke her neck. The baby must have died from the fall."

"Oh no, little bird," Corinne said. "That really sucks. But it's okay, Abby. Please don't be sad."

"No, Corinne, it's just that—" Abby tried to explain, but another bout of sobbing wracked her body.

I thought it was better that she just get it all out before we tried to get her to talk again.

She wiped her eyes after a few minutes and regained her composure enough to speak. She didn't look any of us in the eye. Her gaze was focused on the fire. "It's just that, it reminded me of... I never told anyone this. I didn't even get to tell Grayson before...before..."

My stomach tightened. What was she getting at? Something she never told us? There was a horrid suspicion in my mind that I knew what she was going to say.

"Only my parents knew because the doctor had to tell

them while I was in the coma," she continued. She blew her nose into a tissue that Lorena had handed her. "I...I was pregnant. I lost the baby because of the attack. Because of those monsters who murdered Grayson. I lost our child. I lost the life growing inside of me all because I just had to fight back..."

I was struck utterly dumb by this revelation, as I'm sure the others were as well. We sat motionless around Abby, looking at each other with stunned and astonished expressions on our faces, mouths agape. Everything inside me felt as if had locked up like rusty machinery. Abby fell into another fit of crying as we all sat speechless. My mind was whirring, trying to find something to say, but all I was drawing were blanks.

Why had she never told us? We were best friends. We were all supposed to confide in each other. How come she had hidden this from us?

A sadness then surged through me like a flood of anesthetic. Hadn't I done the very same thing? I had kept everything to myself when my parents had been taken from me. I knew what it felt like to have all that pain bottled up, feeling like you couldn't speak of those things to anyone.

I understood. I really did. And I'm sure Abby had had her reasons for not telling us that she was going to have a kid. Or that she had lost it.

God...She had been growing a child inside of her. And she had lost it! Its life had been forcefully, brutally... *monstrously* wrenched from this world. I couldn't even imagine how devastating that was for her. I could imagine a lot. And I had experienced many things in my life. But not that.

Watching Abby cry next to me, a thought popped into my head. Did she blame herself for losing the baby? She had fought against her attackers. Did she feel responsible for what happened?

"Oh Abby," I said after moments of stunned silence

filled only with the quiet crying and sniffling of our friend. "God. I'm so sorry. I am so, so sorry." I hugged her tightly, Lorena and Corinne joining in as well.

"Abby," was all Lorena could get out.

"Jesus, no," Corinne said with a whimper. "I'm so sorry, Abbs. I can't even tell you how sorry I am. But you didn't have to hide this from us. We're here for you, babe."

By that time, all of our eyes had become misty as we tried to hold back our own tears.

"I—I know," Abby managed to say in a croaky voice. "Thank you. But I just c-couldn't bear to think...to think about it. I tried pushing it all out of my mind. But I never could." She wiped her tear-stained cheeks. "If only I hadn't fought back, then maybe—"

"This is *not* your fault," Lorena said sternly, tears running freely down both her cheeks. "Don't you even think like that. Those assholes who attacked you are the ones to blame. They did this! If the police ever catch them, I hope they get the death penalty."

"Lorena, please," Abby said, stifling a sniffle, "I don't want to hear or think any more about death. Let's...let's just enjoy our weekend here. Okay? It's a Friday night. We should be enjoying ourselves. You guys brought me all the way out here to have a good time, right? We should be having fun. Can we do that, please?" She blew her nose again and smiled weakly at all of us. "Can we just talk about something else, please? I'd like to do that."

"Of course, we can do that." Corinne told her, "We can do anything you want to."

We all smiled back at her, nodding, though I was still trying to take everything in. My body felt like it had been hit by a truck, my brain smeared on the asphalt.

After we held Abby in a tight embrace for a few more minutes—I didn't really want to let go—I got up to get myself a glass of water. On my way to the kitchen, I glanced out of that large east window that opened up to the darkness outside. I decided I would bury those dead birds somewhere out behind the house in the morning before anyone else got up. I didn't want Abby to see them and be reminded of death again.

I silently promised her that I wouldn't let any more bad memories and sadness ruin this weekend. At least I would try my best. I knew those memories would stick with Abby forever. But they didn't have to dominate her life. The time would come when Abby could live normally again, all this awfulness far in the past. Never forgotten, but no longer sucking her into the abyss.

For now, we were going to do our best to help Abby try to be happy. We'd guide her back to happiness someday.

CHAPTER FIVE

Come, sleep. Dream within the cradle of forever. The realities call. Infinity swirls within all. Consume, remake, corrupt.

After blowing our noses, drying our eyes, and Corinne fixing her mascara, we lapsed into talking. Talking the way we used to years ago when we'd sit up at night in Abby's room until the early hours of morning, discussing school, parents, relationships, and our futures. I missed those talks.

It was close to 10:00 pm when Corinne interrupted the conversation to announce, "Look what I got! Time for s'mores!" and brought out a grocery bag filled with marshmallows, chocolate, graham crackers, and metal skewers.

She set about impaling marshmallows and heating them to the exact amount of toastiness each of us wanted.

"So yeah," she went on saying, continuing the story she had begun earlier as she sat by the fireplace, holding the skewers over the flames. "I'd just moved in with Miles like four months ago when I got promoted at the bank."

"Right, I saw your post online about it," I said, ripping open the chocolate package and graham cracker box and stacking them on paper plates, which I handed to each of them. Corinne seemed to be doing well. It had surprised me when she'd chosen to pursue banking as a career. But despite her ditzy demeanor, math and finance had always been her strengths. Many people found it hard to believe just looking at her. And damn, moving in with her boyfriend. Wow. "How's that been going? Big adjustment for you?"

"It's been pretty great, actually," she replied. "I mean, there's some stuff that he does that can...get under my skin."

"Like what?" Lorena asked, smirking, but then held up a hand. "Wait, let me guess. Does he leave his dirty clothes on the floor right in front of the hamper? Leave the toilet seat up? Leave hair in the sink after he shaves? Doesn't close the cereal box after he eats some? Farts way more than you thought he did?"

"How the hell did you know all that?" Corinne said, handing Lorena a lightly browned marshmallow.

"I fucking live with my dad and three brothers, don't I?" Lorena answered, smooshing the glob of marshmallow onto a chocolate-covered graham before closing it like a sandwich. "Don't worry. My mom can give you some tips on how to whip Miles into shape." She winked, and we all laughed, knowing exactly what she meant.

"Freaking Miles," I said. I've always liked the guy, but... "You've been with him, what? Five years?"

"Mmhm," Corinne replied, handing me my own extra toasted marshmallow. "Yep, five years. Almost six."

"Has he dropped any hints about when he's going to put a ring on it?" I wiggled the fingers of my left hand in front of her face.

Lorena made a high-pitched "oooooh" sound.

"Marriage? Ew. Gross." Corinne smacked my hand away and put on an exaggerated expression of mock disgust and gagged. "That shit is way too grown up. Do I look like I—"

Corinne must have realized what she was saying, because her eyes immediately flicked over to Abby, her instant regret obvious.

"I'm sorry, Abbs. I didn't mean to imply..."

Abby waved her words away. "Oh, no worries. It's fine, really." She leaned forward with a half-smile. "Please, don't worry about me." She took a large bite of on her s'more, focused on not allowing any of the white goo inside to leak out. Once she wiped the mess off her lips, she looked at each of us in turn. "I'm really enjoying all of this. All of us together. Please don't feel like you guys have to walk on eggshells around me. Okay?"

Eggshells. As delicate as tiny bones.

An image of the little Wagtail and its mom lying there outside on the grass, lifeless, flashed through my mind. A shudder passed through me. I heard Abby crunch into her graham cracker, and my stomach writhed a little. I set the rest of my s'more on the plate and pushed it aside. Guilt wormed into me again for having stepped on that mama bird and its baby. They were already dead, but it still bothered me. Probably even more so now because of Abby's revelation.

"Okay," Corinne said. Her cheeks were a bit flushed. "Uh, Lorena, how's school?"

Lorena struggled to swallow the bite of s'more she'd just taken before she could speak. "It going goooood." Melted marshmallow coated her lips.

"You're not going to use that sort of grammar with the kids, right?" Abby joked.

Lorena chuckled. "I'll be perfectly professional," she said. "After this year, I can get my teaching certification, enroll in some prep courses. Hopefully I can find a teacher who will let me assist them so I can get some classroom experience."

We all knew Lorena loved kids. She'd been studying her ass off to be a middle school teacher. And I knew she would love to have one or two kids of her own whenever she found that special someone to start a family with. The news of Abby's loss must have affected Lorena in a much more direct way than it had hit me, since I had never really wanted or even thought about having kids.

"Ready to take on a whole class of hormonal middle schoolers?" Corinne asked, spearing another marshmallow.

"Think you can handle that?"

Lorena barked out a laugh. "I've had plenty of practice over the years dealing with you three," she said. "It was like the universe knew that you all needed an extra mommy to watch over you, take care of you, and save you when you got stuck in knee-deep shit. So it sent me to you as your guardian angel in third grade." She put her hands under her chin and fluttered her eyelashes at us. "Where would you guys be today without me?"

I snorted in response. "Oh fuck off with that," I said, chuckling as I shoved her playfully. But I had to admit it was true. Lorena had always prided herself on being the mother of our little group, and each one of us would have certainly been way worse off had she not befriended us all those years ago.

"Rei..."

I swiveled around in my seat. The hair on the back of my neck stood up. A tingle ran up my scalp. I could have sworn I'd heard someone whisper right behind me. My name? But there was no one. I scanned the room as far as the firelight illuminated. There was nothing I could see that seemed out of the ordinary. So why was my heart racing?

"Rei..."

"Huh?" I turned back toward the others.

"I said what about you, Rei?" Lorena looked at me. "Where are you working these days?"

"Oh." It took me a second to reorient myself. "Uh, I'm still making amazing pizzas at Valentina's," I said as if gloating, then sighed. It was a question I'd been dreading.

"Still?" Corinne asked, then looked ashamed when Lorena gave her a look.

"There's nothing wrong with that," Abby said, patting my leg. "Hey, a stable income is no small thing. And you're doing well in your classes, right?"

"Yeah," I said, glad for Abby's reassurance. "I'm taking computer science classes and trying to get the last of my general eds done. God, I can't believe how much time I wasted fucking around after high school and doing absolutely nothing with my life except drinking and slacking off with Tyler."

"Ty-ler!" my friends shouted in unison, as if only now remembering him.

"Why didn't any of you ever tell me how much of a loser he was?"

"We tried," Lorena said, taking a large bite of s'more as if the gesture made its own statement.

Corinne and Abby nodded, and raised their own s'mores in agreement.

"Whatever happened to old Ty-Ty anyway?" Corinne asked, using her obnoxious nickname for him.

I shrugged. "Hell if I know. I never talked to him again after I dumped him."

"And then came Antonio," Abby said.

"Anto-nio!" Lorena and Corinne shouted.

Corinne giggled. "The pothead, right? The one who spent all day smoking in his dad's basement?"

"Look, I know I don't always have the best judgement, okay?" I glared at her. "But I dumped him too. And you know what? Since ditching those clowns, I feel like my life's been right on track."

"That's great!" Lorena exclaimed. "Good for you."

There was a comfortable lull in the conversation as we enjoyed our snacks.

Then Abby spoke, her voice quiet, almost reflective. "Grayson and I were going to..." But she didn't finish. Tears welled in her eyes, and she bit her lip as it began to quiver.

I took her hand and held it in both of mine. A tense silence settled over all of us and stretched on.

"You know what would go well with these s'mores?" Corinne blurted out. She didn't wait for anyone to answer her question. "Wine!"

"Yes, please," Abby said. She sniffled and gave a soft giggle. "Sounds great."

Corinne jumped up and skipped into the kitchen,

returning with a five-dollar bottle of wine in each hand.

I don't know how many bottles Corinne had brought with her, but she continued bringing them out as soon as we polished one off.

I lost count after we opened our fifth.

Or had it been the sixth?

∾⊰⊱∾

I woke up shivering on the couch the next morning with the sun shining brightly on my face. I sat up, rubbing the sleep out of my eyes and yawning. Corinne was passed out in one of the large squashy armchairs near the smoldering remains of the fire, snoring happily and drooling. I snorted quietly at her smudged lipstick and mascara. Lorena must have made it upstairs to a bed since I could hear her incredibly loud snores thundering down the stairs from above.

I could see no sign of Abby, however. Where had she gone off to? Had she made it upstairs as well? Or was she already awake and exploring our tiny island?

I grabbed my phone. The clock read 11:34 am. We must have stayed up pretty late last night. I usually never slept in, especially not to this hour. My head hurt a little, but other than that I felt fine and ready to start the day. Perhaps my body had decided that I just really needed the sleep.

The hardwood floor felt uncomfortably chilly on my bare feet when I stood up. Running upstairs to the bedroom Abby and I were sharing, I retrieved my fuzzy blue slippers from out of my duffle bag and put them on. No sign of Abby up here either.

Returning downstairs and heading into the kitchen, I rummaged around in the plastic grocery bags and found a can of coffee. I set a pot to percolate and went to find Abby in the meantime.

I had searched the entire first floor and was about to head back upstairs to check again when I saw a flash of movement outside the large east window. I made my way outside through the front door and went around the side of the house. I found Abby sitting quietly in the sand by the lakeshore, once again staring out into the serene, glass-like water. She apparently didn't notice me until I was right beside her, causing her to jump slightly.

"Sorry," I apologized as I sat down next to her in the sand, flashing her a smile. The warm sun felt good on my face. I knew I never got outside enough these days. I was sure I had an unhealthy lack of vitamin D. "I didn't mean to startle you. Is everything alright?"

"Oh yeah, everything's fine," Abby replied casually, wiping some of her hair out of her freckled face. Her eyes looked a little puffy, as if she had been crying not too long ago. I wish I had gotten up sooner.

"Are you sure?" I asked. I didn't want to push too hard, but I knew Abby needed prodding sometimes to get things out of her.

"Yeah, I'm okay," she said. "Everyone was still asleep when I got up, so I came out here to look around. After a while I just felt like sitting and watching the water for a bit."

"It is quite beautiful out here," I remarked, deciding not to ask whether she had been crying. I pulled my knees up to my chest and gazed out across the calm lake.

In the bright light of day, I could see all the way across the perfectly still, greenish-blue water to the other side of Devil's Eyes Lake where a beautiful expanse of tall pines and firs sprawled out in every direction in an explosion of deep emerald. It seemed quite a ways away to the far side of the lake, and I was pretty certain that I could never swim that far. Not that I would ever have to.

My thoughts came back to our private little island. It was just so cool. It was small enough that I doubted any other structures besides the house could be built here. But it was large enough and far enough away from land that it felt like you were in another world. A world you could call all your own. And it was all my own. I owned it!

"Such a stunning place," I murmured mostly to myself. "Really takes your breath away."

I closed my eyes and leaned back to let the heat of the sun warm me up, resting my upper body flat on the sandy ground. I kicked off my slippers, and stretched out my legs in front of me, my toes almost touching the water. I felt quite content here. This was a good place to relax and get away from all the hubbub and rushing around in my everyday life. Even if it was only for this weekend. Maybe on my next vacation, I could take an entire week off from work and come up here.

I was drowsily cognizant of the gentle lapping of the water a few inches from where we rested, the gentle rustling of the leaves each time a small breeze passed over us, and the subtle intermittent creaking of the wooden bridge, reminding me of a grumbling old man trying to get out of bed. I inhaled deeply, filling my lungs, feeling them expand with a wonderful stretch. My nose filled with the lovely scent of fresh vegetation, clean air, and—

A painful fit of coughing and gagging suddenly overtook me, choking me for a few seconds. My head swam as I quickly sat up, my eyes watering profusely. I felt as though I wanted to vomit everywhere.

Abby was startled out of her daydreaming by all the sudden noise. "Are you okay?" she asked me, patting me on the back, a look of concern on her face.

"Yeah-yeah, I'm fine," I sputtered, finally regaining my composure, taking in large lungfuls of air.

Confused, I rewound my memories back several seconds. What had just happened? I had been instantly, though briefly, overwhelmed by the stench of something terrible, as if I had inhaled a chunk of rotting, festering death itself. I had never smelled anything remotely like it before in my life; something so repugnant and so rank that I nearly spilled the contents of my stomach as the odor had infected my nostrils. I could even still taste the rot in my mouth.

Fortunately, it had only been for a brief instant. The smell had come and gone so quickly, I couldn't even be sure that I hadn't just imagined it. I couldn't have, could I? How could I have hallucinated something like that?

Before I could say anything more, I noticed Lorena and Corinne striding across the yard toward Abby and me. They carried large beach towels and had their bikinis on under flowy cover-ups.

"Hey, you two. Who's ready for a dip?" Corrine asked with a blissful grin. She pulled off her sarong. "We definitely picked a good time to come. No rain or gloom in sight."

I looked her up and down. I had left Corinne disheveled and drooling on that chair not too long ago. But as always, I was stunned by how quickly and perfectly she could make herself up. It was like her superpower. Hair, makeup, all done in her "all-natural, beach-style" look that suited her for a day of relaxing in the sun by the water.

"Damn. You need some sun," I commented, laughing. I knew, as probably did everyone else, that it was my own self-consciousness trying to find some flaw in Corinne's perfection.

"Hey, your legs are pretty pasty there, too, Rei," she retorted, one haughty eyebrow raised in an arch, not losing her composure for a second.

"So, you're going in the water, then?" I asked, shielding my eyes from the sunlight as I looked up at her from where I sat.

"Of course, I am," she said, then pointed to her face with a manicured finger. "Water-proof makeup, girl. It will last all day."

"I meant, I thought you were scared of going in the water," I said with a snigger as she slathered sunscreen on her arms and legs. "Remember? All the piranhas in there?"

"Pfft, I know you guys were just joking," she said, closing the sunscreen bottle with a snap. Her lips pursed as if she had just eaten something sour. "I know there aren't any piranhas or sharks or whatever other stupid things you said were in there."

Lorena and I couldn't help but laugh.

"Oh, screw you guys," Corinne huffed, though I could see she was trying not to let herself smile. She laid out her towel on the sand next to Lorena's.

"Abbs, come on, let's go get changed," I said, tapping her on the shoulder. I stood up, shaking the sand off my feet, and took a step toward the house. "Come on. Swim time!"

Abby didn't answer, however. I turned around to see if she had even heard me. She still stared fixedly at the water. But now, she was rocking back and forth. I thought I heard her muttering something under her breath but couldn't make out any words. Her back was to me, so I couldn't tell for sure.

"Abbs?" I said, raising my voice a notch.

Lorena and Corinne stared at her now as well, concern clearly etched onto their faces.

I felt an icy dread spread through me. Was Abby alright?

"Yes," Abby said flatly, not looking at anyone. "You are right, of course."

It felt like she was responding to someone else. She abruptly stood up as if a jolt of electricity had run beneath her. But instead of turning back toward the house, she kicked off her shoes and stripped off all her clothes.

"I am ready," she said in an expressionless voice, then turned to face us.

I felt my face become warm and my eyes widen. Growing up together, I had seen Abby in various states of undress several times, having baths together as kids, changing in high school locker rooms, trying on clothes in department store changing rooms, and going midnight skinny dipping at summer camps. But this was just so unexpected and very unlike her, especially with that utterly blank look on her face.

The many still-pink scars from the injuries Abby had

sustained in the brutal attack were clearly visible all over her body. The image nearly overwhelmed me as I stared at her. Something stood out to me, though. Was it my imagination, or did some of those scars resemble...patterns?

We gaped at her for a flabbergasted moment until Corinne, thankfully, ended the awkward silence. "Woo, Abby," she cheered, a mischievous grin trying to cover up her embarrassment at the scene. "You going all hippie on us now? Haha! Well, if it makes you happy, go for it!"

Abby smiled, as if only now seeing her three friends, and proceeded to turn around and run into the water with bounding steps. She splashed at us with her hands when she had gotten waist-deep into the water.

Giggling like a child, she went out farther and dove, coming back up after a few seconds. "Come on in, guys!" she called out as her head broke the surface, her wet hair plastered against her face. "Corinne, Lorena, Rei! I thought we were all going to go swimming? What are you waiting for? It's nice in here!" She grinned and splashed at us again. Her voice sounded odd—like her mirth was forced.

Corinne and Lorena exchanged glances and chuckled uneasily before following Abby into the water. I hesitated for a second, then made up my mind. I ran back into the house and up the stairs, taking them two at a time. I pulled my two-piece swimsuit out of my bag and hurriedly changed into it. By the time I returned to the lakeshore, Abby, Lorena, and Corinne had already swum farther out, splashing water at each other and laughing loudly just like we used to.

My previous misgivings ebbed away. It all looked like a lot of fun, and fond memories of summer camps and pool parties danced through my head.

I strolled over to the edge of the water and laid out my towel on the toasty sand. What Abby had just done kept running through my mind. I had never seen her act so weird before. So...uninhibited. Maybe this was just the side-effect of some medication she had been prescribed.

Or maybe she *needed* to be prescribed something because of what had happened to her and Grayson. I know *I* would have definitely needed something to get over the constant fear of a repeat attack, and the crushing grief of losing a husband—and child.

Abby had suffered some minor brain trauma from the attack as well. But the doctor had seemed confident that there would be no permanent damage. It hadn't even been half a year since then, though. Had the doctor been wrong? Had we just witnessed Abby have some sort of mental episode?

"Rei, come on already!" Abby called out before diving back under the water and resurfacing, spitting water out of her mouth like a stone fish on a fountain. "Hurry up! Get that ass in gear!" Her tone was the pseudo-whining one she had often affected to coerce me into doing something.

"I'm coming, I'm coming," I answered with a laugh, feeling a touch of relief at this momentary glimpse of the Abby of old. Walking toward the water's edge, I gathered up my hair and tied it up into a ponytail before dipping my foot into the blue water. It was refreshingly cool, not too cold at all. It was perfect.

I waded in, the water enveloping me as if it were pulling me into an embrace. Pretty soon I was submerged up to my neck, splashing around with the others and laughing like we were all children again before Abby's world came crashing down into a depressive heap. It felt wonderful, familiar, and comforting. All my anxieties and worries of normal life seemed to be melting away.

After about twenty minutes, we all floated about on our backs about sixty feet from the island, relaxing and taking in the sun with our eyes closed.

"This place is so quiet and peaceful," Lorena said, drifting lazily on the lake's surface, the water droplets on her skin reflecting the sunlight like thousands of glittering diamonds. "I'm so glad that nobody else knows about it, just us. We should make this like our vacation house. You know? Our own private retreat, for when we need to get away from life. I really do like it here." Her voice trailed off dreamily.

"That would be nice," Corinne agreed. "You guys wouldn't mind if I brought Miles up here on a future trip, would you? He's always talking about going camping. But I think he'd settle for this. This beats sleeping in tents on the ground any day."

"I really like this place too," Abby said with a wistful sigh, floating beside Corinne. "I wish we could all stay here forever."

I tensed momentarily as she spoke. Had Lorena or Corinne heard the brief emptiness in Abby's voice? Or was I just being paranoid? Maybe I was still weirded out by her out-of-character actions earlier.

Taking a deep breath of clean, fresh, pine-scented air, I forced myself to relax once more. I stared up at the blue sky, watching the small clouds slowly roll along above us, when I heard a loud splash. I flailed my limbs and righted myself, as did Corinne and Lorena.

Abby had disappeared from view.

"Where did she go?" Lorena asked, looking around with concern.

We all treaded water to keep ourselves upright as we scanned the surface for any hint of our friend.

"She's probably under the water playing a prank on us or something," I said, though I knew I didn't sound convincing. I tried to look down into the water but couldn't see anything except leaves, twigs, and dirt swirling around my pale legs.

Jesus, I really do need more sun.

I realized that we had floated out into a much deeper area of the lake. Though the water was still pretty clear here, the bottom wasn't visible at all.

Without warning, Abby's auburn hair shot through the surface, and she emerged, gulping for air.

Relief washed over me, and I saw the others visibly relax as well.

She coughed out a mouthful of water. "I think there's something down there under us," she said with a serious tone, pushing the hair off her forehead. She looked from one of us to the other. "I saw something."

"Oh ha-ha, very funny," Corinne drawled sarcastically, rolling her eyes. She used a finger to flick some water at Abby. "I'm not falling for that again. Come on, Abbs. How gullible do you really think I am?"

"No, I'm not joking right now," Abby said, a look of utter sincerity on her face. "Really! There is something down there. I heard it."

"I didn't hear anything," Lorena said. "We've all been here with you, and the only sounds have been birds and some bugs flying around."

"That was all I heard too," I said.

How could Abby have heard something coming from *under* the water? That wasn't possible, was it? Wouldn't the water have suppressed the sound?

"I'm going to go look at it again," Abby told us, taking a deep breath before diving back down once more. She disappeared below the surface before we had time to say anything else.

"What do you think she saw down there?" Corinne asked, a hint of growing anxiety in her voice. She kept glancing around her as if expecting some lake monster to appear and drag her under. "You guys don't really think she found something, do you?"

"It's probably just an old boot that looks like her grandpa," I replied, giggling with Lorena. "Remember that picture of him in her dad's study?"

"Oh my God," Lorena said, laughing. "His skin was so leathery. He really did look like a boot. But to be fair, my grandpa kind of looked the same."

We all laughed loudly, but our merriment quickly died.

We weren't amused at all when Abby had not resurfaced after a few moments. We started to worry, looking at each other hoping a solution would present itself. There was no way she could have held her breath for so long down there. I glanced up toward the shore to see if perhaps she had swum back to the island, but there was no sign of her. Panic bloomed inside my chest.

Deciding I had to do something, I drew in as much air as I could and put my face under the water. It wasn't super clear, and bits of vegetation and debris floated around like insects lazily hovering about. The bottom of the lake was too far down to see clearly. All I could make out was vague darkness with no hint of Abby or any human form. I realized I had no idea how deep the lake actually was.

"I don't see her anywhere," I gasped as I came back up for air. "Abby!" I shouted. "Abby, you out there? Can you hear me? Guys, help me look!" The other two frantically nodded their heads.

We all started calling Abby's name and swam in different directions, diving under the water every so often to look for any signs of our missing friend.

Abby, what the hell are you doing? If this is a joke, this isn't funny. But even so...Please, please, please be a joke.

"Abby!" I called out after I had surfaced once more, choking on a mouthful of water. My voice was hoarse from yelling, and my heart now percussed painfully in my chest, beating against its cage of ribs like a bird that frantically sought freedom.

Crazy thoughts swirled through my head. *Was* there really something in the lake? Had it done something to her? What could there possibly be?

No, that is completely ridiculous. There are no lake monsters in here preying on us like in some movie.

Was Abby trying to kill herself? No. I absolutely refused to let myself believe that she would do that, especially here, surrounded by her friends. I knew Abby too well and knew she would never hurt those she loved by doing such a thing. She knew it would utterly traumatize us and completely destroy her parents. But if she wasn't in her right mind...

Frantically drawing in as much air as my lungs could hold, I dove into the water again, trying to reach the bottom. I still didn't know how deep this lake was. How far down could it possibly go down? This wasn't the ocean we were swimming in.

The farther down I went, the colder the water became, as if I now approached the entrance to some frigid underworld. It was gloomier and murkier down here, but enough sunlight still penetrated to illuminate my pale body in stark contrast to the thick mud. After a few moments, I touched the silty bottom. I swam around, trying to expel the air in my lungs in short bursts so I could stay under longer. The water felt icy and gritty against my exposed eyes, but I kept them open, examining everything within my field of view.

Just then, I felt something supple and soft brush lightly past my leg. My body instinctively tried to emit a scream, but all that came out of my mouth was a muffled yelp and a trail of rising bubbles. All of my air was now gone. My emptied lungs burned and ached. I headed up toward the surface, desperate for air.

I breached the surface, choking and gasping for air. "Lorena! Corinne! There's something over here!" I managed to yell at the other two, but before they could respond, I had re-inflated my lungs with fresh air and gone back down into those murky depths once more in search of whatever had touched me. It had to be Abby, right?

I dove straight down to the bottom with as much speed as I could force out of my tiring limbs. Whatever had touched my leg had felt like something alive. It could have been Abby. God damn it. Why had I panicked? Why had I left? So stupid of me. I couldn't let Abby drown down there.

I finally reached the bottom a second time and looked desperately around for any signs of my friend. A few feet from me, through the murk and gloom, I saw a head bobbing with the gentle movements of the water, long auburn hair floating tranquilly, like seaweed, around an expressionless freckled face. I almost gasped in surprise but managed to keep my mouth shut this time, lest I lose my air again. My feet kicked off from the sandy bottom and I launched myself forward, moving as if I swam through molasses. I finally wrapped my arms around Abby's nude and scarred body. She didn't seem to be conscious, but when I tried hauling her up, I couldn't pull her away, like she was attached to something.

As my lungs burned for lack of oxygen, I frantically searched to see if Abby was caught on something. My eyes landed on a strange object. In her hands was what appeared to be a large glass jar that she held in a tight, vice-like grip. The thing seemed to be stuck, trapped between several small white rocks that protruded from the sandy bottom like the grasping claws of some creature. I tried prying Abby's hands away from the jar, but to no avail. Even though she appeared to be unconscious, her fingers remained securely fastened around it and she wouldn't let the thing go. I yanked and pulled at her hands, trying to peel her fingers away. But her grip was just too strong, so I did the only thing I could think of: I began furiously kicking at the finger-like rocks hoping that I could dislodge the jar from their grasp.

I was completely out of oxygen, and my chest felt as if a fire blazed uncontrollably inside of it. But I wasn't going to let either of us drown down here. Battling increasing panic, I kicked as hard as I could at the damn rocks. It was at that moment that I felt the bottom of my left foot explode with a sharp pain. Crimson blood clouded the already-turbid water around me.

Fortunately, Abby's body lurched upward as the jar pulled free from the white rocks, and I was finally able to haul her away from the bottom.

It was unbelievable how heavy Abby seemed to be as I swam upward. I had to marshal all of my strength to drag her with me. My chest blazed with agony, and my cut foot throbbed as I kicked wildly trying to get both of us to the surface. My arm holding onto Abby ached terribly from gripping so hard. My free arm was exhausted and sore as I desperately tried to pull us to the surface for blessed air.

I had to keep going, but my body protested every move; it had reached its limit. I felt that my muscles would just give up at any moment and we would both sink all the way back down to our deaths. I could clearly see the surface, but I didn't know if I was going to make it. I couldn't let go of Abby and let her drown.

It was just...right there...Fresh air was waiting for me to breathe it in. But I was making less progress with each second that elapsed. Time seemed to slow down with each stroke. The pain in my chest urged me to breathe in, almost as if it didn't matter that it would be drowning water that filled my lungs. My arms and legs were going to fail soon. Abby was too much dead weight. I just couldn't...

Two pairs of hands grabbed me, just as my vision began to darken, and hauled me up into bright daylight. I emerged from the water and took in the deepest, most wonderful breath of my life. I never imagined air could taste so sweet. Corinne and Lorena shouted like maniacs, but I couldn't understand any of the words spilling from their mouths like machinegun fire. I felt one of them drag me all the way to shore and lay me down on the hot sand. I looked over to see Corinne dragging Abby out of the water like a drowned child. That damn glass jar was still clutched tightly in her hands.

"Abby, can you hear me?" Corinne yelled shrilly, her eyes wide, and her scraggly hair making her look absolutely crazy. There was no response from Abby, though.

"Watch out," Lorena said, moving Corinne aside and bending over Abby's motionless body. "Fuck. I can't hear any breathing." She proceeded to administer CPR, compressing Abby's chest in a precise rhythm.

I could only lay on the ground, exhausted and shaking, as I watched Lorena trying to resuscitate Abby. I gurgled up the water that had made its way down my throat. I saw

Corinne begin to cry, her hands clenched together as if in prayer.

There was a moment of silence when I thought Lorena had given up, but then Abby gave a ragged cough and jerked upward, retching up water all over herself. She gave a horrible, painful-sounding gasp for breath.

"Thank you, Lorena," she croaked after vomiting even more water all over the sand.

"Oh my God in heaven, are you okay?" Lorena nearly shrieked. "What the hell happened? You almost died!" She sat down beside Abby. Her whole body was shaking uncontrollably.

Corinne wordlessly wrapped a towel around Abby's shoulders and helped her stay upright.

I crawled over to them. "Abby, what the fuck were you doing down there?" My voice was hoarse, though I didn't know whether from fear, anger, exhaustion, or my near drowning. I pointed accusingly at the jar in her hands. "What the hell is that thing? You almost got yourself killed over a jar! Why? Why did you do that?"

Abby looked around at us, clutching the glass jar closer to her chest like a child with her favorite doll. The jar appeared to be completely filled with very dirty, opaque water that had a rotten, greenish-brown hue to it. Little bits of vegetation, sand, and dead insects floated around inside.

"I had to get to her," Abby said looking at each of us. She appeared confused as if she didn't understand why we were so upset.

"What does that mean, Abbs?" Corinne asked in a quivering voice.

"I heard her down there," Abby continued to say as she looked fondly down at the jar. "She was in a lot of pain. She was calling to me."

CHAPTER SIX

Blackness envelopes all. The radiant light withers and rots within the endless depths of frigid darkness. The light shines brightly but blinds the foolish with its fulgent wrath. By lurking in the dark, one can see the true souls of others. The shadow is created by light, but the shadow is the rebel, the resistance to the luminosity. Tendrils of shade seep over the worlds, battling against that which aims to illuminate totality. The light may fester much among the infinite realities, but the emptiness shall prevail. Be not of the accursed and damned, but of the mighty conquerors.

After everyone had caught their breath, we trudged up from the lakeshore to the house where we could sit on something more comfortable than the gritty, sunbaked sand. The four of us dripped water all over the floor and furniture, but that was the least of my worries. I wanted to make sure that Abby was truly unhurt, and I needed her to explain what she had been doing down in that water.

I got some antiseptic and a clean roll of gauze from the first aid kit I always kept in the car to clean and wrap the stinging gash on the bottom of my foot. I then limped over to where the other three sat on the chairs and sofa in the living room.

For what seemed like a long time we all sat motionless in our seats, not saying a word, Abby just in her towel, the rest of us still in our wet swimsuits. I could still feel myself trembling, but it wasn't from being cold.

Finally, Lorena broke the silence.

"Abbs, I need to ask you about what you said outside," she said slowly, her voice calm despite the strain she must have been feeling at the moment. "What exactly did you mean when you say you heard something "calling" to you? Do you need to tell us anything, or do you need help? Is there something we should know? Come on, talk to me, Abbs. Do you think it was that jar? Was that calling to you?" Lorena pointed to the dirty glass container clutched tightly in Abby's lap. "Is there something in there?"

Corinne, Lorena, and I eyed the mysterious jar suspiciously. All I could see was the muddy water swirling around inside the confines of the glass. The water in the jar wasn't the clean, palatable water of the lake. Not at all. Rather, it was thick with sludge, dead insects, and decaying debris, obscuring any other contents it might be hiding.

"She wanted me to find her and bring her up to the surface," Abby said curtly with a casual shrug. "She was calling out to me. It was so loud and clear. She told me that she was in so much pain and that I could help her. That I could save her. Oh, poor sweetie." She then caressed the jar, running light fingers down its grimy side affectionately, her face set in an expression that made the hairs on my arms and the back of my neck stand on end.

"Okay, so you heard something when we were out swimming?" Lorena asked, glancing at Corinne and me. "Abby, how could you hear something deep in the water?"

"I don't know," Abby replied, looking back up, her brow knitted as if struggling to explain not only to us, but to herself as well. "I didn't hear her with my ears, really. It was more like...Well, it was more like I heard it in my head. I think. Does that make sense?" She looked down at her feet and wiggled her toes for a moment like she had just considered something before looking back up at us. "You guys didn't hear her at all?"

"No," we all answered in unison. I was positive I hadn't heard anyone, or anything. This did not make any sense at all. My head pounded with a headache.

"What about last night?" Abby continued, looking a bit frustrated. "That was the first time she called out to me. I just didn't know where she was yet. She was too weak to tell me." She met my eyes directly. "Rei, you heard her, right? You were there."

The memory of last night, standing out by the water, hearing that strange breeze, raced through my mind.

"No," I said. "I'm sorry, Abbs. I didn't hear anything last night except for the wind blowing."

"I haven't heard anything except for the usual noises of nature, like bugs and stuff," Lorena said, forcing a chuckle.

Corinne remained silent, eyes cast downward in thought.

"But you guys *must* have heard her," Abby insisted, a look of utter puzzlement on her face. "Her voice was so loud out there in the water. She was screaming! She was in so much pain, you guys. So much torment." She looked ready to cry at the thought. "I rescued her. I couldn't leave her down there. What kind of monster would I be if I did?" Her expression quickly changed to one of joy. "But she's so happy now that I saved her. Don't you think?"

Corinne, Lorena, and I exchanged more troubled glances with each other. I knew we were probably all thinking the exact same thing: Should we have brought Abby here? Had the attack damaged Abby's mind more than the doctors had initially thought? Did Abby need professional help if she wasn't already seeing someone?

"You keep referring to the jar as 'she,'" I said hesitantly. I truly wasn't sure I wanted to hear the answer. "Can you tell us exactly what, or uh, who, you rescued? Is there some...one in there?" Was I just playing into Abby's delusions?

Abby said nothing. She only held up the grimy jar filled with the sludge in response to my questions. I didn't know what to make of it. It appeared to be a rather ordinary glass jar, about half the size of my head, but the rusty lid—secured with two iron clamps caked with calcified gunk—was made of what looked like very old, pitted metal. Weird.

As Abby lifted it up, the turbid, greenish-brown liquid swirled around inside, so thick with obscuring crap that light couldn't even shine all the way through it. For a split second, I thought I saw something bobbing around inside. Something fleshy and bloated. Corinne made a disgusted noise in her throat.

"Is-Is there something in there?" Lorena whispered. I couldn't tell if she was actually asking or just nervously talking to herself like she sometimes did.

"She's been waiting for a long, long time to come out of that lake," Abby said with a strange and disturbing smile that stretched across her face, distorting her features. I had known Abby practically all my life and she had always had the warmest and sweetest smile of anyone I had ever met. But the half-crazed grimace that played across her lips at that very moment sent a frigid dose of anxiety coursing through my entire body.

For almost ten minutes we all sat there in silence, the three of us exchanging worried looks, or watching Abby lovingly cradle the filthy jar in her arms as if it were a baby, holding it close to her chest. Every so often I could hear her making soft cooing noises at the thing.

Finally, Corinne stood up, declaring loudly that it was time to get out of their swimsuits and into something dry, especially Abby, who was still just wearing a towel. Lorena and I nodded our agreement. I was happy someone had given me an excuse to get away from the macabre scene for a few minutes. I needed time to think about what was going on.

After we had all changed into clean, dry clothes, we sat across the room on the lounge chairs, staring out of the large east window. Abby had also gotten dressed, and was now curled up on the couch on the other side of the split living room, one hand on the dirty jar that she still held close to her. I didn't want that thing on the furniture, but I wasn't going to argue with Abby at that moment. There were much more serious issues at hand.

As I sat on one of the cushy lounge chairs, Lorena and Corinne shared the other. Through the window I could see several of those Devil's Eyes birds flittering around happily outside among the trees, as if they had not a care in the world.

Devil's Eyes, I thought. *What a dumb nickname. These little wagtails are adorable.*

"We should get rid of that nasty jar," Lorena leaned over and whispered to me, taking pains to be sure Abby couldn't hear. "I don't know what's in there, but I don't think it's just lake water. Who knows what kind of bacteria that sludge is carrying. We could all get some disease if that thing is opened. I don't want any of us ending up in the hospital after what was supposed to be a fun, relaxing vacation."

"Yeah, I second that," Corinne said with a pinched look of disgust. "That thing's fucking disgusting. What if there's like a head in there or something else just as gross?"

"Oh, stop it, Corinne," Lorena said, poking at her playfully. "There's no severed head in that thing, or any other body parts. It's probably just some garbage, like a jar of rotting food that someone dropped in the lake fifty years ago. Abby just happened to find it when she was swimming. She didn't hear it "calling" to her, like she said. She's just a little emotional and... unstable right now, I guess. Hell, I would probably in a worse state than she is if I had gone through all the awfulness that she has recently. I can't even begin to imagine the toll it took on her. And is still taking on her."

Corinne and I simply nodded our heads solemnly.

"But," Lorena continued, raising a finger to command our attention again. "We still need to get that jar away from her. I don't know why, but her mind is becoming attached to that thing for some reason. Plus, even with the lid on it, it kind of stinks. And, like I said, we can't allow her to open it. We don't know what hazardous things might be inside. And I don't want to have to clean it up if it gets everywhere." She shuddered.

"I suppose we can try to get it away from her tonight," I suggested. I glanced over the back of the lounge chair to make sure Abby wasn't listening to us. She was still lying down on the couch, her eyes closed. I turned back around. "When she goes to sleep tonight, we can take it and throw it back in the lake, or bury it somewhere around here. Whatever. As long as it's out of this house and out of her reach."

"That sounds good," Corinne replied, looking relieved.

"Yes, it's a plan," Lorena said. "Tonight."

Abby's behavior became increasingly weirder throughout the rest of the day. She frequently stood in front of the large east window, staring with a blank expression out in the direction of the lake, her fingertips caressing the jar she held cradled in her arm like it was some sort of pet. At other times, she would sit on the porch muttering softly to it in hushed whispers, as if she didn't want us to overhear whatever secret conversation the jar and she were having. She had even taken it to the bathroom with her and showered with it. I could hear her singing children's songs to it through the first-floor bathroom door.

Abby was cracking up. There was no other explanation for her behavior. Unless...there actually *was* something inside that jar speaking to her. Had it called out to her through some psychic means to rescue it from the lake? I shook my head at the notion. Of course not. That was ridiculous. Abby didn't need me to start believing her fantasies. What she needed was professional help.

Lorena, Corinne, and I had gathered in the kitchen later that afternoon to talk without Abby. Our friend was deteriorating much faster that I had expected. The creepiness of the situation was increasing at an alarming rate.

"We need to get that thing away from her *now*," I said, agitatedly pacing back and forth in front of the refrigerator. "I don't think we can wait until tonight to do it. We can't waste any more time. Have you watched her? Have you seen what she's been doing with that jar? It looks like she's getting more and more unstable. It's frightening me."

"Yeah, I've seen her," Corinne said as she leaned against the counter, her arms crossed. "She's going mental. She's freaking talking to that thing like it's alive. You know, maybe that jar is leaking and giving off some sort of hallucinogenic fumes? That's a thing, right? She's breathing them in and they're messing with her head. Making her loopy." She shuddered, and neither Lorena nor I could dismiss the notion or offer a better explanation.

Lorena stared down at the tiled floor of the kitchen. She had always been the first to defend someone whom she felt had been ganged up on, especially if it was one of us that was the target. But I knew we were all in accord at that moment.

"You're right," Lorena said, her voice tinged with a hint of sadness. She rubbed the bridge of her nose with her thumb and forefinger. "We must get the jar away from her. It really is messing with her head too much."

"Then it's settled." I motioned for the others to follow me. "Come on. Let's go find her."

We looked around the first floor but there was no sign of Abby or her precious jar. It seemed very unlikely that we could have lost track of her in such a small area. Lorena decided to check around upstairs, while Corinne looked out front by the car and the bridge. I made my way past the staircase and down the small hallway to the door leading to the basement. None of us had gone down there, we had had no reason to. It was probably full of dust, dirt, and cobwebs. Nothing we wanted to deal with. But if Abby were down there for whatever unhinged reason, I had to check.

Grasping the knob, I found that the door was unlocked. I pulled it open a few inches and abruptly stopped. It was as if someone had just poured a bucket of frigid cold water directly down my spine, instantly freezing me. I rubbed my arms in an effort to melt the ice that had been injected into my veins and dispel the goosebumps that had formed on my arms.

I shut the door with a slam.

What was that all about? I wondered. I had felt utterly and inexplicably terrified of going down there. But why? Maybe Abby's head wasn't the only one being messed with. This whole situation had me more unnerved than I had first thought.

I reached out again to touch the doorknob but again snatched my hand back before my fingertips reached it. Now my palm felt hot, sweaty. I felt my breathing increase rapidly, like I couldn't hold air inside of my lungs. I wondered if I might be having some sort of panic attack. I hadn't had one of those in years. I dearly hoped they weren't coming back.

Before I could contemplate my odd reaction further, Corinne came down the hallway with Lorena in tow.

"I found her," Corinne said, frowning, her lips pursed. "She's outside. And she's doing some weird shit."

Corinne led us outside and around to the rear of the house. I hadn't been over to this side of our little paradise yet. I saw a small copse of spruce trees near the ridge of the island that overlooked the northern bank. Resting in front of those trees was a weathered stone slab on top of a stone platform about four feet high and about six feet in length. Its sides were deeply carved with all sort of strange markings or glyphs that resembled nothing I'd ever seen before. Who had put this here? Was this thing some sort of altar?

I pushed those thoughts aside. What demanded my focus at that moment was Abby. She had set the jar on top of this strange stone altar thing and had knelt down in front of it as if in prayer. I could see that her head was bowed, eyes shut, and her arms clasped to her chest in an X formation, each hand grasping a shoulder. Her lips moved furiously, but no words issued forth, or at least none that I could hear.

"Hey, Abby?" Lorena said, her voice sounding calm. She took a few measured steps toward Abby's genuflecting form. Lorena seemed hesitant to get close, and I couldn't blame her. But this was our friend. We had never been afraid of her.

Abby didn't seem to notice us, however, and just kept on doing whatever crazy thing she was doing. Was she merely ignoring us?

"Abbs," I echoed, walking up beside Lorena. My eyes darted toward the jar. Again, for a brief moment, I thought I could see something bobbing around in the murky water. I looked back at Abby. "Could you stop that for a moment, Abbs?" I tried to sound stern, though I didn't quite achieve the effect I wanted. "Please? We need to talk to you right now. It's important."

Still, Abby made no sign of acknowledgment. Could she even hear us? Or was she in some sort of trance? Was this a symptom of some sort of psychotic break?

"Hey, Abby girl," Corinne half-shouted, exuding forced cheerfulness. But her expression was one of worry tinged with annoyance. She started waving her arms. "Hello? Hello! Earth to Abbs! Hey, we're talking to you."

"Can't you see you are interrupting me?" Abby finally replied in a low tone, still not looking up at us. There was an anger, a disgust, in her voice that I hadn't heard come out of her ever before.

"Interrupting what?" Lorena asked, feigning interest.

"The Arch-Githya is in a lot of pain," Abby said with increasing irritation, her eyes still shut. "I am trying to ease her suffering. But until Mother Luminescence arrives to help, I cannot do much. Now stop distracting me from my duty. The Githya needs me."

I tried to wrap my head around everything Abby had

just said. What on earth was she talking about? What the fuck did any of that mean? She really was going off the deep end.

"What the hell is a Githya?" Corinne asked turning an inquiring look on Lorena and me, but we both just shrugged.

"I've never heard the word before," Lorena said, scratching her head. "Abbs, what does that word mean?" Her tone inflected a deep curiosity that her expression utterly lacked.

"This is stupid," Corinne cut in, rolling her eyes. She took a few steps past Lorena and me, her determination obvious. "Abby, snap out of it."

Corinne had reached out to grab the dirty glass jar, when her hand was stopped short midway there. Abby had taken hold of Corinne's arm with alarming speed. And I had never seen such a hateful look expressed on Abby's face in all the years we had been friends. It scared me in a way I couldn't describe properly.

"Don't you ever fucking dare touch her, Corinne," Abby growled, opening her eyes and slowly turned toward her like a turret taking aim.

Out of nowhere, Abby punched Corinne hard in the stomach, causing her to double over and crumple to the ground, her face reflecting shock and agony, the wind knocked completely out of her.

Lorena and I stood still for a long moment, completely stunned at what we had just witnessed.

"You think you're worthy to touch her with your filthy, blasphemous hands?" Abby sneered, her teeth bared at Corinne like an animal. She spat venom with every syllable. "You have no idea what's going on. No idea what's coming. The truth is too much for your simple minds."

Snapping out of my stunned daze, I ran over to Abby and held her back as she prepared to hit Corinne again, where she now rolled around on the grass, clutching her stomach in pain. Lorena went to Corinne, kneeling down and helping Corinne to sit up. For a minute there, Corinne looked like she was going to throw up.

"What the fuck?" I demanded of Abby, whom I had difficulty holding back. I wanted to get her back into the house, but I was surprised at the strength she was demonstrating. I wasn't sure how long I could hold on to her. "Corinne is your damn friend! You hit her!"

"She is unworthy!" Abby snarled, spit flying from her gnashing teeth. "She was going to take her away from me!"

Abby broke out of my grasp to run over to the stone altar. She grabbed her jar and stalked away, all the while glaring at Corinne.

Halfway to the house, Abby froze in mid-step. She lifted the glass jar to her ear like she was listening for something. She nodded a few times before turning back to look at us.

"She says she will see you all soon," Abby said, smirking, then walked through the back door and disappeared into the house.

CHAPTER SEVEN

Do not ever doubt the Master of Totality. You have seen the truth, the one path. Those who are blind shall be guided by your hand, your tongue, and your blade. Violence is not only the answer, but a necessity.

Abby stalked off into the house with her damn jar, hopefully to cool off. I thought about going after her, but instead rushed to help Lorena escort a teary-eyed, whimpering Corinne back into the house where we sat her on the couch.

"She..." Corinne wheezed.

"You're fine," I told her, patting her back. "You're not injured. It's not that bad."

"You're not the one who got beaten up!" she protested. "It hurts! I could have internal bleeding or something!"

"You'll be okay, Corinne," Lorena said, then gave a strained chuckle. "Now you know what a punch feels like." She studiously looked away from Corinne to avoid seeing her scowl.

About an hour later, I went upstairs to the room I was sharing with Abby. I knocked, but when she didn't answer, I opened the door. Abby sat on the bed, staring at the wall. The jar was on the bed next to her, and she had one hand resting on top of it.

"Abbs?"

No response.

"Abbs," I said again. For some reason, goosebumps

prickled my arms and legs. "Can you come downstairs, please?"

After a short beat, Abby finally turned to look at me and said, "Sure."

She followed me down to the living room.

Corinne, Lorena, and I sat on the couch facing the armchair where Abby sat down and waited patiently for someone to speak. She still had the glass jar with its murky contents clutched firmly in her grasp. She definitely wasn't going to give the thing up without a fight. I had no idea how we were going to get it away from her.

"Abbs," I said, trying to push the hesitancy from my voice. "I'm not sure what you were thinking out there. I know you have gone through a lot. Hell, I know you're still going through a lot. But what you did was very uncalled for. You really hurt Corinne, both physically and emotionally. She's your friend. You know that, right? I think you owe her an apology."

"An apology for what?" Abby asked, giving us big brown doe eyes as if nothing at all had taken place.

"Because you freaking punched me in the stomach!" Corinne bellowed, rising from her seat.

Lorena put a hand on her arm, pulling her back into the couch. "Come on," Lorena said, gripping her arm firmly. "Yelling is not going to help anything. Just settle down. We can talk this out. We're all friends here."

Corinne huffed, shook off Lorena's hand, and crossed her arms. "Yeah, well none of my friends have ever attacked me before today!"

"You shouldn't have tried to take the Githya away from me," Abby answered with a slight sneer on her face, her tone matter-of-fact, as if everything were self-explanatory. "That was a cruel thing to do."

"We really don't know what you mean, Abbs," Lorena said before Corinne could yell again. She spoke to Abby as she would a disturbed child. "We're having a little trouble understanding the situation here. Could you explain it to us?"

Abby stared straight into Lorena's eyes, then Corinne's, then mine. She held my gaze for a few moments, but it seemed like hours. I felt oddly entranced by that stare, like her gaze was sucking me into some spiraling vortex.

"It will be my pleasure," she said. Then, with no change of expression or other warning, and before any of us could stop her, Abby suddenly pried open the jar's lid and emptied its terrible contents onto the coffee table with a disgusting plop. A malodorous, brown sludge splattered everywhere, and the three of us recoiled in horror.

The unholy stench that permeated the room was by far the worst thing I had ever smelled in my entire life. At first, the fetid odor vaguely reminded me of that awful smell I had experienced this morning when I had been sitting with Abby at the lake's shore—the smell that had caused my coughing, gagging fit.

But this... Dear Lord and holy mother of God. This was so much worse. The diabolic stink of what I imagined to be a smoothie of raw sewage, sun-cooked roadkill, and rancid, diseased flesh, mixed with other filth I couldn't even begin to comprehend, filled every damn inch of the living room like a physical presence.

Trying desperately to breathe, I vomited until my stomach was completely devoid of any contents, even retching a few more times though nothing came up. Corinne joined me, emptying her belly, the rank miasma growing thicker around us. Lorena's hands had shot up to cover her mouth and nose as she dry-heaved. That lucky lady managed to keep everything down, however.

When I was finally able to lift my head up again without tasting bile rising in my throat, I saw poor Corinne leaning back in her chair. She was sweating profusely, and the front of her blouse was stained an awful muddy-yellow color. Lorena seemed to have fled into the kitchen. I could hear water running in the sink under the sound of her gagging noises.

Somehow, Abby alone appeared unaffected by the

horrid stench or our violent reactions. She sat and watched as the vomit-drama played out in front of her.

"Jesus Christ," I hacked out. I desperately wished I could scrub out the inside of my nose and mouth with a pad of steel wool. "What the hell is that?"

As I glanced at the blob on the coffee table, my stomach turned itself inside out again. I felt my stomach wanting to heave once more.

There was something lying on that table, weakly squirming and undulating in the dirty puddle of putrid water. The abomination before me was something that even my most awful nightmare couldn't have conjured up. I desperately wanted to get away from it. I wanted to never lay eyes upon it ever again. But, despite the vehemence of my desire to distance myself from it, I found myself unable to tear my transfixed gaze away from the thing on the table.

"What in God's name *is* that?" Lorena demanded in a hoarse voice. She had returned from the kitchen, her eyes staring over a cloth that she was holding to her nose and mouth.

Corinne's eyes opened—her stomach having finally emptied all of its contents—and she looked down at the table and let out a tiny shriek when she finally noticed the fleshy thing that had come tumbling out with the jar's water. She tried to scramble over the back of the couch to get away.

"I just... Oh Christ, is that... What is it?" I sputtered incoherently. The words didn't want to come out, and it felt like my tongue was glued to the roof of my mouth. My mind couldn't understand what I saw. The thing was truly revolting. "Is it alive?"

Through all the muck that covered it, the thing looked like a soft, fleshy, grotesque tumor about the size of my fist, with rudimentary limbs and a fifth lump that I guessed to be a malformed head of sorts. An early-stage fetus was the only thing I could liken it to, although whether human or animal, my brain just couldn't decide. Maybe it didn't want to? Maybe the same part of my mind didn't want to have anything to do with what was going on?

A fetus... I received a quick flash of memory: an image from months ago when I had hallucinated a nightmare in the elevator.

The creature squirmed lethargically on the coffee table, making awful choking noises as if it were in constant pain and struggling to breathe. Its slimy skin was red, raw-looking, and completely hairless. I could discern no true facial features on its head-lump-thing, although there did seem to be a ragged slit from where it garbled out horrendous sounds. Was that a mouth?

"Isn't she absolutely beautiful?" Abby said smiling, her voice as soft, loving, and full of pride as anyone I had ever heard. "I never imagined she could be so perfect. That she could be so wonderful." This was like some horrific, hellish corruption of what I imagined a mother seeing her child for the first time to be like.

Gently scooping the thing up, Abby cradled it in her arms, looking down at the thing as if admiring her own flesh and blood, and wiping some of the muck from it with her shirt. This was a total nightmare. It had to be. None of this could possibly be real. Could it? Maybe I was still passed out from the previous night's wine debauch?

Yes, that was it. I wasn't going crazy. I closed my eyes, willing myself to wake up.

"Oh God, it's so disgusting," Corinne blurted out as she moved away. She heaved again as she watched Abby rock the fetus-thing in her arms, which seemed to soothe it. Corinne's face was literally green. "Abby, get it out of here. Please! I can't stand that damn smell! Oh God, it's so gross. It's so gross!" She had backed up to the opposite wall and now frantically fumbled with the window latch before throwing the window wide open.

"Don't talk about her like that!" Abby snapped, her face contorted with fury now.

What had happened to her? What sort of brain damage

could affect this kind and sweet person?

"Your constant cruelty toward this precious gift is unforgivable, insulting, and evil! How can you say such things? Have you no heart? Have you no soul? You piece of shit bitch." Her voice rose in volume and pitch as she glared at Corinne.

"Abby, listen to me," I said, demanding her attention. I got shakily to my feet. "Look, just calm down, okay?"

What a stupid thing to say, Rei. Who in the history of being told to calm down had ever calmed down?

I felt light-headed from the noxious fumes that still enveloped the room, but I managed to remain standing.

"Abbs, just give it to me, whatever it is," I said as I picked up the now-empty jar that she didn't seem to care about anymore. "Put it back in here. Can you do that for me? We'll go back outside and get rid of it. You shouldn't be handling it. Especially not with your bare hands. We don't want you getting sick. That thing is probably festering with who-knows-what."

Abby turned her furious gaze on me. I almost lost my grip on the jar as I saw the hatred burning in those eyes. A hatred now aimed directly at me.

"No!" she screeched, gnashing her teeth in animalistic rage. "Stop calling her a "thing." She needs my help! Why can't you guys understand that I'm only trying to help her?"

Everything inside of me wanted to increase the distance between me and the grotesque lump of flesh Abby carried, but I knew I had to get it away from her. My mind conjured up horrible lists of diseases and plagues that the fetus-looking lump might be carrying. Not to mention the mere fact that it was revolting just to look at—and to smell. I wanted it sealed back in that jar and disposed of as soon as possible.

My desperation to have the thing gone caused me to move precipitously. I lunged for Abby, but unfortunately, she saw me coming and jumped up and around to the back of the chair, evading my grasp.

"Damn it, listen to me, Abbs," I said, trying to keep my voice calm as I inched my way around the armchair toward her. I forced my body to be sure each step I took was gradual and steady. I didn't want to make any more sudden movements, but my intentions must have been crystal clear.

Abby's gaze flicked between the doors and the windows, looking for an exit like a cornered fox. She had a wild look in her eyes that frightened me more than I would have thought possible.

"We're not trying to hurt you, Abbs," Lorena told her, inching closer as well. "We're just trying to help. You know us. We're your friends. We've always helped each other, right?"

"Just hand the...just hand her over, okay?" I tried to sound as unthreatening as possible, though I felt a little like a doctor in a mental institution trying to coax a patient into a straitjacket. "You're not well. We're just trying to help you, that's all. Trust me, we're your friends. We only want what's best for you."

"Sweetie, give Rei the...the thing," Lorena said, approaching Abby from the opposite direction. "Come on, Abbs. You can listen to us. You can trust us." Her voice was gentle and pleading, though the effect was ruined by her constant gagging as she inhaled the lingering reeking haze.

Abby darted away.

Lorena leaped forward and seized her by the arm that held the fetus-thing. I tried to grab Abby's opposite arm, but she slipped out of my grip and raked her nails across Lorena's face, drawing blood. Corinne quickly leapt to our side after Lorena yelled for assistance, trying to help subdue the flailing Abby.

I think I could safely say that this was definitely not, in any conceivable way, how I had pictured this weekend going.

"Get that fucking thing away from her!" I commanded

Corinne as I held the glass jar in one arm, ready for that fleshy abomination to be sealed back inside, my other hand latched onto Abby's right limb.

"I can't!" Corinne squealed, a nauseated look on her face. "I don't want to touch it!"

"Just help me!" I ordered and tried to pry the fetus-thing out of Abby's protective grip. It was slimy and warm. I swore I could feel a pulsing, like a tiny heart beating inside of it somewhere beneath its skin.

As I touched it, my body shuddered, but I kept my mouth firmly shut, lest I retch again. I didn't give up. I kept trying to loosen Abby's fingers around her treasure in an attempt to get it away from her.

I heard Lorena shriek as Abby grabbed a fistful of hair.

Eventually, I thrust the jar at Corinne so I could use both of my hands to pry open Abby's steel grip. It took all of my willpower not to let go every time I touched that horrid, grotesque thing's rubbery flesh.

Abby thrashed violently around, trying to protect her precious treasure. While Lorena held onto Abby's left arm, still trying to get her hair free, I was prying the thing out of Abby's right hand.

In the scuffle, we all slipped in the dirty, slimy water that covered the floor. Abby, Lorena and I all went down hard, landing in a heap on top of each other. A sharp pain dashed through my ribs. The air had been knocked out of my lungs as I fell on my back, but I refused to let go. I was quickly on my knees, still straining to loosen Abby's grip. When had she gotten so strong? Lorena freed her hair from Abby's sticky fingers and was now helping me force open Abby's arms like they were rusted hinges on a door that we needed to get through. The three of us continued to struggle on the ground, wrestling as if the championship belt was at stake.

In her flailing about, Abby kicked out wildly and her foot struck Corinne's, who had been standing next to our heap, stunned and unsure of what to do. Corinne's leg buckled from the blow and she crashed to the ground, joining us on the floor.

A loud shattering sound and a shriek of pain pierced the air. Corinne rolled over onto her side, her hands bloody with pieces of glass from the broken jar sticking out of them.

"Oh shit," Lorena said. I echoed her sentiment.

I felt so angry at seeing Corinne hurt so badly that I did something I had never done, or even thought about doing, in all of my life. I briefly let go of Abby and rose to my knees. I cocked my hand back and slapped Abby hard across the face as she writhed on the floor. The smacking sound echoed throughout the house.

Abby was stunned, more from surprise, I think, than actual pain. I was completely shocked as well at what I had just done. I had never hit anyone before. Let alone out of anger. Especially not one of my friends!

Luckily, Lorena recovered quickly from her shock and took the opportunity to finally wrest the fetus-thing from Abby's now-weakened grip. She sprinted out the back door with it and disappeared from view.

"Abbs, I'm...I'm so sorry," I said as the adrenaline began to wear off. The palm of my hand still stung and I could see a big red handprint welling up on the side of her face.

Abby said absolutely nothing. Her eyes were large and completely round. She just stared ahead blankly, as if her mind was somewhere far, far away. For a few moments she was utterly motionless, nothing but the steady rising and falling of her chest indicating that she was even alive. Suddenly, she burst into tears, covering her face with her hands and loudly sobbing into them.

I wanted to say something. Anything. But I had no idea what I could say that would make the situation any better. Things were beyond words at this point.

I moved over to Corinne and helped her stand up, taking her over to the couch where the late afternoon sunlight that streamed through the west-facing windows

illuminated her shredded hands. I retrieved a pair of twee-
zers, alcohol pads, and some gauze from the first aid kit,
along with a bowl of warm water and a soft cloth from
the kitchen. I carefully remove the shards of glass from
her palms, then set about disinfecting and bandaging her
wounds as best I could. All the while, we could hear Abby
crying piteously from where she still lay on the floor. I had
to resist the powerful urge to yell at her to shut up.

⁂

About twenty minutes later, after I had finished bandaging up Corinne's hands, Lorena came back inside, looking
sweaty and grubby, but resolute. She glanced at Abby, still
on the floor, who had finally stopped sobbing. Stepping
past her, Lorena sat down next to us on the couch.

"I buried the thing out in the back," she whispered to
us, making sure Abby couldn't hear. "Out by that stone
slab, just so I could remember the spot. I...I don't know
what that shit in the jar was. In fact, I don't think I ever
really want to know."

Corinne and I nodded in agreement.

"But I think it might have been alive. I mean, you guys
heard it. It was making those awful mewling sounds...But
it wasn't moving anymore when I took it outside. Did you
get a real good look at it?"

"It was utterly repulsive," Corinne said in a low, harsh
voice. "It looked like a diseased bear fetus or something."
She shivered, then stared at her bandaged hands.

"I don't know what it was," I whispered. I couldn't get
the image out of my mind. Picturing the way it had writhed
on the table made me feel nauseated again. "Maybe it was
some deformed animal? Maybe even something that had
mutated? But that wouldn't make sense. Either way, I'm
glad you got it out of here. That damn smell is still lingering around, but I think most of the stench went with it,
thankfully. Though, I'll still have to wipe down the table
and floor and open all the windows so we can sleep tonight,

and the whole place is going to have to be professionally cleaned and disinfected eventually. God, I think just the memory of that stench is going to haunt me for the rest of my life."

"Rei, I don't want to stay here anymore," Corinne said, tears sliding down her cheeks. "This has all been a disaster. I want to go home." She reached up to wipe her face with one of her bandaged hands. "Ow...."

"We will go home," I reassured her. "First thing tomorrow morning, I promise. We'll leave this place. Tonight we'll—"

Abby abruptly stood up behind us. Her puffy face was red and tear stained. Her clothes were dirty and torn from the struggle in the slime water. Through a big rip in her shirt, I could see the scars and wounds from the assault that covered her torso, making my heart feel heavy. The scars seemed somewhat pinker and rawer than when I had seen them earlier. I even noticed some spots of blood here and there along the length of the scars, but I couldn't tell whether that was actually just Corinne's blood.

"I'm going up to bed," Abby said in a dull tone completely devoid of any emotion. She climbed the creaking staircase without another word.

All our eyes were on her as she disappeared into the dim upstairs hallway.

"Are you okay?" Lorena asked Corinne once Abby was gone. Corinne simply nodded timidly with a loud sniffle and rested her head on Lorena's shoulder like she used to do in high school.

"Well, this whole weekend definitely isn't going as planned," I said, snorting derisively at my own amazing understatement. I put my head in my hands. "Everything's gone completely to shit. I don't even understand what happened, really. Who would've thought Abby would flip out and go off the deep end like that?"

"Her husband was murdered, Rei," Lorena said, wrapping a comforting arm around Corinne. "She was beaten almost to death. And she lost her baby, for Christ's sake. Who can say what toll that took on her? Both mentally and physically. I can't say I know in what ways I would be affected if that had happened to me. I'd maybe be acting even crazier than she is right now. It's not right to blame her for acting irrationally. Even this irrationally. She's obviously depressed and probably traumatized among who knows what else. Let's just let her rest for now." Her face reflected the strain and exhaustion I knew she felt, but her eyes shone with concern.

"I know you're right," I said, sighing heavily. Ashamed by my lack of compassion for my friend, I turned to examine the bandages covering the wound on the sole of my foot. The blood had begun to soak through the gauze. I considered rebandaging it, but decided it hurt too much to mess with at the moment.

"We're her best friends," Lorena continued, her maternal, protective tone soothing. "We have to be there for her and support her no matter how she behaves. She would do the same for any one of us, right? Rei, you know what it's like to lose someone you love. I don't mean to bring up bad memories, but out of the three of us, you're probably the one who can best relate to her pain and help her get through all of this. Don't you think so?"

"Yeah, I suppose so," I replied, rubbing the bridge of my nose to ease the headache that had begun to pound. Still irritated, despite knowing that I sounded like a truculent brat, I heard myself say, "But back when I was grieving, I didn't swim into a lake and dredge up some disgusting whatever-the-hell-that-was. And I certainly didn't threaten and then attack my friends." Meeting Lorena's eyes, I felt even more sheepish at my words.

"Let's just be patient with her," Lorena replied as she stroked Corinne's blonde hair. "I know it may sound like I'm asking too much after what happened just now. But let's try. This is really hard for all of us to deal with. It's tough to see someone we love crumble like that. But just remember, this is even harder for Abby."

"All I know," Corinne said matter-of-factly, all the anger and hurt drained from her voice, "is that when we get back, she definitely needs to see a shrink. If she's already seeing one, then maybe she needs to see two. And maybe I need to go see a shrink after all of this too."

I was pretty sure she wasn't making a joke, and I nodded. I could feel my heartbeat throbbing in my left foot. The pain helped me focus.

"We should get rid of that thing from the jar," I said, staring into the cold, empty fireplace for a moment, counting the soot stains.

"I *did* get rid of it, Rei," Lorena reminded me. "I told you I buried it out back. Do you want me to show you?"

"No," I replied, shaking my head. "That's not what I mean. I want to destroy it. I don't know *what* the hell it was, but I don't want it around. Even if it was a hundred miles away, I'd still feel uneasy knowing it...existed somewhere. I want it utterly gone. We should burn it or something."

"I understand what you're saying," Lorena said, nodding in agreement. Then, a disgusted expression spread across her face. "But I don't want to handle it again."

"I don't want to handle it either," I said. Just picturing that thing made my stomach writhe and my nose wrinkle. "But I won't be able to rest easy knowing it's nearby. And I don't want Abby somehow getting a hold of it again. We all know she's going to try to go look for it. That's inevitable." I got up off the couch, my foot instantly reminding me to take care while walking, and I hobbled over to the window. I looked around as far in each direction as I could, making sure Abby hadn't managed to sneak outside.

"I agree with Rei," Corinne said, sitting up. "I want that crap out, away from here. But why the hell was it down in the lake in a jar in the first place? Someone had to have put it down there, right? And how long has it been there? How can it still be alive? It definitely wasn't a fish, and it was breathing. Wouldn't it run out of air? The jar was filled to the brim with water. None of this makes any sense at all." She took a deep breath as if trying to suppress the panic rising in her voice.

"I don't know what to tell you," Lorena said. "I have no answers for any of those questions. And I don't know that I really care to know the answers."

I stared out of the window at the calm lake and nearby motionless trees. I fervently hoped that Abby had actually gone to bed and was sleeping off whatever craziness had infected her today. Ever since she had come out of her coma and found out she had lost both her husband and her baby, Abby had been in an almost constant state of deep depression. It was completely understandable and expected. Sad, definitely, but it was a normal reaction for her to have. But what had happened today was neither normal nor reasonable.

"Rei," Lorena said from the hallway.

I hadn't realized she had gone to the closet and brought out the broom and mop.

"Hey, are you listening to me?"

"What? Oh, sorry," I said, turning back from the window. I ran a hand through my sweaty hair. "What is it?"

"If you don't mind, could you go get changed and help me clean this mess up?" she asked as she swept up the shards of glass littering the floor into a neat pile. "We can't leave all this here or we'll end up with it all in our feet." She paused. "Wait, what's this?"

"What is what?" Corinne asked with a note of concern, but not getting up from the couch where she cradled her injured hands.

"It's the lid from Abby's jar," Lorena replied, carefully picking it up and examining it. "There's some sort of symbol etched onto the inside. Looks weird." She held it out to me.

I hobbled over to her, careful to avoid stepping on the broken glass. She handed me the lid, and I studied it. The lid appeared to be made of some flaking, rusty iron, like the kind you would see on ancient artifacts in a museum. Turning it over, I saw that there was some character or rune etched on the inside. I stared at it for a long moment, but it meant nothing to me. I didn't even recognize what language or culture it might belong to. I had never even seen anything like it before.

Or had I?

I felt a vague but growing sense of familiarity. I realized the symbol kind of looked like something I had seen on... what? Abby's body? Her scars? Or maybe had it been on that stone altar-thing outside?

The longer I stared at the rune, the more its shape seemed uncannily familiar and it ...shifted or altered its form in some way I couldn't identify. I was sure that it undulated in rhythm with the beating of my heart. But as soon as the thought coalesced in my mind, I blinked, and the symbol was back to normal. It filled me with a strong sense of uneasiness and made my eyes hurt. My head swam, and I felt like I stared into some swirling vortex that drew me in, piece by piece, down into an infinite abyss. It told me things, things I had to do. It moved once more—

I quickly handed it back to Lorena.

"It's probably nothing," I told her, rubbing my eyes and ignoring her quizzical look. I hobbled over to the staircase, preparing to somehow get myself and my wounded foot up the steps so I could change my clothes. I turned back to Lorena and Corinne. "You know, it was probably some kids out here in the boonies who got bored and decided to perform some Satanic ritual that they read about on the internet. Something like that."

"Abby said that thing called to her," Corinne said as I climbed the first step. "It's crazy, I know. It's impossible. But how else did she find it? You didn't hear anything, did you?"

"No, I didn't," Lorena replied, almost angrily. "Everything that happened put Abby under a lot of emotional and mental strain. That's all. She didn't hear anything. Nothing called out to her except maybe a voice in her own head."

But how *had* Abby known that the jar was there, deep under the water? She had to have known it was there somehow. Did she plant it there? Or could she have really heard it calling to her? Had I heard something outside the night before?

I glanced up to the top of the staircase. I was exhausted and on edge. That had to be why I thought I had just heard someone call my name, a voice floating on the wind.

CHAPTER EIGHT

The life blood flows, swirling, roiling, amassing into an ocean of crimson. The tides bring a miasma of death and fetid corruption. Viscera, decayed and blackened, rises to the red surface to be picked and eaten by the winged varghuls. The breeze of one billion shrieks tears across the sky, wishing to escape the torturous sun.

I sat on the lounge chair in front of the large east window that looked out over the small island and the lake, nursing a warm beer and elevating my injured foot. The sun had begun to set, causing the clouds to turn from a fiery red to darkening indigo, as if hell had been pouring in from the heavens and was now flooded in a sea of twilight. I had no idea what time it was. I felt too lethargic to get up and check my phone, which lay on the dining room table, and none of the clocks on the walls had working batteries yet. But I could have sworn that yesterday the sun hadn't set until much later in the day.

"I just checked on Abby," Lorena said as she returned downstairs. "She's sleeping. Which is good. Hopefully she'll be in a better state of mind when she wakes up." She stood in front of me. "Anyway, what's wrong? Besides everything with Abby, of course. You have a...look on your face. What are you thinking about? Is there something else bothering you?"

"No, there's nothing," I said, rubbing my eyes. I was tired from today's events and I probably wasn't thinking straight. The beer wasn't helping the thought process, obviously, but the buzz felt good. I stared up at Lorena. "Do you know what time it is?"

"No, I don't," Lorena said listlessly. She began patting the pockets on her jeans. "I don't even know where my phone is, actually. I thought I had it. It's probably upstairs somewhere." She let out a sigh and plopped herself down heavily in the lounge chair next to mine. "Well, Corinne's napping on the couch. Her hands are pretty messed up. I feel so bad for her."

I could see new tears forming in her worried eyes.

"Me too," I said, running fingers through my tangled hair. "But I think her hands will be okay. It looked worse than it actually was, I think, because of all the blood. None of the shards went in too deep. The cuts all looked pretty shallow when I was removing the glass." I peered over the back of my lounge chair at the couch. I couldn't see her, but I could hear Corinne's soft, rhythmic breathing.

"Rei, she still needs to see a doctor," Lorena said earnestly. "All of you need a damn doctor. I saw your foot. That puncture is definitely not shallow."

Out of the corner of my eye, I could see that she was looking at me with even more worry. I turned and flashed her a weak smile. "I'll be okay. Don't worry about me."

"We need to go," she continued. "I would rather leave right now."

"I know," I said after another sip of warm beer. I didn't really want to admit how unnerved I was of the thought of driving through those woods with nothing but the car's headlights to illuminate our way. Everything that had happened so far had set my nerves on the very edge. My entire body felt like a tense, coiled spring ready to explode. The image of the figure I thought I had seen on the bridge the first night flashed in my mind, adding to the anxiety that everything with Abby had caused. And truthfully, besides all of that, I *was* extremely tired. "I would rather leave now too. But it would be better if we left in the morning. You can't tell me you're not exhausted. We're both very tired.

We need to try to get some rest before making the drive. Corinne certainly won't be able to drive with her hands like that. And we definitely can't rely on Abby either. I wouldn't trust her behind the wheel at the moment."

"Neither would I. But, Rei..." Lorena began, but stopped with a heavy sigh when she saw the look in my eyes. "I guess you're right. I don't like it. But I *am* pretty exhausted. Plus, I suppose you shouldn't be driving right now either, even if you weren't tired." She glanced at the half-empty beer in my hand.

"This is only my second one," I said to her, my tone a little angrier than I had intended.

Lorena sighed again, as if trying to clear her mind. I thought she said something else, but I wasn't paying attention. At that moment, my thoughts were fixated on Abby, sleeping upstairs. At least I hoped she was sleeping. I'm sure she needed even more rest and recuperation than the rest of us did.

My mind drifted restlessly. Abby was our friend. She was my friend. I was so desperate to help her in any way that I could. But how? What could I do? I put the bottle of beer to my lips and took several long swallows. I felt devastated for her and for the suffering she was still experiencing. Once again, I wondered how I could possibly help her get through all of this to be strong, loving, happy Abby again.

I had a sudden realization. A part of me was not only afraid for her and everything that had happened. But also felt afraid *of* her.

I expelled that disturbing thought from my mind. It was quite unhelpful if we were going to help Abby get past the toughest time of her life. How could I help someone I was scared of?

"We'll leave as soon as it's light tomorrow morning," I said, tearing my eyes from the strange beauty of twilight over the lake, turning to look at Lorena. I met her eyes and forced another small smile. "I promise you we will. I want

Abby to get the help she needs just as badly as you do. Let's just both get some good sleep tonight so we can start the drive back home with clear heads. Okay?"

"Okay," Lorena replied, nodding slowly. She seemed satisfied. "I guess we should pack up our things tonight before we go to bed. Get everything ready for the morning. We can pack Corinne's and Abby's stuff for them too. I'm sure they won't mind."

I nodded in agreement as she stood wearily and went back upstairs, turning on the house's lights on her way to dispel the lightlessness that had enveloped us. A great sigh escaped from me as I stared out of the window at the iron clouds that masked the sky now. So much for our Amazing Girls' Weekend. I sighed.

This has to be the dumbest thing I've ever done, my angry, hypercritical inner-voice berated me. Abby needed doctors and meds, not road trips and s'mores. I was furious with myself for such an idiotic idea, thinking that all Abby needed was Corinne, Lorena, and me. It was now obvious that she was much more damaged than any of us—perhaps even her doctors, who had medically cleared her for the trip—had realized. She was certainly beyond our ability to provide any meaningful help on our own. What would Mr. and Mrs. Brennan say about everything that had taken place here these past couple of days?

A hot tear slid down my cheek, but I quickly wiped it away as Lorena returned, dropping back into her lounge chair.

"Abby's still snoring away up there," she said. If she had noticed me wiping my eyes, she didn't say anything, and I was grateful for that. "She looks really peaceful and relaxed at the moment. I hope when she wakes up, she's back to the same old Abby that we know and love."

"Yeah, you and me both," I said and chugged the rest of my beer as I stood up. "I'm going to go outside for a bit and get some fresh air." I let out a loud, wet burp.

"Nice one," Lorena said flatly. "Be careful out there,

Rei. Especially with that foot of yours. I don't want to have to carry you back inside."

I nodded and waved at her dismissively as I put on my jacket. Curiously, the house didn't stink at all anymore, the stench from the fetus-thing gone. But I just needed to get out of there for a minute. I grabbed my phone from the dining table and headed outside.

Be careful indeed. At least there were no annoying neighbors around here to bother us.

I closed the door behind me and carefully descended the porch steps, holding tightly to the railing and trying not to put too much weight on my wounded foot. I knew I shouldn't be walking at all on it, but I just needed some open space to think.

I slowly made my way to the lakeshore where so much had happened earlier today. At the moment it was perfectly quiet with no breeze to disturb the smooth water. It looked like a completely different place. The lake resembled a gigantic mirror, silently reflecting the unbroken gloam just like it had the night before. Other than the lighted windows of the house and the porch lights, there was no other visible source of illumination anywhere around. We were completely alone and isolated. I would have found it quite peaceful and relaxing. That is, if this had been a normal trip and not some out-of-control spiral into crazy-ville.

I walked along the shore around our tiny island, admiring the lake and the trees that grew around the house, big beautiful pine trees, their fallen needles crunching with a satisfying sound beneath each limping step I took.

A thought struck me, and I took a few steps closer to the side of the house with the large window. Using my phone's flashlight, I examined the ground, but didn't see any sign of the small black bird and its baby. With everything that had gone on since this morning, I had completely forgotten about them. But it was too late now. Some animal must have gotten to them before I could bury them.

Oh well. Nothing I could do.

I stared up into the trees above me, wondering which one it had been from which the baby bird had fallen. There wasn't enough light to make out anything among the branches beyond shadowy, vague shapes.

Limping back over to the shore, I continued my circuitous path around the island to the back side of the house. The copse of spruce trees that formed a small circle around the stone slab-altar came into view. Once again, turning my phone's flashlight on, I hobbled over to the altar and knelt down, where I could make out writing on the heavy stone base.

Even after pulling away some of the obscuring shrubs and leaves, I could not even begin to make out what the writing said. It seemed to be in a foreign language that used strange, elaborate characters and symbols. It kind of reminded me of Egyptian hieroglyphics, but the glyphs looked different than anything I had ever seen in history textbooks. Another archaic language with a writing system similar to Egyptian, perhaps?

Even if I had possessed the knowledge and ability to read the inscribed text, the stone was extremely weathered making the carvings indistinct. I ran my fingers across the engraved symbols, feeling the cold indentations. The etchings looked extremely old, ancient even. But the house certainly couldn't have been here that long. My parents had purchased it only about nine years ago. They had shown me pictures of it, how it looked when they first saw it. Sure, it was a little run down before they had renovated it, but it hadn't looked very old at all. It had been no more than ten or twenty years old.

Had someone deliberately moved this stone here? Maybe the previous owner had eccentric decorating tastes? Or had the altar already been here when the house was built? That was more probable. The builders hadn't wanted to disturb it.

I was suddenly overcome with a powerful, eerie feeling, as if I were being watched. I looked around but saw no one. Of course, the darkness obscured much, but I couldn't sense any movement.

The sensation dissipated quickly, but when I looked back at the stone and trees, I felt it again. It was so strong this time that the hair on my arms and neck bristled. I stood up, my body tense, ready to flee, regardless of the pain in my foot. But something in the back of my mind turned my gaze back down to the ground. I shined my phone's light downward, studying the earth for a moment before my eyes fixed themselves on a spot to the left of the stone where several tree roots rose out of the ground like giant, withered fingers.

I don't know how or why, but I felt—I knew—at that moment that this was the very spot where Lorena had buried the thing from the jar.

In shocked revulsion, I quickly took a step back. Pain shot through my foot as I carelessly put too much weight down on my injury. My leg buckled, and I fell backward onto my ass, landing hard in a sitting position on the grass.

Stupid! I shouldn't have walked around so much with a deep puncture wound in my sole. The inside of my shoe had become warm and wet. The gash must have opened up and started bleeding again.

"Son of a bitch," I muttered to myself, trying to push the agony out of my mind. I was glad the others hadn't been out here to witness my embarrassing fall. "Fuck this place." I wondered how much I could get if I sold this damn house.

The wind picked up as I sat massaging my backside. I had fallen on my tailbone pretty hard. I hoped it wasn't badly bruised, or the drive home would suck even worse.

"Rei..."

I froze, then looked around. I was sure I had heard someone calling my name.

"Help..."

Did someone just say—

Nope. I shook my head in vehement denial. I knew

it was only the stupid wind, just like it had been before. Everyone has heard stories about being in a creepy place and hearing voices. It was a well-known cliché of almost every horror movie I'd seen. It was just people's overactive imagination, combined with some fear they were already experiencing, that accounted for ghostly voices. Especially when the person was already on edge.

"Just the wind," I reminded myself out loud and forced out a giggle. I listened to the soft blowing of the breeze, but it did not form any more words. "Just—"

But the words abruptly caught in my throat. I shone my phone's flashlight up at the trees. Not a single leaf was moving. I looked over at the lake, but the water was as smooth as glass. My hair hadn't even been ruffled, I realized.

But I had heard the wind. I know I had.

I felt...out of place. That was the only description that seemed to fit. It was so quiet now that I felt as if the silence were physically pressing against my eardrums, trying to penetrate the thin membrane and get inside my head to grab hold of my brain.

Putting my hands tightly over my ears, my whole body grew even more tense, my muscles turning into stone as they contracted. I kept looking around me more and more frantically. I didn't quite know what my eyes searched for, but I could sense something around me. My hands pressed harder against my ears. My vision began to blur.

I then started to choke, like an invisible force was pressing against my throat, crushing my windpipe. I removed my hands from my ears and clawed at my neck. I couldn't breathe, couldn't think, couldn't get more air into my lungs.

It was like I was back in the lake, drowning all over again. The pressure was too great—pressure against my throat, against my ears. I gasped as I suffocated, and I still couldn't hear anything.

But then I heard a loud splash from the other side of the island. The silence and the feeling of oppressiveness vanished. I could now hear the gentle lapping of the water on the shore, the chirping of crickets, and the far-off howl of some dog or wolf. Cool, life-giving air flooded into my chest. My lungs inflated. My eyes snapped back into focus.

"What the fuck..."

I crawled over to the stone altar and used it to pull myself up right. As I stood up, I realized that the stone had been warm and moist under my palms. But it wasn't moisture from the air, it was as if the altar had been...sweating.

I backed away, wiping my hands furiously on my jeans trying to cleanse them of some imagined infectious agent. Without warning, the grass to the left of the altar bulged and opened up. It was the spot I had identified earlier as the fetus-thing's burial spot. Some sort of viscous liquid oozed upward out from the soil like a broken sewage pipe. It definitely wasn't water. And whatever it was, it gave off a familiar, yet still-revolting, putrid stench.

The ground bulged farther upward, as if something were trying desperately to escape from underneath. Something was down there. Something wanted out.

That was it!

I didn't want to see what might be digging its way out. I turned around and bolted, sprinting—more precisely, limping—as quickly as I could around the house to the porch and burst through the door, causing Lorena and Corinne to jump out of their seats. I slammed the door behind me. I fumbled with the lock, but eventually managed to slide the bolt home. I then collapsed onto the floor, leaning against the door and crying.

"Rei, what the hell happened?" Lorena cried out, running over to me, Corinne right beside her. They knelt down and half-carried me to the couch, where I lay, sobbing into my hands. "Rei, talk to us."

Corinne noticed the blood dripping out of my shoe and, as best she could with her bandaged hands, retrieved some wet paper towels from the kitchen and fresh bandages from the first aid kit. Lorena gently removed my shoe, causing me to hiss in pain between sobs. My sock was soaked through with blood. After pulling off the sock as well, Lorena set about carefully cleaning my foot, reapplying butterfly bandages to hold the gash closed, and rewrapping my wound. Meanwhile Corinne tried to help clean my dirty hands and wiped my sweaty brow.

"Can you tell us what happened?" Lorena asked again once my sobbing had quieted down enough.

"I-I don't know," I stammered, trying to calm my breathing. What *had* happened out there? "I'm not sure what it was. I think I'm losing my mind. Am I going crazy?" I looked up at my friends, searching their eyes for the truth.

"No, you're not going crazy," Corinne said, dabbing my forehead with the towel as she let my head rest on her lap. Lorena finished wrapping and tightening the bandages on my foot.

"You're alright now," Lorena tried to reassure me as she released my foot. "Just tell us what happened. Did you trip on something and fall? Was there something out there? An animal? Did it chase you?" Her eyes were still watching me intently, and I realized how badly I must have frightened them when I came in.

"No, none of that," I said, shakily. Nothing was clear enough in my head to explain. "No. Maybe. I don't know. I can't explain!"

"Do your best, Rei," Corinne said calmly, stroking my hair. The scent of the lotion she always wore comforted me, helping me calm down.

"I don't know," I said again, trying to focus my thoughts. "I was just walking outside, having a look around. I wanted to get some fresh air. I just had to get out of the house for a minute. I walked along the island's ridge, and eventually I got to that altar stone out in the back. While I was standing there, I thought I heard—I thought I heard some noises. Then I tripped and fell. Then something came out of the freaking ground!" Tears threatened to burst from my eyes once more. I used all my willpower to hold back the incipient panic I felt. I had always hated appearing out of control in front of people, even my best friends.

"Something came out of the ground?" Lorena asked, looking at me with concern. "What kind of something?"

"Could it have been a mole, maybe?" Corinne suggested. "They burrow in the ground. Do they have those around here?"

"Is Abby okay?" I asked suddenly, ignoring their questions. Some thought about Abby had just popped into my mind. I wasn't sure why.

"Yeah, I think so," Lorena said. "Corinne went upstairs to check on her while you were outside."

"She was fine," Corinne said, nodding. "She was still sleeping when I looked in on her. It was, like, five minutes ago."

I tried to sit up, but Corinne and Lorena held me back.

"Relax, Rei," Lorena said, holding me firmly.

"I have to go look!" I said, irritated that they were preventing me from getting up from the couch.

"Rei, stop it," Lorena said, her voice now stern. "Calm down. Abby is fine, okay?"

"Just let me go look," I demanded, still struggling with them.

Lorena and Corinne exchanged glances. With mutual sighs of defeat, they helped me up.

"Be careful with your foot," Lorena said. "I don't want it bleeding again."

I ignored her and headed for the stairs. My foot throbbed and burned with constant pain, I wouldn't let it stop me. I grabbed the wooden railing and hopped up, stair by stair, as best I could. Lorena and Corinne were close behind.

"Abby!" I yelled. A growing feeling of dread coiled itself in the pit of my stomach.

I kept going. The pain traveled from my foot up my leg. My body desperately wanted me to stop, but I needed to see that Abby was fast asleep, safe in her bed.

I finally reached the top of the stairs and limped down

the hallway to the bedroom Abby and I shared. I staggered over to the door, grasped the doorknob, and threw it open.

The room was chilly and the window was wide open. Everything else lay in complete gloom. I fumbled around the wall, groping for the light switch. Once I had found it, I flipped it on. The bulb flickered for a second, but eventually stayed lit, illuminating the room.

There was Abby's bed, the covers twisted in a mess.

But Abby was not there.

CHAPTER NINE

The Children and Harbingers of Corruption require souls and meat. The blind and the unworthy shall be theirs to feast upon. For not all can be welcomed onto the path of truth.

I limped out of the bedroom and down the stairs as fast as I could with Corinne and Lorena right on my heels. In unison, we all yelled Abby's name at the top of our lungs as we frantically searched the first floor.

"Where could she have gone now?" Corinne panted, her brows furrowed in concern, as we made our way toward the front door.

"I don't know," I replied breathlessly. "The bedroom window was open. Maybe she climbed out. She has to be outside." I grabbed the doorknob and threw the door wide open, exposing the chilly night beyond. "Maybe Abby—"

"Yes?" Abby stood before me on the porch in her robe and slippers, her hand stretched out as if reaching for the doorknob. She looked at us with vague surprise and an innocent smile. "Maybe I what, Rei?"

"Abby?" I said, gawking at her in stunned confusion, having barely stopped myself from crashing right into her. For a moment, the relief of finding her safe and sound pushed everything else from my mind. But why had she gone outside? What had she been doing out there? She hadn't been looking for her mutant jar-creature, had she?

"That's my name," Abby giggled after a few seconds, throwing up her hands in a shrug. "Don't wear it out."

"What the hell are you doing out here?" Lorena asked, pushing past me and putting a motherly arm around Abby's shoulder's, leading her inside. "Oh my God, you're freezing! You feel like you've been out there for hours." She led Abby over to the couch, sitting her down and pulling the blanket from the back of the couch to cover her legs and feet. She rubbed her hands to warm them.

"But I just checked on her not that long ago," I heard Corinne whisper to herself.

"I was just taking a stroll by the water," Abby said, smiling at all of us. "It seemed like a beautiful night for a walk."

Lorena went over to the fireplace and soon had a warm blaze going. "You stay there," she told Abby. "I'm going to make you some hot tea." She then headed into the kitchen to put the kettle on the stove.

"Abbs," Corinne said, scooching closer to her on the couch. "How did you get outside exactly?"

"Well, that's a silly question, Corinne," Abby let out a laugh. "With my arms and legs of course!"

"No," Corinne replied with irritation. "That's not what I meant. We didn't see you leave the house."

Abby just shrugged again and continued to smile. The stupid grin on her face—a grin that clearly told us she was just playing dumb—had started to irritate me. I felt anger rising inside me. But I forced it all back down. I didn't want to yell at Abby and lose my cool again. I had already let my emotions get the best of me once today.

"I was just now outside," I said to her, my voice steady and calm. "I didn't see you at all while I was walking around. I did hear a splash, though." I looked down at her fuzzy slippers poking out from beneath the blanket. They were dirty and soaking wet. "Were you throwing something out into the lake?"

"Throwing something?" Abby asked, looking genuinely confused. "What would I be throwing into the lake?"

"I don't know," I replied, looking fixedly at her. What *would* she have been tossing in there? Rocks? Coins? I felt uneasy. "I'm just trying to figure things out, is all."

"What's there to figure out, Rei?" Abby asked, giving a little shrug. "I told you guys. I was taking a stroll. Why is everyone so suspicious?"

My eyes locked onto hers, trying to decipher what was going on. Did Abby have something to do with whatever had happened to me outside? Why the hell had she been outside in the first place? I hated the fact that I now felt so mistrustful of my best friend. But there was definitely something strange going on here, and I could not dismiss the way she had been acting earlier or the way she was feigning ignorance now. I kept staring into Abby's eyes, as if I could discern the truth from them. The truth, I was more and more convinced, that she was hiding from me.

She simply looked back at me with one of her sweet smiles. Maybe—

A sudden loud whistling almost launched me off of the couch. Lorena stood and went into the kitchen to take the boiling kettle off the stove.

"Here you go," she said, returning from the kitchen to hand Abby the steaming mug. "Be careful, it's really hot."

"Oh, thank you, Lorena," Abby said, smiling up at her and taking the tea.

Lorena settled onto the arm of the couch next to Corinne, making eye contact with me, trying, it seemed, to convey some message. My mind overflowed, full of swirling thoughts, however, and I was unable to divine what she wanted me to understand.

All was quiet for a while, except the crackling of the burning logs and the soft sound of Abby sipping her tea.

"How are your hands?" I asked Corinne after a few minutes of silence. "Can you move them at all? Do the cuts still hurt a lot?"

"They still hurt," she replied, looking at them as she flexed her bandaged fingers. "But not as much as they did before. I don't think any of the shards went in too deep. They're a little numb, though." She frowned at them.

"After we leave here tomorrow morning, we'll get you to a doctor, first thing," Lorena reassured her, leaning over to kiss Corinne on the top of the head.

Corinne mumbled her thanks.

"You and Rei both need to get your injuries looked at. Rei, you probably need stitches."

"Ugh, great," I said, shuddering at the thought of needles.

"I can't tell you how grateful I am that you guys brought me up here," Abby said cheerfully.

We all turned to look at her. She smiled, taking another sip of tea as she regarded us for a moment. "I know it hasn't been the best vacation for you guys, and I'm sorry for that. But I've actually been enjoying our time up here so far. I'm glad we came."

None of us responded. Corinne and I went back to staring into the fire, while Lorena rose from her seat and headed back into the kitchen.

"I think I'll start cooking us some dinner," she called from out of the kitchen. "How do grilled cheese sandwiches and tomato soup sound? Is that alright?"

We all said it sounded perfect. I really hadn't noticed my stomach rumbling until Lorena had mentioned food. I couldn't find my phone to see what time it was—I had had it with me outside and could have sworn I had put it in my pocket—but I guessed it was around 8:00 pm. I hadn't eaten anything all day. It would do us all some good to have a warm, comforting meal in our bellies.

I tried to relax, letting my mind zone out while I waited for dinner. I had heaved my leg onto the footrest to let my throbbing foot soak in the heat of the dancing flames. I sank a little lower in the cushy sofa and let my eyes close. The heat on my aching sole felt wonderful. Maybe I would just sleep down here by the fire tonight, then I wouldn't have to climb the stairs again, the thought of which I very much dreaded. The headlong rush down the stairs to find Abby had hurt more than I'd realized in my panic.

My eyelids became heavy. I must have dozed off for a moment, caught halfway between the waking world and the dream world, for I thought I heard a faint, unfamiliar voice that sounded far away.

"Face of metal, heart of malice, mind of corruption…"

"What?" I whispered back, a sense of dread prickling my skin.

"I said, have you guys seen my phone?" Corinne asked in a frustrated tone.

I opened my eyes to see her looking around the couch and coffee table, turning over pillows, looking under furniture. But she came up empty-handed.

"Nope," Abby said, sipping her tea, watching Corinne with apparent disinterest. "I haven't seen it since yesterday."

"No, sorry," I said, shaking my head. Then I remembered my own misplaced phone. "Actually—"

Thump!

"What the hell was *that*?" Corinne squeaked, freezing in place. Her shoulders hunched as if she expected an attack at any moment.

"Don't know," I said softly, slowly sitting up in my seat.

"Oh man," Corinne whispered. "I hope another bird didn't crash into the window."

Shaking my head, I pointed upward. That sound had come from above. There was another *thump,* and I had no doubt that it had come from up on the second floor.

Goosebumps sprang up on my arms and my chest tightened. Whatever it was, it had sounded heavy, like someone jumping down off a chair.

"Rei," Corinne said, her voice trembling with fear, her eyes glued to the ceiling.

"Shh!" I put a finger to my lips. If someone was up there, they had to know that we were here. But I didn't want whoever it was to know that we were aware of his or her presence.

"Rei," Corinne said again, this time in a whisper, her

voice still shaking. She crept over to me. "Is someone up there?"

I looked at her. Tears of fright welled up in her large eyes. I glanced at Abby. I couldn't believe it, but she was still sipping her damn tea, staring into the fireplace, and smiling as if nothing were happening. Was she freaking deaf? There was no way she hadn't heard that noise.

Fuck it. I didn't care if the intruder knew we had heard him.

"Who's there?" I shouted, scaring a squeak out of Corinne. If someone had broken in, I decided that I wanted the stranger to know that we were *very* aware of their presence. Hopefully that would spook him enough to just leave.

Lorena came out of the kitchen with a bread knife in her hand, looking confused. "What are you guys yelling about?"

"Shut up," I whispered to her and pointed to the ceiling.

All our eyes shot upward as we heard the faint creaking of floorboards from directly above us. There could be no doubt now. Someone *was* up there, and the four of us were all down here.

There's not supposed to be anyone around here for miles. I dismissed the thought. Did it matter anymore what things were "supposed" to be?

I hobbled as swiftly and silently as I could to the bottom of the stairs, trying to ignore the stabbing pain in my foot. The inky darkness permeated the second floor like a solid cloud of pitch. The light switch for the upstairs landing was at the top of the stairs.

Of course, it's at the top. What a stupid-ass design. Okay, what do I do?

Turning to look at Lorena, I hobbled over to her, snatched the bread knife from her hand, and returned to the foot of the stairs. This knife would have to do. I gingerly put my good foot on the first step, slowly letting all of my weight settle onto it as I stepped up. The wood creaked mournfully.

I glanced back. Lorena stared with huge eyes up at me. Corinne hid behind her, peeking over her shoulder. Abby still sat on the couch, paying no heed to the proceedings going on.

I motioned for everyone to stay put and used the wooden handrail to pull myself up to the next step. This one groaned much louder than the first, causing my heart to beat faster. I held the knife out in front of me in case the intruder decided to jump out of the shadows. When no one did, I climbed to the next step, which, thankfully, made no noise. I let out a painful, shivering breath that I hadn't realized I had been holding.

A stray thought passed through my mind. *You're walking into the darkness alone. The same thing you make fun of people in movies for doing. What are you thinking?* But I wasn't just afraid, I was also pissed. How *dare* someone break in here?

I heard movement behind me. Turning around, I saw Lorena climbing the first step.

"No," I mouthed soundlessly at her, gesturing for her to stay. I didn't want them to come to harm if something were to happen. I was determined to do this, but we didn't all need to act foolish.

The very top of the stairs was still too dim and obscure for me to make out any shapes. That pitch blackness seemed almost tangible, as if I would crash into it once I reached the top. Oh, how I wished for some city street lights—some light pollution leaking in through the windows—at that moment. I had never been afraid of the dark, but I had never been in a place so lacking of light as this island. It was almost overwhelmingly frightening.

A flashlight would have been smart, I chided myself, unable to keep my thoughts from buzzing inside my skull. *Too late now, dumbass. You really think that bread knife is going to fend off anything?*

I was shaking. I only hoped that it wasn't as obvious to an onlooker as it was to me. I gritted my teeth to keep them from chattering.

The small window at the top of the staircase usually offered some light, but the clouds had decided to cover the moon at that moment to ensure almost total darkness.

I climbed a few more softly creaking steps, all the while reminding myself to breathe. It's amazing to realize how much noise one could make when trying to be fucking silent!

Freaking hell, my foot hurts, I screamed internally. *Good, focus*. I just had to focus on the pain, not the fear. Don't let the fear spread.

Pausing for a moment, I realized I hadn't heard any more thumps from the second floor since I had started up the stairs. But, of course, that didn't mean anything. Whoever was up there could just be hiding in a shadowed corner, behind a door, under a bed, or two feet in front of me for all I knew. My heart was practically in my throat, kicking like a frog to escape. My hand slipped a little on the handrail with each step I climbed. My palms were sweating like crazy, and my fingers were going numb with their death grip on the bread knife.

With one final step, I arrived at the top. I had reached the second floor.

I could see nothing. The glow of the lights and fire from downstairs couldn't penetrate this far. The light switch had to be here somewhere. I wracked my brain, trying to picture it in my mind, but like so many seemingly inconsequential details of daily life, I had no conscious recollection of its location or position. I turned to the wall, knowing my only recourse was to feel for it.

At that moment, the clouds decided to get out of the way of the moon. A square panel of moonlight from the window appeared on the wall, casting welcome illumination, however dim, a few feet in all directions.

My hand froze mid-grope as the clouds blanketed the moon once more. I could have sworn I had seen—sensed?— movement out of the corner of my eye.

Beads of sweat ran down my face. Someone hiding, not wanting to be seen. I couldn't keep myself from shivering, no matter how hard I tried. Someone was lying in wait. I struggled to breathe. Someone was waiting for just the right moment to attack me.

I turned and fixed my gaze to where I was sure I had seen...something...slip into the cover of even darker gloom. Was something *moving* there in the darkness? Or were my eyes playing tricks on me?

I realized the thunderous pounding in my ears was my own racing heart. I reached out behind me, without turning my head, my hand once again slapping against the wall, trying to locate that damn light switch. That profoundly oppressive silence enveloped me again as it had done outside. I felt as if someone had stuffed cotton into my ears. I could hear nothing except the overwhelming sound of my own thundering heartbeat.

But no. That wasn't all. I could also hear something else.

I stared at an area of somehow deeper blackness and suddenly realized I could hear soft inhaling and exhaling. Someone was standing right in front of me, though my eyes could not locate a form.

Soft whispers of breath emanated from that lightless corner. Images of pure nightmare raced through my mind, overwhelming my brain, conjuring up horrors that could be lurking just a step out of my view, ready to pounce on me from some hellish dimension. The utter absence of light. The inability to see, to know what could be crouching right in front of me. What could be lying in wait in that terrible shade? A monstrosity ready to gut me, ripping me open like a pig...

I lifted the bread knife like a dagger, pointing it in the direction of the breathing. My hand shook so badly, I was afraid that I would drop my only means of defense.

"Who-Who's there?" I tried to say, but the only thing I managed to utter was a strangled choking noise.

The breathing grew heavier, more labored. It took on a raspy quality, as if the person struggled to take in lungfuls of air. Ragged, monstrous. Through the unnatural silence, I heard the slow creak of a floorboard right in front of me.

With each strained breath that came from out of that tenebrous cocoon, I felt as if the air in my own lungs was being sucked away, being stolen. Bullets of sweat rolled down my face like miniature rivers, but I couldn't wipe them away. There was no way in hell that I was going to lower my weapon. The sweat dribbled into my eyes. It stung like acid. My other hand was—

I finally flipped the switch on. A scream that had been growing inside of me like a dam ready to burst, exploded forth from my dry mouth as the second-floor landing light flickered on momentarily before instantly winking out again.

For the briefest, most fleeting of moments, a figure stood right before me. It had worn the dirty and torn remnants of what looked like robes. Its face and its entire head had been obscured by cloth wrappings, painfully bound by dirty ropes and rusted wires. Everywhere on its head and body were reddish-brown stains, and I knew what they were. The person's exposed arms were covered in deep gashes that wept crimson streams.

It had stood right before me, illuminated for a split second.

But as the light flickered back to life and stayed on, there was no one there. I was alone on the landing.

The oppressive silence that had been clogging my ears had fallen away. Lorena and Corinne charged up the stairs. They were no doubt reacting to the shriek I had shaken the house with. When they reached me, I still held my arm outstretched, the knife gripped tightly in my hand, and my knuckles turning white.

It took Lorena several tries to pry the knife from my hand. I fixed my eyes on the spot where I had seen the figure, a fading phantom image of it still burned onto my retinas. Unformed, incomprehensible thoughts swirled around in my brain as I tried to glean some sense from what had just occurred.

"What happened?" Corinne asked, gripping my arm. I could see my own terror reflected in her bulging eyes. "Was there something up here? Did you see someone?" His voice was barely a squeak.

"I-I don't kn-know." My mouth didn't want to form words properly as I stood there.

Corinne's arm encircled me tightly as I shivered uncontrollably. My throat had constricted as if a snake had wrapped itself around my neck to choke me.

Realizing we couldn't all just stand on the landing the rest of the night, Lorena and Corinne reluctantly searched the upstairs rooms but found no one and nothing out of the ordinary. They checked in all the closets, under the beds, behind the shower curtain, and then made sure all the windows were closed and latched. They found nothing.

"Maybe there was a raccoon in the walls or something," Corinne said with forced cheerfulness, putting an arm around me once more. Her expression told me that even she didn't believe that explanation.

It took some cajoling to get me to move away from the spot to which I had been rooted. I wasn't sure if my paralysis stemmed from fear that the figure might came back, or if I just physically couldn't move my legs.

When we eventually descended back to the first floor, Abby was still sitting peacefully on the couch, her feet tucked underneath her, her damn mug of tea still cupped in her hands as she took an unnecessarily loud sip.

"Did you guys find anything?" she inquired pleasantly, as if she somehow knew we would find nothing. She watched me hobble down the steps, supported by Corinne and Lorena. We walked back over to the couch and armchairs.

"No," Corinne said irritably as we all sat down. "We found jack shit. There was nothing up there."

"I didn't think so," Abby said with an overly sweet smile. I could almost imagine sugary honey dripping from the corners of her mouth.

Lorena stared at her, mouth open, for a minute. By the look on her face, I knew she wanted to say something. I wished she would, but instead, Lorena got to her feet.

"I'll get the food," she said. "I think we could all use some food in us."

She turned and headed to the kitchen.

The plates and silverware clinked as Lorena prepared the food.

I locked eyes with Abby. We stared at each other, not speaking. I didn't want to break contact, but I was eventually forced to blink. Abby winked at me as Lorena returned with a tray of sandwiches, a pot of soup and laid it all on the dining table.

"Dinner," she called out timidly.

We all made our way to the table and sat down, serving ourselves.

I nibbled on a sandwich. Despite having been hungry earlier, my stomach didn't like the idea of food anymore. My insides felt like they had been twisted and tied into a knot, then finally turned to stone.

Corinne and Lorena didn't eat much either. Lorena slowly chewed a mouthful of grilled cheese while staring down at the table, tracing some scratches in it with her fingertip. Corinne had a bowl of soup in front of her face, a spoon held awkwardly in one of her bandaged hands. After every shaky spoonful, she looked anxiously around, almost as if expecting some ax-wielding maniac to burst out from a door or through a wall.

Abby was the only one of us with an appetite. She tore into her sandwich like a lion feasting on a recent kill and loudly slurped up her soup. I had never been fond of people's eating sounds, but the noises that emanated from her would have made anyone feel both nauseated and angry. I desperately wanted to slap her face again as she chewed her food with her mouth open, turning the grilled cheese into wet mush in her gnashing maw with sickening squelching noises that echoed throughout the room. Each bite sounded like a pig snuffling about in its trough and devouring its evening slop. I wanted to fling the bowl of tomato soup away from her when she noisily downed it with loud, irritating gulping that was unnecessarily deep and audible. I almost gagged at the sight of the orange soup dribbling down her chin and the front of her robe.

I resisted the furious urges, though. It took everything within me to refrain from slapping my palms to my ears and screaming for her to stop. I certainly didn't want to seem like I was the one going crazy, even though I felt like I was.

Abby is the one who needs help, I kept telling myself as we ate our dinner. But was she the only one? *I am not going crazy. I'm not hallucinating all of this. I really did see someone upstairs. Didn't I? But Lorena and Corinne didn't find anybody. They checked all the doors and windows. They were all locked and latched from the inside. Are they all playing some elaborate prank on me? No, they have never, and would never, be that cruel. All this Abby stuff is getting to me. I'm going to need a vacation after this vacation. Jesus tap-dancing Christ, now I'm having full-on conversations with myself.*

"I'll clean this all up in the morning," Lorena said quietly, pushing away an unfinished sandwich. "I don't feel like doing it right now. I'm just so exhausted."

I think she just didn't want to be alone in the kitchen, a feeling I understood completely.

"Besides, my dog's not here to get into the food." She gave a low chuckle that quickly faded away.

"You girls barely ate anything," Abby declared, hitting her fist against the table like a king demanding more. "It was all so delicious. Thanks for the food, Lorena." She then let loose an explosive belch and rubbed her belly.

Corinne turned a disgusted look on her but seemed to

bite back whatever it was she had wanted to say.

"You're welcome," Lorena said stiffly with a hint of revulsion in her expression.

"Well, I think I'm going to turn in for the night," Abby said, jumping up from her seat. The sudden movement knocked the chair backward, clattering onto the floor. But she didn't seem to care.

"We'll see you in the morning, I guess," Lorena said to her.

Abby climbed the stairs and turned to face us when she got to the top. She stared down at us for a minute, then flicked the landing light off and disappeared from view.

"Sweet dreams," her disembodied voice said.

CHAPTER TEN

Lies! So many untruths flying around from mouth to ear. Those of inferior logic cannot possibly grasp the meanings of the corruption. Denying the weak their existence is a mercy one can grant them, for they strain against our cause like a fragile dam attempting to hold back the floodwaters. But we shall prevail, for our harsh words, our black hearts, and our eternal wisdom shall engulf the totality of existence in the infinite realities.

Had I lost my grip on my sanity?

All the things that had happened so far on this trip seemed completely surreal. Had Corinne "accidentally" spiked our food with a mind-altering substance again, like she had on our high school class trip to Washington D.C.? Had some of the food Lorena cooked not sat well with me? Or perhaps I was actually still in the process of drowning in the lake, and this was all some grand hallucination caused by extreme oxygen deprivation that my brain was concocting in the final moments of my life.

No, I didn't believe it was any of that. It couldn't possibly be. All this fear, all this anxiety...everything just felt all too substantial for this to be anything other than reality.

It was real. All real.

I was utterly exhausted and absolutely drained, both physically and emotionally. But I couldn't fall asleep. My body didn't *want* to fall asleep. I didn't even know if sleep was possible after what I had experienced at the top of those stairs. My palms became sweaty every time I thought about the lightning-quick image of that figure just standing there, somehow staring at me with cloth-covered eyes.

There was no way in hell that I would go up there to one of the bedrooms and try to sleep, even if Abby was sharing the room with me. If I was honest with myself, the thought of sleeping near her actually added to my anxiety.

A bed might have been comfier than the armchair where I was currently reclining, but I wanted to stay in the circle of cheery warmth beside the crackling fire. As it probably had for my prehistoric ancestor, the fire seemed to provide not only light, but protection from the horrors that lurked within the shadowed corners of this damn house.

"You should get some sleep, Rei," Lorena said, gently brushing the hair back from my face. "If you're going to insist on being the one to drive tomorrow, you need your rest. I don't want you falling asleep at the wheel."

"I can't sleep," I said, clutching a pillow to my chest the way I used to cuddle a plush fox my dad had given me as a child. "I can't even keep my eyes closed. Not after... Not after everything that just happened." I pointed to the stairs. I needed that staircase light on. "Please, let's just leave the lights on. All of them. Okay?"

Lorena simply nodded and flipped every switch on.

Those dreaded stairs were no longer draped in obscuring gloom. "What if it comes back, Lorena? What if it comes back while we're sleeping?"

"Rei," Lorena said, her voice full of worry, yet still stern. "There wasn't anyone up there. Corinne and I checked all the rooms. We didn't find anybody. Everything was securely locked. No one could have gotten inside without us knowing."

"What about Abby's open window?" I rebutted.

"How would someone have scaled the side of the house to reach it?" she asked.

Though like me, she probably hadn't figured out how Abby had gotten down without hurting herself.

"Anyway, it's locked now."

"I'm not lying about this!" I shouted, tossing the pillow across the room. "I don't care what you and Corinne didn't find. I know what I fucking saw!" As soon as all the words had escaped my lips, I immediately regretted my outburst.

"Just try to get some sleep, Rei," Lorena replied in her usual calm tone, ignoring my sudden tantrum. "Listen, I'll stay up tonight if that makes you feel better. I'll keep watch until morning. I can sleep during the ride home tomorrow. How does that sound? You can stay all night there in that chair if you want. It looks comfortable enough. I'll be right here, and I'll make sure nothing happens. Okay?"

"I don't think I can fall asleep," I said, rubbing my temples. "I want to. My body desperately needs to recharge. My stupid brain just won't let me."

"I got something for you." Lorena pulled a small orange bottle out of her purse and popped open the lid. She dropped a small white pill on my outstretched hand. "Here, take one of these. I gave one to Corinne a little while ago." She nodded at the other armchair where Corinne dozed peacefully, her head back, drool sliding from the corner of her mouth.

"I was wondering how she could fall asleep so easily," I said, watching Corinne, curled up like a cat and softly snoring away in dreamland. My gaze shifted back to the pill in my hand. "What is it?" I asked, examining it. I never expected Lorena to have drugs on her, let alone offer them to me.

"It will help you sleep," she replied and left it at that.

I always trusted Lorena. And I *was* pretty tired. My eyelids felt heavy, but they didn't want to remain shut, springing back open once my brain realized I wasn't paying attention to my surroundings. My body yearned for rest, but my mind was on high alert.

What did I have to lose? Lorena said she'd keep watch all night. She'd wake me up if any actual issues arose. So, I popped the tiny pill into my mouth and swallowed it without water.

"Promise me you'll wake me if there's a problem," I said after a few minutes. I could already feel myself starting to relax.

"I promise," Lorena reassured me, a gentle smile on her blurry face.

"Alright," I mumbled. Or at least I think I did. I rested my head against the back of the chair and closed my eyes. My lids twitched as if protesting, but they were too weak to force themselves open.

I was floating.

The next thing I knew, I was standing alone in a long hallway full of creeping shadows. The walls were wood-paneled, covered in what looked like decades of accumulated grime and sprawling brown stains that struck me as obscene.

The only sources of light in this unfamiliar hallway were candles resting within iron sconces that were secured every few yards along the walls. Every here and there among the sconces stood identical heavy wooden doors coated with crimson paint that was peeling off in jagged strips to reveal rotten, damp wood underneath. Their brass knobs were corroded and looking ready to fall apart. These doors were just as dirty and decrepit as the walls, and a filthy red carpet lined the entirety of the floor on which I stood.

As I made my way down the hall—for no other reason than I felt compelled too—I could hear the sounds of terrified screaming or crying coming from behind several of the doors. From one door in particular came a ferocious pounding from within, rattling the entire thing, its hinges sounding as if they'd pop off at any moment. From another door, there was no sound, but its doorknob whipped back and forth as if someone were frantically trying to escape some hellish prison beyond.

The inside of my skull felt like it was full of fog. Where was I? This wasn't the lake house, was it?

Looking down to what I presumed was the end of the

hall, there was utter darkness, a space too dark for the candlelight from the sconces to penetrate.

"H-Hello?" I said, my voice echoing down the hallway, bouncing every which way and amplifying itself strangely until it sounded mocking.

An icy chill overcame me. A carpeted, wood-paneled hallway wouldn't produce an echo, would it? My thoughts were interrupted by the realization that everything had gone abruptly silent. No more terror-stricken crying. No more screaming bloody murder. No more relentless pounding and crashing from the doors. Even that one doorknob stood motionless.

"Is anyone there?" I called out, a bit louder, though still tentative. I wasn't entirely sure whether I wanted my presence to be acknowledged.

No answer came from my echoing query. There was just the peculiar, spine-tingling silence that hung in the air like a heavy curtain.

I took several slow steps down the hallway and noticed that I wore no shoes. In the preternatural stillness, I could hear my naked soles squishing into the carpet—some foul wetness sliding between my toes. I shuddered at the thought of what might have soaked the carpet, but I braved a glance downward at the floor.

Now that I looked directly at it, I couldn't tell if the carpet was actually red or if something had seeped—nope, never mind. I looked up and away. I didn't dare kneel to examine the carpet more closely. I told myself I didn't care what it was soaked with. I walked on, trying to disregard the cringe-inducing sensation that accompanied each step.

The flames of the candles flickered, reaching for me as I passed by them, almost as if trying to grab my shoulders. An arctic chill emanated from behind each door I passed, as if my skin could sense whatever unnatural thing awaited me on the other side should I venture to open one.

A thought jumped into my brain, and I froze mid-step. I looked down at my foot, and I realized that I had been walking normally. I wasn't limping at all. There was no pain in the foot I had injured. In fact, it wasn't even bandaged anymore.

That's weird. But beyond that, my mind dismissed it, not caring to pursue this mystery any further.

Before I could take another step, two leather-colored candles burst to life at the end of the hallway, giving off a ruby-colored light. They illuminated a door that had been hidden in the inky murk. Unlike the other doors lining the hall, this one was curiously made of what appeared to be dull gray steel.

A sound crawled into my ears with icy, probing fingers, intruding on the unnatural silence. I immediately spun around to look behind me. I thought I had heard breathing. The same heavy, ragged breathing I had heard earlier at the top of the stairs. But all I saw was the hallway that stretched on forever into another wall of blackness. I strained my ears to catch the slightest hint of a sound while I took a cautious step backward.

Was that an exhale I just heard? But from where? I was alone here as far as I could see. There wasn't anyone else in this hallway. I strained to listen even more closely—

BOOM!

A thunderous explosion roared through the hallway, shaking me down to the very marrow of my bones.

"Get away from me!" a shrill voice screamed from behind one of the doors. Together these noises caused me to nearly vomit out my heart and go into cardiac arrest.

All the doors exploded into life once more with the racket they had been making previously. Perhaps even louder and more vehemently now. The roaring clamor of dozens of people crying out in rage and anguish resonated through every inch of air that hallway contained.

The steel door that had been hiding in the obscurity at the end of the hall squeaked open halfway, revealing a lightless yawning abyss of utter nothingness.

Between that unknowable void and whatever was

behind the red doors trying to get out, the steel door seemed like the safer—for lack of a better word—option.

I couldn't just stand in the hall forever. If nothing else, the indescribably horrible din coming from those red-doored rooms would drive me insane if I had to listen to it for much longer.

Forcing my legs to run, I approached the open steel door. I shivered in nauseating revulsion with each step as my bare feet squished into the swampy carpet. The closer I got to the steel door, the colder the hallway became. A chilly draft blew into me from behind, pushing me, as if the doorway were sucking in air and drawing me toward the void.

Could this doorway possibly lead outside?

I stopped before the open door, my nose mere inches from its surface. Its reinforced metal was streaked with rust and deep, claw-like scratches. My eyes could not penetrate the tangible gloom that lay beyond the threshold.

Gathering my courage, I took a single, hesitant step forward through the doorway. The darkness was so palpably oppressive and heavy that I felt if I stretched my hand outward, I could seize it.

Without warning or any discernible trigger, a switch flipped on in my brain. I was no longer safe. Solid dread washed over me, freezing me. The sudden overwhelming reek of festering decay violated my nose. I knew, beyond a doubt, that there was something in the room that I would not want to see. Ever. My sanity screamed in protest.

Get away, my brain demanded of me, and I felt no reason to argue with it.

But as I made to step backward from that doorway, a torrential vacuum of air pulled me forward, forcing me to take several steps over the threshold. My heart seemed to stop and freeze solid as I heard the steel door swing shut behind me.

I stood in that sunless space, unable to see even the faintest glimmer of light. Unable to hear or feel. I was in such a state of complete sensory deprivation that it made me feel physically ill. I couldn't even tell if I was still standing on a floor. I seemed to be suspended in the most profound depths of starless space where nothing, not even time, could reach. I deliberately clamped my molars down on the inside of my cheek just to be able to feel something. Pain flared through the soft tissue in my mouth.

That was when I heard it. All around me, I heard the harsh intake of breath. Someone was forcefully taking in air, inflating their lungs to the limit as one does when preparing to bellow as loudly as possible.

The sound of air intake ceased, and I tried to prepare myself for the clamorous explosion that was to come.

"Rei..." The merest tingle of a whisper echoed hotly into both of my ears simultaneously.

A fraction of a second after my brain registered the word, there sounded a deafening crash from all around me, a cacophonous eruption like tires screeching on asphalt, glass shattering, and large bodies of metal crumpling. A pair of blinding orbs scorched my eyes as they flew at me.

I caught myself screaming hysterically. I could make out absolutely nothing around me, just the white-hot light that engulfed me. That loathsome, putrid odor returned to ravage my nostrils and my feet suddenly felt as if they had just violently slammed onto solid ground. My legs crumpled and a cold, tiled floor flew upward to meet my flailing body.

I heard a loud buzzing click. After a few moments, my eyes adjusted, and I realized that there were harsh fluorescent lights overhead that must have been shining directly into my eyes. Vague outlines of objects began to take shape.

Retrieving myself from off the floor, I was in what appeared to be some sort of medical facility, with two metal gurneys in the center of the room, various instruments lying about on stainless-steel tables in neat rows, and what looked like some sort of a large filing cabinet built into the walls.

"Hello?" I called out, finally able to coax my vocal cords into working. I desperately hoped someone would hear me and rescue me from this awful place. How I had gotten here, I had not the faintest of clues.

The only answer was the loud steady buzz of the overhead lights, as the suffocating feeling of dread inside me intensified.

I made my way around the room.

There has to be some other way out, I tried to remain calm and rational.

When I turned my gaze back to the center of the room, the gurneys, which had previously held absolutely nothing, now featured two large shapes completely covered in white sheets. The lumpy shapes looked like human bodies.

"Oh, fuck that," I said aloud as I realized what this place must be. I glanced over at the large drawers set in the walls, and then turned my gaze back to the draped figures on the gurneys.

This was a morgue.

How the hell did I get here? I asked myself again, wracking my brain for an explanation. Why was I here at all? I remembered being in the lake house. I had been sitting by the fire, then—

All the rationalizing thoughts were immediately swept as I caught the most miniscule hint of movement from under one of the sheets. The white material rose a fraction of an inch. I froze for a moment..

"Screw all of this," I muttered under my breath, and hurried over back to the steel door though which I had come. I didn't care that the door led back into that hallway. Being here was worse.

I grasped the cold steel handle and pulled, but it didn't budge. Likewise, pushing produced no results. There was no visible lock on the door, so I didn't know why I couldn't move it. I put all my weight into it, alternately pushing and pulling, each effort more frantic than the last. But no amount of force moved the damn thing at all.

As I stood panting from my efforts, my sweaty forehead resting against the chilled, unyielding steel, I heard a sound from behind me. A cough. I froze and felt my stomach tie itself into a hard knot. I forced myself to swallow the lump in my throat and drew in a deep, shaky breath.

There's no one else here, I told myself. *There's no one else here. There's no one else here. No one...alive.*

Ever so slowly, I turned around and looked at the white-sheeted figures.

There was a brief indistinct movement under the sheets.

At first, I thought my eyes must be conspiring with my overactive imagination to play tricks on me. But there was no denying it. The figures writhed under their coverings. I attempted to back up as if a few more feet between me and the corpses would be safer, but there was nowhere to go. I pressed my back against the door, feeling the cold of the metal through my sweat-soaked shirt. I watched in horror as red splotches appeared all over the white sheets, like ever-growing inkblots. Blood streamed down the sides of both gurneys, creating little crimson pools on the white tile floor.

Both figures sat bolt upright, the sheets still clinging to their bodies, and they let out simultaneous bloodcurdling screams of agony. I closed my eyes and clapped my hands over my ears, but the shrieking was over as quickly as it had begun.

When I reopened my eyes, the heads of both figures turned in my direction, as if staring at me through their white masks of blood-stained linen.

"Rei, sweetie," a soft voice came from one of the corpses, drifting over to me.

"We miss you," the other covered figure said in a deeper voice. The words caressed my ears.

The voices triggered warm, fond, and mostly happy memories. Yet, I could not describe the complete horror that shot through every fiber of my being at that moment of pure insanity.

"N-No, it can't be," I said, tears running down my cheeks, holding my hands up and palms out as if trying to fend them off. "This isn't possible. This isn't right. Mom... Dad...you're dead. You've been dead for years..."

"We're here for you, Rei," the voice of my father said. The father I knew could be strict, but had always been loving, and there had always been a distinctive warmth in his voice. A warmth that the voice emanating from the thing now before me lacked. "We came for you. We love you so much. It has been so difficult without you."

It couldn't be him. I refused to believe it. This was not real. This was not possible.

The draped figures swung their legs off of the gurneys with stiff movements, and stood up with painful slowness as if their bodies hadn't moved in years.

The bloodied sheets fell away, revealing the corpses of my parents. But they weren't the parents I remembered. Their bodies were mangled. Torn to shreds. Bits of flesh hung off their bones like old, peeling wallpaper. Limbs were bent at sickening, unnatural angles. Once-familiar faces were now severely battered and deformed. A large chunk of skull and brain was missing from my mother's head, perhaps still a stain beneath the bridge she had thrown herself off. And my father's chest was caved in where the steering wheel had been jammed forcefully into him when he lost control of the car and crashed into a tree on the side of the road.

My stomach roiled and heaved at the sight of them.

"Come be with us," my mother said to me. There was a malicious undertone in her words that sent a piercing chill through my very core. Her bruised broken jaw stuck out at a sickening angle, though it didn't affect her voice as she spoke. "I left this world to be with your father. But you never followed. Did you not want to be with us anymore? Did you not love us? We've waited for you for so long."

"S-Stay the hell away from m-me," I stammered, taking several steps to my left, almost falling over a metal table. I wanted to be as far away as possible from these creatures.

"You'll enjoy it here with us, Rei," my father said. He had a gash across his forehead and one eye bulged from its socket. They advanced toward me on awkward legs. My father smiled at me with a mouth of broken teeth. "Don't you want to be with us again? We want to be with you. Remember all the good times we had? That day when I got you, Lorena, Corinne, and Abby out of school early and took you to the water park. That was a fun day. Or remember when we all went to Japan to visit your grandma? You loved that trip. But it seems that you have forgotten us. You don't want to remember us anymore. Your love for us has dried up. Your love died when we did. Is that it?"

"That's not true!" I shrieked, backing farther away, my eyes searching around for an exit as the ghouls drew ever closer with their slow, shambling gait. The door I had come through was probably still sealed shut and there didn't seem to be any other way out. "I loved my parents. I still do. But you are not them! Get the fuck away from me!"

"Rei, that's no way to speak to your parents!" my dad's corpse roared. He sprang forward and lunged, arms outstretched. But I jumped out of the way just in time before his dead, waxy hands could grab me.

"Go away!" I yelled, grabbing instruments from the tables and throwing whatever I could reach at them.

They didn't seem to react at anything that struck them.

"Your corpse will lie within the corruption for all eternity as the worms chew your rotting flesh," he spat at me, then threw his head up, laughing hysterically. His guffaws were abruptly cut short, then he looked back at me, meeting my eyes. "Rei, no... What is this? I'm so sorry. Please, no!"

I didn't understand. He looked at me with eyes and an expression that I recognized.

"Ungrateful child," my imposter, corpse-mother snarled. "Little bitch who sucked the lives from us."

"Stop it!" I said, covering my ears, trying to block out

her words. "Why are you saying this? Stop it! Stop it! You're not my parents!"

"Of course, we are," my dead father said after his brief moment of clarity. His expression had returned to its previous one full of malice, his eyes brimming with hate. "Although I did often wish you had never been born."

He began that awful laughing again as they both advanced, my improvised projectiles still having no effect on the walking cadavers.

"It wasn't the death of your father that made me kill myself," the corpse of my mother interjected. "It was your own miserable pitifulness that drove me to suicide. After he died, I realized that you were all that was left of my family. I couldn't accept that. Throwing myself from that bridge so that my head exploded on the rocks below was a better alternative." She grabbed a chunk of brain from her damaged skull and flung it at me, missing my face by inches. "Death came as a relief compared to the thought of having just you." She dug two fingers into her broken head and pulled out another chunk of brain matter, crushing it in a fist before joining in with my father's maniacal laughing.

The sounds grated inside my head like a knife was digging deep into my ears.

"No! Shut up!" I screamed at them, but they continued their infernal cackling. "My real parents wouldn't be doing this to me. They wouldn't be telling me all these lies!"

Out of the corner of my eye, I noticed a sudden movement by the wall. My head snapped to the spot, and I saw one of the cadaver storage drawers slowly swing open, revealing a lightless aperture. Out of the open drawer, the face of a small boy with wispy, brown hair, pale skin, and striking jade-green eyes appeared. He stuck out a thin, emaciated arm and frantically waved me over.

"Hurry," he urgently mouthed while the corpses of my parents were busy focusing on me.

Without thinking, I upended the metal table beside me,

sending it crashing into the legs of the ghoulish corpses, knocking them down, autopsical instruments flying everywhere.

I fled toward the boy, who had disappeared back into the confines of the storage drawer. Without thinking, I scrambled headfirst into the open chamber sliding on my elbows onto the cold metal rack as the door inexplicably shut behind me.

What now? I couldn't hide in here forever. Those monstrous, living corpses out there would be able to drag me out. It wasn't like I could lock myself inside.

"Don't worry," said a tiny voice ahead of me as if the boy were reading the frantic thoughts racing through my panicking mind. "They won't be able to get in here. I made sure of it. Come on. Let's go."

His small body scrambled away.

There was a complete, impenetrable lightlessness in the cadaver storage drawer. I couldn't even see my hand when I passed it in front of my face. I couldn't really turn around either. The space was too restricting. I had to focus on calming myself. The intensely claustrophobic and morbid nature of where I lay threatened to overwhelm my sanity.

"Come on," the small voice said again. "I'm not going to wait for you forever."

"Come on t-t-to where?" I choked out as I moved toward the nothingness ahead of me. My only options were to move forward or to move backward. I definitely didn't want to go backward into the waiting clutches of those walking cadavers. But wouldn't I just hit the end of the drawer if I moved forward? I didn't imagine these things were that long. And where was this kid anyway?

"This way," the child said, sounding as if he were several feet beyond me. He shuffled as he moved away.

I had no other choice but to follow. I wriggled myself through the confines of the drawer that seemed to inexplicably tighten around me, using my hands to pull and my feet to push against the sides and metal bottom. I didn't understand how, but the storage drawer didn't end. I kept on going, following the sounds of the boy.

It had been chilly in the morgue, but now whatever sort of shaft it was in—for that's what it had to be—became quite warm and somehow even more confining. It was as if the walls themselves now pressed against me, hugging me, making it difficult for me to breathe.

Panic set in once more. The thought of suffocating in a dark, squeezing space filled me with witless terror. I dragged myself along as quickly as I could. Rivers of sweat from the ambient heat that radiated from the walls poured down my face and back, causing my elbows and knees to slip and slide.

Why am I going farther into this infernal rabbit hole? Why am I trusting this kid to lead me out? I don't even know who he is.

I hadn't realized it immediately, but the metal in the shaft on which I had been crawling had gotten gradually... softer. When I attempted to get a firm grip to drag myself forward another few inches, instead of the smooth bottom I expected, my hand grabbed a fistful of what felt like warm, moist flesh. I snatched my hand away, stifling a sound of surprise and disgust that blossomed in my throat.

"This way," the boy said, breaking his silence. He sounded as if he had put more distance between us. "We're almost out. Just a bit more. Come on."

"Okay, I'm c-coming," I stuttered. I took a deep breath, trying to settle my nerves.

I had to have faith in this mysterious child. I hoped he wasn't leading me into even more insane danger. I was about to say something to him when my seeking hand met air instead of the squishy floor of the shaft, and I abruptly plummeted face-first into an empty space that had opened up before me.

Only a half-second scream erupted from my mouth before I hit the ground, which consisted of the same fleshy substance through which I had been crawling.

Sitting up, I realized I was in some sort of chamber. In the center of this new "room" was a massive, translucent, bulbous growth that radiated a soft white light. It grew from the floor like a hideous tree with membranous tendrils rooting it to both the spongy floor and the ceiling above. By the faint illumination the growth gave off, I could see red walls that curved upward into a dome. It was made of the same fleshy material as the floor.

My shirt and pants stuck fast to my sweat-drenched skin.

I could see no sign of the child. Where had he gone?

"Hey, kid," I whispered, unsure of what else might be around to hear me. "You there?"

But there was no answer, only a steady, muffled thumping coming from above me. There were no other tunnels leading out of this place. And as I turned to look back at the way I had come in, I saw that the hole I fell through was completely gone. I spun around, looking at every inch of the wall, hoping I had just looked at the wrong spot. But there was no exit. No way out. The hole I had come through had simply disappeared, closed up.

"Kid, where are you?" I whispered again, desperate for an answer.

"Don't let her do it," his voice suddenly echoed around me.

"What do you mean?" I asked, unsure of where he was.

Instead of an answer, my surroundings began to pulsate and close in around me, as if I were in a giant, deflating balloon. The red, fleshy walls began to collapse and lose their structural integrity.

I was going to be buried alive.

"Kid, tell me where you are!" I screamed, no longer caring if anything else heard me. "Help me get out of here!"

"Please don't let her," the boy said again.

I could not tell from which direction his voice came.

"Please keep the Metal-Faced Lady away from her."

The chamber was now half the size it had been just moments ago. My chest tightened, and I struggled to breathe, from lack of air, fear, or both, I couldn't tell.

"Get me out of here!" I shrieked. The chamber was even smaller now. I couldn't expand my lungs properly. There was not enough space, not enough air. The walls pressed unyieldingly against me. They had partially engulfed the luminescent growth, making its faint light even weaker.

I tried pushing back the walls, but they just folded around my arms like silly putty. There was nothing I could do. I was trapped. I was going to suffocate and die in this place. The chamber enveloped me. I tried to cry out for help, but the sagging flesh filled my mouth, choking me.

"Don't let her. I beg of you, Rei."

My vision left me.

And I died.

CHAPTER ELEVEN

Now, jealousy and vindictiveness festered within...

My eyes flew open as I woke up, feeling as if I were choking on my own tongue.

When I realized I could actually breathe, I took several deep, shuddering breaths as I stared up at the shadowed ceiling. I lowered my hands to my sides, which, for some reason, had been scratching desperately at my throat in my sleep.

Someone had covered me with a blanket—probably Lorena. It was now soaked through with my sweat.

I sat up straight in the armchair, rubbing my eyes and letting them adjust to the dim light of the room. The fire had burned down to nothing but faint, glowing embers in a cradle of ash. I wondered why Lorena had let it go out. Wasn't she supposed to be keeping watch all night?

It was then that I noticed her asleep on the couch in an uncomfortable position she had probably affected to keep herself awake.

Corinne still snored softly in the other armchair.

"Damn it, Lorena," I muttered to myself, but then sighed. I couldn't fault her for falling asleep. This weekend had been a drain on all of us, mind, body, and soul.

I quietly got out of my chair, stretching as I stood, enjoying each pop and crack my back and shoulders produced. I picked up my sweaty blanket, thought better of it, and got a fresh blanket from the back of the couch, covering Lorena with it. I could stay up the rest of the night if need be. I was just surprised that whatever drug Lorena had given me had worn off so quickly. The nightmare must have had something to do with shocking me into full wakefulness.

As much as I tried, I couldn't exactly remember what I had dreamed about. My parents? No, I didn't think so. A boy, rather. Going through a door, maybe? The harder I tried to remember, the fainter and more elusive the memory of the nightmare became, like I was trying to grab the wind. But just concentrating and thinking about the dream caused my body to shiver, so I eventually stopped trying to recall the details. Something kept nagging at me as if I was supposed to remember it, but it was no use. I couldn't nail down the events that had occurred in my romp through the dreamlands, so I just let it go.

A hot cup of tea sounded really good at that moment to help clear my head. I headed over to the kitchen and set the kettle on the stove.

Whispering again floated around me.

I could make out the sound of leaves moving outside of the kitchen window, but nothing else. I closed my eyes again and rubbed my temples with my fingers. The stress of everything must have been getting to me, cracking me even further. Either that, or this was just a remnant of the elusive nightmare replaying inside my head.

But as I waited for the water to heat up, the whispering returned, louder this time.

I'm not going crazy, I kept telling myself.

At that, a heat blossomed in my chest, and I felt a sudden sharp anger clawing from inside my gut.

That was it! I was *done* with this creepy shit. Fists clenched, I walked into the living room and listened, trying to determine where the noise had come from. Straining my ears, I followed the murmuring trail of sound which led me down the rear hallway to the basement entrance.

"How fucking, incredibly wonderful," I muttered to myself. I had watched enough horror movies with Abby over the years, to know that going down into the basement when unexplained creepy things were going on was about the dumbest thing I could do.

But this was real life. This was not a movie. There were no ghosts or monsters in real life. They existed only in stories.

I repeated those assurances to myself like a mantra. I needed to prove to myself that I had been making normal things into something they weren't. The whispering sounds were just a draft coming through a loose window or under a door. The caretaker better fix that as soon as possible. The figure I had seen upstairs had been a pure figment of my imagination as I had been already completely on edge and momentarily blinded by the bright light turning on. I'd tell Mr. Neilson to have the caretaker install a light switch at the bottom of the staircase. The putrid sludge coming out of the ground outside could have been a problem with the septic tank, which would need to be inspected.

Everything was easily explained.

I kept these thoughts in mind as my trembling hand grasped the doorknob and pulled the basement door slowly open. The hinges creaked ominously, of course. I had known they would.

How cliché, I thought, trying to repress my anxiety.

A vague, coppery, rotting odor wafted up, stinging my nostrils and causing my stomach to heave like a ship tossed about in a storm. I peered down into the blackness of the basement with one hand held protectively over my nose and mouth, trying not to breathe in the rank stench. I could see nothing past the first step. It was as lightless as an abandoned mine down there.

Luckily, this time, the light switch was much better positioned. I stretched my arm out and flicked it. Anxiously, I put one foot through the doorway, the wood moaning under my step as if asking why I would want to go down there.

At that moment, the light dimmed before extinguishing completely.

"You're freaking kidding me," I hissed, clenching my

teeth in annoyance. *Who did the electrical in this place?*

I stepped back, not wanting to stand in the pitch black that had reclaimed the stairs.

The bare bulb had a cord. Perhaps that would turn it back on. To reach it, I would need to step over the threshold.

As I contemplated making that one step, I realized my entire body was shivering. I tried to calm myself by regulating my breaths. In and out. I only had to grab and pull. Easy. But my legs refused to go forward. I tried reaching out, my fingers grabbing for the bulb's cord.

The thin string was right there. Why couldn't I touch it? It was as if the thing were keeping away from my fingers on purpose, staying just barely out of reach like it was teasing me.

All I needed to take was one small step over the basement door's threshold and I could easily grab it. I kept telling myself to just *do* it. Just step in there and yank it. But my body stubbornly refused to go any nearer to that shadowed pit, It was like my heart was pumping dread through my entire body in place of blood.

Argh, shit, shit, shit, shit, my mind yammered. *Just do it. Just do it. Just do it.*

It took all my willpower, but I leapt over that damn threshold and pulled that stupid cord, almost ripping it down from the ceiling in my haste.

Nothing happened.

"Screw it!" I said aloud and quickly spun away, intending to head back to the living room as fast as I could.

It was then that I ran right into something solid. Something that should *not* have been there.

I bounced off, stumbling backward through the basement door. My foot slipped off the edge of the first step, but with a panicked grab, I managed to catch hold of the doorframe.

My throat constricted in abject terror as I looked up, trapping within my lungs the scream that wanted to burst out, as I beheld a tall figure.

Not just any figure. It was *the* figure. The person I had seen upstairs on the second floor for that split second.

My heart pounded so furiously that I thought I might actually be having a heart attack. This was definitely no figment of my imagination. No interplay of light and shadow.

I had run into it. I had felt its tangible body.

Who is this person? my horror-addled mind demanded.

Even though the figure's face was still covered with white cloth, I could feel it sneering at me as it swiftly stepped back and grabbed the basement door.

Instinctively, I pulled my hand away as the door swung toward me. I slammed my body against it, preventing it from closing. My mind could not even comprehend the horror of being locked alone down in the basement. I could not allow the door to shut.

I struggled, but the force on the other side was too strong. I couldn't budge it back an inch. I felt as if I were pushing against a brick wall.

"Let me out!" I screamed, hoping the others would hear me and come to my aid.

At that moment, the door swung open, away from me, taking me by surprise and throwing me off-balance. The figure stood silently within the doorframe, its covered gaze staring blankly at me like a store mannequin.

It was too late when I saw the figure raise a leg and thrust its heel into my stomach. The impact flung me backward, and I fell into the empty void. The door slammed shut, with a deafening *bang*, echoing loudly. It was a nail being driven into the lid of my coffin.

I was suspended in the air for a fraction of a second, or an eternity, I couldn't tell. Eventually, I fell against the stairs, my back hitting them with a loud smack. I grunted and yelped in pain as I bounced off each step, tumbling and rolling every which way all the way down until I came to land face-first onto what felt like a hard dirt floor.

There was not one single source of light down there. I could not tell if I was blind, or if I had blacked out. I did not know how much time had passed until I was finally able to move. I felt like I had been thrashed into one gigantic bruise. Warm blood dripped down my face from under my hair. Two of the fingers on my right hand were unnaturally stiff and painful. My scrambled brain told me they were probably broken.

A groaning cough forced itself from my mouth, puffing up dirt from the earthen floor. I inhaled the dust, which caused me to cough again. The temperature down here was noticeably warmer than it had been upstairs. I would have expected the opposite, but even the earthen ground had an eerie warmth to it, as if it had somehow absorbed the sun's rays all day.

The odor of rancid putrefaction stung my nostrils with a greater intensity, making my stomach wrench. I tried not to breathe through my nose. Whatever the reek was, it made me feel dirty and infected, like I was inhaling purulent air filled with hundreds of diseases.

I tried to heave myself up to a standing position. I only got halfway before I felt dizzy and collapsed back onto the warm ground. Tears began to stream down my face as pain—mingled with waves of dread and hopelessness—washed over me.

Why was all of this happening?

Why had I suggested we come to this damn place?

I waited a few moments to let the dizziness subside before attempting to push myself up again, finally managing to get into a sitting position. My scalp wound leaked, the blood running down my face and mixing with my tears before I wiped it all away with the back of my hand. I was certain that the gash on my foot had opened yet again and now bled once more.

I had no idea which way the stairs were from my current location. And because my head pounded and swam so severely at that moment, I couldn't even be positive which way was now up.

I hadn't hit my head and gone blind somehow, right?

"Help! Anyone!" I yelled with as much volume as I could muster. But after sitting in the unbroken silence for several minutes, I doubted Lorena or Corinne had been able to hear me. What if that tall figure got to them too?

"Guys! Please..."

"They won't hear you," a small, wispy voice said from somewhere in the fortress of darkness.

I gasped and jolted away from the voice's direction, accidentally smacking my broken fingers across my thigh. I yelped in agony, and a torrent of fresh tears flooded my eyes.

"Who are you?" I asked, my voice sounding weak to my ears. I gritted my teeth against the pain in my fingers. "Don't come near me." My eyes scanned uncontrollably—but uselessly—back and forth across the blackness.

"Rei, it's not me you have to worry about," the voice said, sounding almost sad. There was something familiar about it, but my throbbing head made it difficult to remember at that moment.

"Wh-Who are you?" I tried to demand, but the words came out trembling, imploring.

"I am truly sorry," the soft voice said, ignoring my question. "I realize now that I was too late with my warning. I tried reaching through as quickly as I could. I first attempted to contact you months ago in that elevator. It takes so much energy. I'm so sorry. But you should not have come here. You should have at least left, all of you, while you still had the chance. This isn't a good place for anybody to be. There are things here." There was a long pause. "But it's too late now, I'm afraid."

"Just tell me who you are!" I shouted, my voice sounding shrill to my ears.

"You have met me in the past. Long before coming here. But you didn't know at the time that I was there, right in front of you." There was a deep melancholy to the voice, as if longing for something that was forever out of its reach. "You could say I was hidden. But I know you. And I know

Corinne and Lorena. I've listened to you talk many times. Your voices were so warm and loving and... comforting."

Recognition dawned on me. The memories of my nightmare came flooding back, rushing into my mind to remind me of the terror I had felt. "You're the—the kid from my dream! But how are you here?"

"It's too late to leave now," the young voice said again, ignoring my question. "Abigail was tricked. She was tricked into accepting Her into her mind." Any sadness in the voice was lost, replaced by anger as he spat words out like rotten morsels. "She let that disgusting parasite deceive her and now it has infected her with its corruption. It is using Abigail like a puppet. Her mind was too vulnerable to resist."

"I don't know what you're talking about," I wailed in frustration. "Who is using Abby? What do you mean? How are they using her? Why is this happening?"

"The jar!" the child's voice raged. "You should have left that thing where it was. But you let Abigail open it. Now She has been let out! You shouldn't have come down here. You stupid people! Why did you let her open it? You should have stopped her! Damn you, Rei! I'll tear out your entrails and feed them to your friends"

A shriek escaped my mouth as something rushed across the earthen floor towards me. What felt like tiny hands began to close around my throat, but then were quickly pulled back. Something scampered away from me.

"S-Stay away from m-me!" I uttered, my voice trembling.

There was a long moment of oppressive silence.

"I am sorry," the boy whispered after a few minutes. There was no more anger in his words. "I didn't mean to do that. I have no intention of hurting you. It seems like the longer I'm in this awful place, the more I... lose control. There is an infection in this place that twists everything. This land isn't good for the living or the dead."

"What?" I wasn't sure I had heard the boy's words

correctly. "What do you mean the "dead?""

But the kid did not answer. Instead, the silence was broken by a soft susurration. It grew louder and louder, as if the source of the sound were drawing closer. It was louder than I had ever previously heard it. It was whispering no longer. It sounded like dozens of people all speaking at once, trying to talk over each other. I couldn't make out any of the words that floated around me. They were muffled, as if the people uttering them held something over their mouths.

"Oh no," the child said quietly, the fear evident in his voice. "They have come."

"What is it?" I asked hesitantly, my chest beginning to thump wildly. How much more could my heart take? "Who's come?"

"There are those who dwell here. Those who have been dead far longer than I have," he breathed as if not wanting to be heard. "And there are others. Others who are not among the living but who have never died."

Even with the warmth that permeated that basement, chills ran down my spine at the boy's words. Although I didn't quite understand what exactly he had been trying to say, none of it sounded good. I had to get out. Of that I was certain.

"The Metal-Faced Lady will return to herself soon," he said. "She has been waiting for longer than you can imagine."

"Who is the Metal-Faced Lady?" I whispered, biting my lip. "What does any of that mean?"

No answer came. I could still see nothing, but I somehow no longer sensed the boy's presence around. However, I got the very distinct feeling that something else was nearby.

"Is someone there?" I asked. Had I even said it out loud?

I listened, trying to hear over the rapid drumming of my heart. Blood or sweat or both dripped down my forehead, but I was afraid to make any move to wipe it away.

There was the sudden sound of shuffling. Had something just taken a few steps to my right? I instinctively turned my head in that direction, but the blackness around me was unbroken, unyielding. What sounded like a tired, heavy sigh emanated from my left. I clasped my hand over my mouth to stop myself from screaming.

Even with my body almost paralyzed with fear, I forced myself to scooch backward along the floor as slowly and soundlessly as possible. I didn't know what it was that stood next to me in that sunless pit, but I sure as hell didn't want to find out.

More sounds around me grew audible. I whimpered deep in my throat, desperately hoping that whatever was there couldn't see or hear me as I cautiously made my way backward. I had no idea if it was the right way to go, but it was imperative that I distance myself from the sources of those sounds as quickly as possible.

Like a clap of thunder, I was surrounded by the clanking and screeching cacophony of metal on metal, followed by loud mournful groaning and the creaking of what I could only identify as stiff limbs moving about.

"You!" a deep angry voice cried out amidst the racket, causing me to jump and let out a shriek, covering my head with my arms. It was a voice full of such pain and rage that my heart froze in pure terror.

"I knew it all along!" another man's voice bellowed.

"Get away from me!" a woman shrieked from nearby, with a voice like knives.

For only a second or two, everything went completely silent as if I had gone deaf. But then, the voices exploded all around me, again making the basement sound like it was packed with hundreds of people screaming all at once.

"I will murder you!"

"I'll tear off your skin and eat it!"

"I am going to rip out your eyes and shove them down your own throat until you choke to death!"

Dozens of hands like talons grabbed me from all sides, pulling me up off the ground. They clawed at me viciously as I screamed so loudly I thought my throat would bleed. The hands tore at my body, arms, legs, and face. It seemed as if some of them were wielding razor blades as they gouged my limbs and torso. White-hot pain erupted when a large chisel plunged into my shoulder, slicing and digging into the muscle, before being roughly yanked out. At the same time, teeth like jagged, broken glass bit into my thigh, tearing out a chunk of flesh.

In my extremity of terrified panic, I screamed until I could no longer pull breath into or out of my lungs. But still I tried to shriek.

The basement lights burst to life all around me. For a few seconds before they flickered out again they illuminated the room with their weak fluorescent bulbs.

In that brief moment of illumination, I saw that it was people, so many people—if they could still be called that—who were assaulting me. Their bodies were rotten and covered in bloodied, diseased-looking flesh, macabre tapestries of wounds covering them from head to toe. Bits of metal, some small, some large, had been embedded into their festering wounds, seemingly at random. Razor-like blades embedded in fingers, metal rods sticking out of chests and backs, steel plates grafted to limbs. None of them wore any clothing to hide the corruption of their mangled flesh. Only their heads were covered in dirty white, ragged cloth bound to their skulls with thin, bloodstained ropes and rusty wires that cut into their skulls. It was a mercy when the basement was flooded with darkness once more.

They crushed me into the floor under their assault. My arms and legs flailed wildly as I tried to fend the creatures off in the hot oppressiveness of the basement. My own warm blood flowed all over my body as more and more wounds opened up in my fragile, delicate flesh.

I yelled for help one last time. At least, I think I did. I

couldn't tell for sure. The sound of these creatures' cacophonous shrieking was deafening and my throat was numb. I pulled myself to my hands and knees, in an attempt to crawl away.

Two distinct pairs of hands grabbed my arms and shoulders and dragged me backward. I screamed and thrashed around like someone being electrocuted. My limbs were like live wires, hurting myself with my own desperate flailing. But I couldn't let them take me. I couldn't!

But I wasn't strong enough to stop them from pulling me away into the inky void.

CHAPTER TWELVE

They would twist all of creation into what it was truly meant to be. Corruption would infect, decay, reform, and recompose the unending cosmos into something worthy of existence.

"Rei, calm down!"

"Oh God, look at all those gashes..."

"Rei, can you hear me? Ouch! Stop flailing!"

I was shaken violently. As I gasped for breath, two frightened faces gradually came into focus. They stared at me in confusion, the utter worry clear in their eyes. I knew those eyes, one pair pale blue like a cloudless sky, the other a brown that always reminded me of golden amber.

They were my friends. And I was out of the basement, lying on the couch in the living room. There was light.

"Lorena? Corinne?" I said meekly. "Where are they? What happened?"

"Take a breath, Rei," Lorena said, wiping sticky strands of hair off my face. "What happened? Why were you down in the basement all night?"

All night? That couldn't be.

But as I looked out of the large window, I could see a gray and cloudy, yet obvious, morning sky.

"We've been looking for you all night! Didn't you hear us calling for you? Where did you go? You weren't down in the basement when we first checked there. Did you fall?" Lorena continued to pile question on top of question, not giving me a moment to respond.

My head pounded, and I looked away from the window and down at my bruised and bleeding legs and feet.

"Hell...You're bleeding all over the place. Corinne, get the first aid kit. Christ."

"There are things down there," I said quietly, my throat raw as I examined other parts of my battered body.

Something dripped down my face, but I couldn't tell if it was tears or blood.

"Things living in the basement. They attacked me! They tried to kill me!"

"What things?" Lorena asked, sitting down next to me and—steering clear of my injured fingers—holding my other hand gently and reassuringly in both of hers. "Like an animal? Did an animal attack you?"

I could tell from neither her expression nor her tone whether she believed me or was simply humoring me.

"No. Yes, th-they were like animals," I sobbed, unable to keep my voice steady. I gripped her hand in a vice with my convulsing fingers. "They were people, but something was...something was very wrong with them. They were crazy." I pulled my knees up to my chest, resting my forehead on them for a moment before looking back up. "Didn't you guys see them? Or even hear them? Didn't you smell them? That wretched stench. All that blood." I found myself unable to continue.

"We need to get the hell out of here," Corinne declared as she handed Lorena the first aid kit. Like a caged lion, she then proceeded to pace back and forth in front of us. "I don't care what time it is, or if we're packed, or how much gas we have. We need to leave right now." She looked at Lorena. Her tone was not requesting.

"I agree," Lorena said with a slow nod. She began pulling alcohol wipes and bandages out of the kit. Before this weekend, I don't think I had ever gotten so much use out of it.

After cleaning the dirt and blood off my hands, Lorena created a splint for my broken fingers with some tongue depressors, gauze, and tape. When she was satisfied it would hold, she set about bandaging every other wound she could see on me.

"We need to get everyone to a hospital as soon as possible," she said with a heavy sigh. "Something is very wrong here. We shouldn't have come here at all."

"I didn't want to come here in the first place!" Corinne screamed, her teeth bared in a furious grimace. "I wanted to go to Vegas! This place...This place has been getting weirder and weirder by the minute! Rei says she got attacked by crazy people down in the basement! And Abby's acting like some sort of insane—"

Corinne's tirade faltered as she realized Abby stood at the foot of the stairs, her hair still sleep-tousled. All the yelling must have woken her up.

"What's going on down here, girls?" she asked in an overly sweet, saccharine-infused voice. "I heard a lot of shouting going on. Is everyone okay?"

"No!" Corinne said in a voice so choked with emotion that I knew she could break down crying at any second. She strode over to Abby. "Everyone is definitely *not* okay! Has anything been okay since we got here? Haven't you been paying attention to everything that's been going on around you?"

Abby turned away from Corinne without saying a word. She looked at me curiously for a moment before striding over to where I sat, her fuzzy purple robe swinging lazily over the shirt and shorts she had slept in. She knelt down and examined my wounds intently. I pulled my right hand away before she could touch my broken fingers.

I couldn't quite figure out what the strange expression on Abby's face conveyed. She took hold of my arm and gently turned it this way and that to get a better look at the slashes and cuts.

I winced a little, wanting Abby to stop. But I couldn't seem to find the words to tell her to leave me alone.

Abby lay a light finger next to one particular ugly gash

and traced it almost tenderly with her fingertip. She then looked up at me, her eyes shining and a wide smile on her face. "Wow," she said, her voice full of awe. "These designs are amazing. Such beautiful carvings. You're so lucky. The Githya says that pain is a blessing, it helps strengthen those of us who are devoted to the truth. You've been strengthened, Rei. I can't wait for my own body to be adorned to its fullest. I know I'll have to wait, but it will be worth it. The Githya promised me that. She would strengthen me *herself*!" She let out a joyful giggle almost, it seemed to me, in anticipation.

"What the ever-loving hell is wrong with you?" Corinne growled, the venom heavy in her voice. She walked over and abruptly pushed Abby away from me, causing her to tumble backward onto her ass. "I don't know what's gotten into you. But you seriously need to see a shrink. I can't take this anymore."

I could see pain and fear underlying the rage on Corinne's face.

Abby stared up at Corinne for a few seconds, calmly meeting her hateful gaze with an expressionless face. She then burst out with mocking laughter.

Corinne was taken aback by the unexpected reaction.

"Oh, sweet Corinne," Abby giggled. "If only your pathetic little brain could understand what was going on here. I told the Githya you were pretty much useless and that She shouldn't waste Her time with you. But She is far wiser than I am. She told me She actually has a use for both you and Lorena. Can you believe it? You should consider yourselves most fortunate that the Githya even acknowledges your pathetic presence."

"Will you shut *up*?" Corinne bellowed. Her bandaged hands were pressed against the sides of her head as if she were ready to tear out her own hair at any second. "Shut up! Enough with your psycho rambling bullshit! Shut up! Shut up!"

Abby stood up. Her eyes rolled up into the back of her

head as she surged with laughter. Only the whites of her eyes remained visible, making her face resemble some grotesque, demonic mask.

Corinne's shouting, Abby howling in glee like a psycho, the pain wracking my body; it made the scene so utterly surreal.

As if this all weren't enough, at that moment there was a thunderous boom as every single door and window in the house burst open. Projectiles of splintered wood and shards of glass flew through the air from the force of the impact. A great wind roared and shrieked through the house, sounding like a tornado of tortured souls screaming out in unbearable pain. Lamps smashed against the wall, heavy furniture was overturned, books went flying, and we were all physically tossed about like ragdolls.

Just as suddenly as it had begun, the terrifying cyclonic gale ceased, and the house fell deathly still and silent.

I looked up from the floor near the hearth where I had been tossed, cautiously searching for any more surprises. Corinne moaned in pain close by. It looked like she had tried to take shelter under the large coffee table, but the thing had overturned, smacking her in its tumble. Corinne lay on the floor between both halves of the now broken table.

"What the hell just happened?" Lorena asked groggily.

As I sat up, I noticed a shallow laceration on her fore-head where something must have hit her during the... what? Freak windstorm? Poltergeist?

"Where...where did she go?" Lorena whispered after a few moments of deathly silence. Her eyes bulged from her skull.

"Where did who go?" I groaned, using the couch to push myself into a sitting position. My body was on fire with all of my cuts and bruises, the newly inflicted ones overlaying those from the basement. I found it increasingly difficult to corral my thoughts.

"A-Abby," Lorena answered, her voice almost inaudible

now. "I don't see her."

Corinne and I glanced around. Abby was nowhere in sight.

"God damn it," I muttered with very little energy. My broken fingers felt like they each had their own heartbeat. "Where the hell did she go now?" I pulled myself painfully the rest of the way to my feet.

"Who cares where she went? She's crazy!" Corinne insisted, her voice rising in a shrill pitch. "Let's just leave! Whatever all this is, I'm positive it started with her. When we reach town, we can send someone back for her. Let's just go!" Tears of anger and terror wet her face, sliding through some fresh cuts on her cheeks.

"No, we can't leave without Abby," Lorena said, but there was a conspicuous uncertainty in her voice. "It doesn't matter how erratically she's acting. We can't just abandon her here."

"Right," I agreed automatically, but without much conviction. Did I really want to stay for Abby? If they had both decided to leave right now, would I have wanted to stay behind?

"We wouldn't be abandoning her," Corinne protested. "We'll have someone come get her. We can't deal with this ourselves any longer. It's way over our heads now!"

"We are not leaving without her," Lorena insisted, putting her foot down.

"Fine! Screw you guys, I'm getting out of here then!" Corinne got to her feet and grabbed the car keys from inside my purse before turning and flying out the door.

"Damn it!" I growled as Lorena and I chased after her into the overcast day. Truthfully it was Lorena who did the actual chasing, and I limped after the both of them, my sliced and battered body protesting each movement I made.

As I stepped onto the porch, I saw that the gloominess wasn't due solely to the hazy sky. A fog so thick it was opaque blanketed the land around us, an impenetrable wall of gray, as if every cloud had descended to surround our small island.

Corinne stood motionless at the lakeshore just past the car. She stared out into the unending fog.

"Where did all this come from?" I asked as I caught up to them. I shivered and wrapped my arms around myself. Tendrils of ice caressed my spine. Every which way I looked, the view beyond the island was obstructed by the bulwark of fog engulfing us.

"It...it must have just rolled in recently," Lorena said with tense uncertainty. "It was clear and sunny when I got up this morning."

"It's not here..." I heard Corinne whisper in a defeated voice. She still stared out into the dense fog.

"What did you say?" Lorena asked, walking over to Corinne's side. I followed in silence.

"It's not here anymore," Corinne said again, not looking at us. "It's gone." I saw fresh tears begin to fall down her cheeks.

"What's gone? What are you talking about?" Lorena asked in a calmer voice, instinctively reacting to Corinne's change of mood. She followed Corinne's gaze and merely stared for a moment until her eyes widened in realization. "Oh my God."

"The bridge is gone," Corinne said, more to herself than to us. She sank to her knees then, as if a great weight had been placed upon her shoulders and her body lacked the strength to hold her up.

"Oh, come on. It's just covered by the fog," I said, dismissing her words. But I felt more than a twinge of fear in my stomach. I walked over to the shore's edge where we had driven across on the bridge, but there was nothing there except gently lapping water.

I must have been mistaken, and the bridge was a little to the left or right of where we stood. I had been stuck in fog like this a few times when I had spent a semester in England. It could get so thick, you could be standing a few feet from something and not even see it. I walked first in one direction along the shore, then the other, but could find no sign of the bridge.

"Rei, it's gone," Corinne said pitifully.

I could barely make out her fuzzy silhouette through the nebulous gray mist.

"It's not gone!" I yelled at her. "Bridges just don't disappear. It's not possible. It...it's just the fog. It's too thick to see through. It's just playing tricks on our eyes. It can do that."

I heard a frustrated sigh, but I couldn't tell if it came from Corinne or Lorena. They believed my explanation about as much as I did. I couldn't even find the tire tracks the car must have surely made when we had first arrived. What the hell was going on here? And—

"Where's Abby?" I said more to the fog than to my friends. "Abby!" I called out. I doubted she would come even if she heard me. I had no idea what state of mind she was in or what she might be up to.

"I don't want to be here anymore," I heard Corinne sob, her voice muffled by the almost-solid wall of gray. "I hate this place."

My brain felt as if the fog had started to seep into it through my ear canals. My head was clouded and heavy, and I had trouble thinking clearly. Things like bridges just don't disappear into thin air. They can't. It wasn't physically possible. Then again, was any of what had happened here logical?

"Maybe," I said, trying to clear my mind as I walked back over to the other two. "Maybe we can just swim back across to the other side. The bridge was what? About hundred feet long? I can make it."

"That sounds like a good idea," Corinne sniffled, a little hope returning to her voice.

"No, it doesn't sound like a good idea," Lorena said firmly. "You'll get totally lost in that fog. We can't even see the far side of the shore from here. You won't be able to see where you're going, and we won't be able to keep an eye on you or help you if you get in trouble. It's a bad idea."

"Lorena, it's the only way," I replied, eyeing her with determination. "I can make it across and then go get help."

"You almost drowned once already in that lake," Lorena pleaded. Her eyes were full of that motherly worry she always had for all of us. "Plus, look at you! You look like you've been through a meat grinder. I can't let you go. We have to try something else. We'll find another way."

"For fuck's sake, we're running out of time!" I shouted, trying to impress on her the urgency of the situation. "Things are getting worse by the minute. We're *all* injured. And who knows where Abby is and what she's got up her sleeve."

Lorena opened her mouth to argue with me some more, but whatever she had been about to say, it never came out. At that moment we heard panicked screaming coming from the shore. It was then that we noticed that Corinne had disappeared into the fog. Where she had been kneeling on the ground lay only the hoodie she had been wearing, and next to it her socks and shoes.

"Corinne!" Lorena and I both yelled and I found myself squinting into our gray surroundings as if I could push the misty wall away through sheer willpower.

What had happened now?

Please let Corinne be okay, my brain repeated over and over.

We ran through the heavy curtain of grayness toward the water and Corinne's inchoate shape became increasingly solid in front of us as we neared. She lay on the ground on her back, crying and shrieking. We fell to our knees beside her.

"Oh God, oh God, oh G-God," she kept saying as tears streamed down her face. She clawed at her leg. "I-I was going to g-go across...g-get help. I j-just p-put my foot in the wa-t-ter..."

She passed out.

Lorena and I looked down at Corinne's feet. Lorena choked back a scream.

I was on the verge of throwing up. My mouth opened and closed with little more than a gagging sound.

I couldn't tear my eyes away from Corinne's left foot. Most of the skin was gone, as if haphazardly torn off. And a large chunk, along with her pinky toe, was missing, leaving behind splintered bone and ragged muscle that bore the imprints of sharp teeth.

CHAPTER THIRTEEN

Rip the flapping tongue from your gaping maw. Tear the unseeing eyes from their sockets. Rend the muscles within your meat, letting the fibers snap with the music of the cosmos. Break every bone, let their jagged edges pierce through. Monuments to pain in the land of your flesh.

"This can't be happening," Lorena said tearfully as she and I—though I couldn't help much—carried the maimed and unconscious Corinne back into the house.

"Oh shit, oh God," I spluttered repeatedly. "What the hell did that to her? There's something in the lake!" My mind flashed back to memories of teasing Corinne about dangerous animals in the water.

We managed to lay Corinne carefully onto the couch. The various lacerations, stabbings, and bite marks covering my own body screamed at me in pain. But I ignored them for the moment, overcome by the sight before me.

There was blood everywhere, all over the floor, all over our clothes. Corinne's foot was horribly mangled, as if someone had taken a jagged razor blade and had sliced off large portions of her skin. Stringy tendons and torn muscle fibers hung limply from the flayed flesh like dead worms.

"She's going to die," I cried, tears flowing down my cheeks uncontrollably. My stomach churned. "She's going to die. She's going to die."

I had never felt so utterly helpless.

"Rei, shut up!" Lorena snapped at me. "Get me bandages! Are there even any left after everything that's happened? Fuck! Get towels, T-shirts, anything! Just help me. We need to stop the bleeding!"

There weren't any more bandages in the first aid kit, so I gathered up as many T-shirts and towels as I could find, plus a handful of pads from my bag, bringing them back to Lorena. She hesitated for a moment at even touching the foot, obviously afraid to damage it more. After a moment, though, she carefully wrapped several of the T-shirts around the wet, red, nauseating remains of Corinne's foot.

"She still isn't moving," I whimpered. I placed a shaky hand on Corinne's forehead, unintentionally leaving red blotches on her skin. "She's ice cold but sweating so much."

"She's lost a lot of blood," Lorena said as she finished wrapping Corinne's foot tightly in a towel. She was trying to remain brave and calm. "She's in shock."

"What are we going to do?" I asked, staring in hopelessness at Corinne's motionless face. Her lips—always smirking and coated in brilliant lipstick—had turned so pale.

"I don't know," Lorena said, the fear finally creeping into her voice. "She needs a hospital, badly. We all need a damn hospital. But we can't get off this fucking island now." She dropped her face into her blood-stained hands, allowing herself a moment of despair.

"There has to be a way out of here," I said, trying to convince myself as much as Lorena as I wiped my cheeks. "Bridges just don't disappear. Maybe it collapsed into the water."

"So what if it did?" Lorena replied, rubbing her temples. "That doesn't help us. What could we do? Pull it out of the water and rebuild it? We need to find another way across to the mainland. We obviously can't swim. There is...there's something swimming around in there. Maybe lots of things. We won't stand a chance if whatever's in there did that to Corinne when all she did was dip her foot in the water."

We stared at each other, each trying to draw strength from the other.

"There has to be a way," I said, more to myself. *There just has to be.*

"Where the hell is my phone?" Lorena demanded as I racked my brains for ideas.

"Maybe we can float across?" I suggested. "We can make a raft or something. Will a mattress float?"

"Maybe at first," Lorena said as she looked under the broken pieces of the coffee table for her phone. "But I think it will soak up the water and sink quickly."

"Then we can build a raft out of logs and stuff," I said, my voice rising to a slightly more desperate tone.

"What logs, Rei?" Lorena demanded. She sat down in an armchair and put her head in her hands once more. "There are only a few trees on this whole stupid island. Besides, do you have something to chop them down with? Do you know how to make rope to tie them all together?"

"I'm just trying to come up with solutions," I retorted irritably, crossing my arms.

"Well then come up with something that's not stupid shit!" Lorena roared, jumping to her feet. "We shouldn't have come here in the first place! I suggested we go to a weekend spa, remember? Massages, mud baths, pedicures? But do you guys *ever* listen to me? No, of course not. You never do what I suggest. And then in the end, I'm always the one who has to bail everyone out!" She threw her arms up in frustration. Her eyes blazed with fury.

I took an involuntary step backward, a bit frightened, my mouth hanging open. I had never heard Lorena yell like that before. She had always been the calmest and the most serene person I knew. The reliable and sensible one, the one to help everyone else, the one to solve all of our problems. Now she stood in front of me, her chest heaving, her jaw tight, a vein throbbing in her neck.

"I'm sorry," I whispered, realizing how unfair it was to always expect these things from her.

Suddenly her face changed back to the Lorena I knew. "I'm sorry too," she groaned, sitting back down. "I don't know what just came over me. I didn't mean that."

"I think you did," I said, though there was no anger or hurt in my voice. "But it's okay. We do always expect you to be the one to rescue us from our problems."

Her hands shook as she clasped them together in her lap. This was the first time I had seen Lorena lose it like that and yell in anger. But I suppose, considering everything we had experienced in this damn house this weekend, Lorena yelling was nowhere near the strangest thing to happen.

I knelt down beside her chair and wrapped my arms around her, hugging her tightly. We both wept for a long time, neither of us willing to let go of the other. I felt almost afraid to let go. What was going on here? Was this house haunted? Aren't haunted houses supposed to be old with a rich and violent history? Or was all of this just a figment of my imagination? Maybe I actually drowned in the lake and I was now in some sort of hell? Had I simply lost my grip on my sanity?

I didn't think so. But I hugged Lorena tighter just to make sure.

"I'm still sorry that I flipped out," Lorena said softly as she finally pulled out of the embrace.

"It's okay," I murmured, rubbing my puffy eyes. The pain from my gashed, clawed, and slashed body—and I couldn't forget my broken fingers—slowly seeped back into my consciousness. I was a mess, but at that moment, I had other things to worry about.

"The raft idea actually sounds solid," Lorena continued, her tone more confident now. "We just need materials. I'm almost positive I saw some old tools and some lengths of rope down in the basement when Corinne and I..." She cleared her throat. "When we had to go down to get you."

My eyes widened in terror at her suggestion. "No. No way," I said, holding my hands up in protest. "I'm not going down there again. Not with all those maniacs crawling around!" I looked down at the various injuries that tapestried my arms and legs. My entire body shook at the mere thought of returning to that lightless pit. "And there's no way I'm letting you go down into that hell hole."

"Rei, I didn't see anyone else other than you when I was down there," Lorena replied in a reasonable tone. "There was absolutely no one besides you. There's no way that many people could have hid from us. But I do believe something happened to you," she said. Holding up a fore-stalling hand before I could argue. "However, if there is stuff down there that can help us get out of here, then I think I have to go down and get it."

"No," I insisted, replaying my assault in the basement. "Promise me you won't go down there. Please, Lorena. Please promise me." I gripped her hand tightly, locking eyes with her.

"Okay, okay," she conceded, sighing. She patted my hand. "I won't go down there."

When I didn't loosen my grip, she went on.

"I promise, Rei. We'll look for things we can use up here. Or we'll think of something else." Rising from the armchair, she walked over to the couch to gaze down at Corinne, whose breathing was rather shallow and stroked her hair. "Hang in there, girl."

I gazed down at our friend whose foot was a butchered mess. A fresh surge of anxiety and regret washed over me. Oh God, why had I brought us here? The ever-present question punched at my conscience. How could I have brought my friends into such danger? And speaking of friends...

"Lorena," I said softly, turning to her. "Where do you think Abby is?"

"Honestly, right now, I don't care," she said in a somber voice, her eyes never leaving Corinne's face. "I hate that I feel that way. But, she has to be around here somewhere, right? She can't just leave the island any more than we can. There's no bridge. And she'd get attacked in the water too. At least, I assume so. She's probably holed up in the house somewhere or outside looking for where I buried that disgusting thing from the jar."

The thing from the jar. The image of its pulsating body and rank odor deepened my sense of anxiety. I shuddered with revulsion at the thought of that thing. But what had it been? Did it have anything to do with all of this? Maybe when Abby opened it in the living room and spilled those sickening juices everywhere, it spread some sort of disease? What if we all got infected and were now in the throes of fever-induced, dream-like states?

I looked down at a particularly gory gash on my arm and lightly touched it with a fingertip. I winced and let out a whimper. That was certainly real enough.

"You okay?" Lorena asked, glancing over at me in concern.

I nodded. "I just...I need to go take a shower," I said, suddenly feeling incredibly dirty, like the grime covering me was fusing to my skin. "I just need to get clean." I paused for a moment. "I'm going to use the downstairs bathroom. I don't want to be upstairs by myself."

"Alright," Lorena said, still standing over Corinne, watching her. "You go do that. I'll be here with Corinne."

I retrieved some fresh clothes from the pile of stuff I had brought down from the bedroom when Lorena had ordered clean wrappings for Corinne's foot and brought them with me to the bathroom by the kitchen, feeling relieved I didn't have to climb the stairs again.

Flicking the lights on, I shuffled into the bathroom, setting my things down on the small vanity. The floor was made up of brown, marbled tile, while the walls were slats of polished wood. The interior of the shower was covered in gray stone. I remembered my mom saying that it felt like you were showering in a forest under a gentle waterfall.

Opening the glass shower door, I reached for the knob and turned it on. The water warmed quickly, steaming up the mirror.

I undressed as gingerly as I could. I peeled my shredded T-shirt and shorts off. It was quite painful since they were sticky with sweat and blood and had adhered to my wounds, tugging at the gashes as I stripped the cloth away. I found myself wincing each time I grazed a laceration or when my broken fingers got caught in the fabric. But finally, I managed to get everything off and stepped into the shower's embrace.

The hot water stung my body at first. But after a few minutes, the sensation was mostly pleasant. The warmth of the water seeped into my skin and muscles, relaxing away the pain and the stress. The dirt, grime, and blood that was plastered all over my skin from the attack in the basement slid off my body in small waves, leaving raw, pink wounds behind. A puddle of dirty red water accumulated around my feet.

As I looked down at my skin, I almost felt that I could see a pattern in the injuries covering me. It was almost as if they weren't random, but rather purposeful markings.

Hadn't Abby said something about being marked?

I shook my head. No. I didn't want to think about that stuff anymore. Lorena was right. There were probably no people down there in the basement. I had gotten hurt by falling down the steps. That had to be it, right? I had hit my head hard and imagined the entire thing.

After letting the water pour over my face for a while, I slowly lowered myself down and sat on the smooth stone floor of the shower, bringing my knees up to my chest and letting the hot water fall all over me like rain. I wanted to stay forever in that moment of peace. It was so warm, so comfortable. I felt relaxed for the first time in what seemed like forever. I turned my face upward with my eyes closed, the water pattering down onto my face.

Something spluttered, like a wet cough, and my eyes snapped open. My heart began to pound, but I saw nothing.

I'm hearing things again.

I then noticed that the shower drain seemed to be draining very slowly, and I now sat in a half inch or so of water.

Great. All of this weirdness and now a clogged drain.

I almost laughed at the banality of the problem.

I shifted from my sitting position to my hands and knees, being careful of my injuries, and took the little metal cover off of the drain. I could not see through the overflowing water down into the pipe.

Probably just a ball of hair.

My parents had probably used this shower when they had been here renovating.

I stuck my fingers down the drain, fishing around for the obstruction. When I touched a disgusting, wet hairball and extracted it, I made a repulsed noise in my throat and tossed the wad of hair onto the shower floor.

That should do it.

I prepared to sink back into the relaxed state that the hair clog had interrupted. But I was wrong. The water still refused to go down. Maybe there was more hair? I reached down into the drain again, my fingers searching for another blockage.

That's when I touched something that wasn't hair.

Something soft and quivering.

A short gasp escaped my throat, and I yanked my hand away. What the hell was in there? Did I even want to know?

I hadn't soaped up or washed my hair yet or anything, but I was definitely done with my shower right then and there. I couldn't deal with any more surprises.

I backed away from the drain, sitting back on my feet. Before I could stand up to get out of the shower, some sort of writhing, membranous polyp burst out of the drain with a wretched squelching pop.

I pushed myself away from it, my right hand slipping on the wet floor, causing my elbow to slam into the ground. Searing hot pain shot up through my arm. I scrambled back into a corner as I watched the thing squeeze itself out of the drain. It stood about three feet high, rising out of the drain, and its slimy, pulsating flesh was the nauseating color and texture of raw-liver.

My stomach turned violently, and icy-cold dread filled

my insides. Goosebumps erupted over my skin even with the hot water still pouring down on me. I felt like my mind was going to tear itself apart, as if this were the last straw to break my sanity.

"This isn't happening. This isn't happening," I kept repeating to myself as the polypous thing continued to writhe out of the drain. I was paralyzed, and though the monstrosity utterly revolted me, I could not tear my eyes away from it.

It remained there, looking like a demonic plant that had crawled out of some dank, hellish pit to take root in the shower floor. For a moment it stopped moving, and I thought—I prayed—it was dead.

All of a sudden there came a sound so awful and so sickening, it burned itself into my brain; a memory that I knew, whenever recalled, would cause my own brain to writhe in furious agony as I spiraled just a little bit further into madness.

It was the wettest, grossest rending, flesh-tearing sound.

The tumor-like polyp-thing ripped itself open like a time-lapse video of an overripe fruit. The top split wide to reveal a ragged cavity. What I first thought was a wormy, bruise-colored tendril burst forth, thrashing around in the air.

My hand shot to my mouth as I realized what this actually was—a tongue. For when the cleft in the polyp-thing widened even farther, I saw circular rows of long, brown teeth lining the inside. Every so often, the horrible, slimy tongue retreated into the creature's mouth to greedily lick at its wet, rotten-looking gums.

Something snapped inside my head. Was I losing my mind? Or had I already lost it? This couldn't be happening. My heart leapt into my throat and everything else inside me melted into the bottom of my stomach. My skin prickled and itched. All the happiness and hope drained from my soul, as if my mind was cracking apart and leaking out everything within. I couldn't deny the horrifyingly maddening events happening any longer. They weren't just nightmares conjured up by my brain. There was something truly beyond understanding occurring in this house. Something was here that did not belong in this world.

"Help!" I finally managed to scream. "Lorena!"

But there was no answer.

I managed to steady my mind for a moment. If I could just manage to jump around this thing and get out of the shower...

But my thoughts were interrupted by a retching sound that reminded me of my grandma's elderly cat about to upchuck a hairball. The drain creature choked and heaved violently as though it was trying to get something out of its throat. Was it drowning in the slowly rising water?

The monster gave a powerful retching heave upward, straining against its grip on the drain, and spewed out several white, maggoty worms each about the size of my forearm. I glanced back to confirm the small size of the drain...How could things that size...None of this made sense!

A shriek was wrung out of me as one of the pale, squirming worms latched onto my ankle. A stinging pain shot through my foot. The thing was sucking blood out of me. I kicked and thrashed trying to dislodge the maggoty horror, but it held firmly onto me.

In the next moment, the long, black tongue of the drain-creature whipped out and grasped the white worm on my foot. It tore the thing off leaving a gaping hole in my skin with blood dripping down my ankle.

The drain-creature pulled the large maggot into its waiting mouth. It made a chomping and popping sound like someone biting down on a ripe tomato. A small spurt of blood—my blood—came out of its mouth as it ate the maggot.

The rest of the worms advanced on me, wriggling their slimy forms across the flooding shower floor.

I lifted my least-injured foot and brought it down as hard as I could, stomping on the nearest maggot with all of my strength. The pale white flesh burst open, and a yellowish bile covered my foot, getting between my toes. A stench that reminded me of decaying farm animals infected my nostrils.

I didn't care, no matter how much my stomach protested, I brought my foot down again and again on the remaining worms. Each one popped like an overfilled water balloon. White membranous flesh and bile splattered everywhere.

The drain-thing squealed in anger and lashed out at me with its whip-like tongue. I tried to dodge the whip, but it caught me on the cheek. I was able to avoid the next lash entirely, however, the tongue missing me by mere inches as it slammed the glass wall of the shower.

The glass shattered. It must have injured the thing's tongue, for it squealed in anger again and withdrew the black, writhing appendage back inside its mouth. I took the moment of distraction to leap around the thing and get out of the shower.

A small shard of glass lodged itself in my already injured foot. I screamed in agony and quickly extracted it, jumping around on one leg for a moment, trying not to slip.

Stupid glass!

Stupid house!

Stupid crazy shit that shouldn't be happening!

I threw open the bathroom door and flew out, slamming it behind me. I couldn't tell if I was laughing, crying, or both. But it didn't matter. I had gotten away.

"Ah, he didn't get you, eh?" a strange voice said from behind me.

I spun around so quickly, I made myself dizzy. I stood there naked, wet, and vulnerable, and before me now was not one of my friends, but an old woman wearing a silky red and gold shawl.

"Y-You?" I sputtered, confused out of my mind.

It was the squat old woman we had seen walking on the side of the road as we drove up to this accursed place. The old woman I had almost run over.

The woman who had been in Abby's hospital room months ago.

In response to my question, she hit me on the side of my head with something heavy and everything faded away.

CHAPTER FOURTEEN

But you can come to learn. Forsake the falsities of what has been driven into your skull since the beginning of forever.

I slowly opened my eyes, but immediately closed them again to block out the blinding-hot light that pierced my retinas. My head throbbed like it had been split open and now everything inside was leaking out of it onto the dirty floor.

The floor?

Yes. I seemed to be on the floor.

I tried to reach up with my fingers to examine my head wound, but I couldn't move either arm or any part of my body at all. The image of the old woman flashed through my mind. I could even hear her voice, with its hint of some strange and unidentifiable accent, as the memory replayed itself again and again in my brain.

No, the voice wasn't in my mind.

Pushing back against the excruciating pain, I eased open my eyes, letting them gradually adjust and focus. Blurry shapes slowly sharpened, and I realized I lay in one of the upstairs bedrooms. The short old woman clad in the same crimson garments that she had been wearing back in Abby's room in the hospital held up an ancient-looking, wrought iron lantern. She bent over someone else on the floor a few feet from me.

Lorena!

"Where is She?" the old woman spat, giving Lorena

a hard kick in the hip. "The Somas do not tolerate hindrances, girl. You will cooperate, or you will suffer."

"Please, stop!" Lorena cried, her face and voice both conveying the terror and pain she must have been feeling.

I was paralyzed. My hands were fastened behind my back with rope. But there was something else pressing against my mind that forced me to remain immobile, despite my desperate urge to help my friend. I could only watch through half-open eyes. I could see a plethora of crying, red lacerations all over Lorena's skin. The old woman held a large, blood-stained knife in her hand.

"I don't know who you're talking about! Is it Abby? I don't know where she is!" Lorena pleaded with the woman, her voice rising in desperation.

"No, I am not speaking of Abigail," the woman snarled, her tone indicating that Lorena already knew this. "She is already with the other Somas. Stop pretending to be too stupid to understand. Do you really think that is a useful tactic?" She waved the knife in front of Lorena's face. "Where is the Arch-Githya? What have you done with her?"

"I don't know what you're talking about!" Lorena screeched, the sound of her voice turning from terror to agony. "I'm telling you the truth!"

I shuddered as the old woman sliced deep into Lorena's thigh, fortunately not near the femoral artery. I yearned to help my friend. I wanted to bash this old lady's face in. But my body was held in stasis by some force, in addition to the rope, that I couldn't see. My only option was to lie there, feigning unconsciousness until I could move or formulate some plan. I hoped the old bitch didn't try to get answers out of me next.

"For the last time, child," the old woman said, shuffling over to the bedroom window, opening it, and looking down at the back of the house. The dusky sky was still heavily clouded and thick with the mysterious fog that encased the island. "Tell me where Arch-Githya Kamilla is!" Her tone left no doubt that she had almost exhausted her patience and would soon take more drastic measures.

Just then, I thought I could hear the faint sound of people speaking coming from somewhere outside, below the window.

"Abigail told us how you cruelly took the Arch-Githya away from her," the old woman continued, tuning back to face Lorena. "Abigail found our Kamilla down in the water, trapped in that accursed vessel. But when she freed the Arch-Githya, you took Her away and hid Her. We know Kamilla is not dead. We would have felt it. So, tell me where She is!" The old woman slapped Lorena hard across the face, the sharp smacking sound lingering in the air for several seconds.

Lorena looked stunned, befuddled, but then comprehension dawned on her face. "The...the thing from the jar? That's what you're after? The thing that Abby found in the lake? We got rid of that—"

There was another scream as the old woman jabbed the knife into Lorena's left bicep. I strained my jaw in an effort to shout out, wanting to draw the attention away from Lorena, to help her. But I could do nothing. It was like a spell had been cast over me to turn me to stone. I felt wracked with guilt at my inability to act.

I'm so sorry, Lorena.

"How dare you do such a thing to the Arch-Githya?" the old woman hissed in a deadly whisper. "You will come to respect Her, unless you wish to suffer pain like you've never even imagined before. Now tell me where She is hidden before I start removing your fingers and toes. I'll feed them all to your friend over there, making sure she chokes down every last one of them."

"Please don't!" Lorena begged, her voice hoarse from crying and pleading. "I b-buried it outside behind the house. It's by that stone altar thing. It's there in the ground!"

"Now that wasn't so hard, was it?" Out of my half-closed eyes, I saw the old woman straighten up and walk toward me. I let my eyelids close—the only part of my body I could control—hoping she hadn't noticed their movement.

Thankfully she walked past me, out of the bedroom, without a glance. The stairs squeaked as she waddled down to the first floor.

At her departure, I felt some great oppressive weight lift. My arms were still bound painfully behind my back in the same manner as Lorena's were, but at least I could now squirm around.

I waited a few minutes, listening hard to see if the old bitch was coming back. When there was no sign that she would, I managed to roll onto my stomach and use my bound legs, shoulder, and the side of my face to push myself up into a kneeling position before shuffling over to the crying Lorena.

Before I had been knocked unconscious, I had fled from the bathroom covered in nothing but water—the sudden memory of the shower and the drain-creature flashed before my eyes, sending a lightning bolt of terror through me to settle as a queasy knot in my bowels. But now I wore some sort of dress or tunic that reached down to my knees. It was made of a rough, itchy fabric, dyed a deep red and covered with golden embellishments that formed eerie, unfamiliar patterns and pictographs. Lorena was wearing an identical garment.

"Lorena," I whispered, scooching closer to her so that our shoulders touched. I tried to ignore how the coarse fabric made my skin itch and caught and pulled at my wounds. "It's okay, she's gone. What happened?"

Lorena just lay there with her eyes squeezed shut, unmoving.

"I blacked out. I think that asshole hit me when I came out of the shower. Lorena, what's going on? Talk to me."

"I don't know," she managed to whisper after choking back sobs. "I was looking around the house for stuff we could use for our raft, when they burst in through the front door."

"They?" I asked, my fear clicking up a few more notches. "So, there's more than just the old lady?" I remembered the voices I thought I had heard coming from outside the window when the old woman had opened it.

Lorena sniffled and nodded, looking at me out of the corner of her eye as if afraid to turn her head. "They call themselves the Somas of Light."

"What the hell? Do you know how many there are?"

"I don't know. Maybe a dozen, I think," Lorena replied, sounding utterly exhausted. Finally, she turned to look at me. "Rei, these people are insane. We need to get out of here. Now!"

She didn't need to tell me twice.

I shifted around on the floor, turning around and lying back-to-back with Lorena so I could begin to work on untying the bindings that held her hands together. My mind leapt forward, trying to concoct a plan. How were we going to escape the island while also avoiding those psychos and whatever was in the lake?

Lorena squeaked as I accidentally pinched her skin. I whispered an apology, but I knew I had to get these ropes undone as quickly as possible. Our lives depended on it.

"I almost have it," I said after about what seemed like an eternity of working to untie Lorena's knots.

I finally managed to loosen it enough for her to slide her hands out of the rope and she began to untie mine. After our bonds were off, we hugged each other fiercely, but briefly, my shoulders sore and stiff from the position they had been held in, my body still in agony from the wounds suffered in the attack in the cellar. There was still a slight throb in my head, but luckily, all the paralysis seemed to be gone.

"We have to get away," Lorena whispered urgently, her eyes red and teary, her hands on my shoulders shaking. "They are going to kill us. I know they will!"

"You don't have to convince me," I replied.

There was no doubt in my mind that these crazies would

try to kill us. But they hadn't. Not yet, at least. They had tied us up and dragged us upstairs. They were saving us for something. But what? Maybe just until they recovered the thing from the jar. What they wanted it for, I couldn't fathom, and didn't let my mind linger on it.

We needed to get far away from these people as fast possible and alert the authorities.

"They got to the island somehow," I said as the thought occurred to me.

Lorena nodded in agreement. "Maybe we can leave the same way. But we can't leave here without Corinne and Abby."

My thoughts jumped to Corinne. Was she still downstairs on the couch? Was she even still alive? She had lost a lot of blood. *So much blood.* And then Abby...The old woman had said that she had spoken with Abby. Was Abby helping these people? No, I couldn't believe that. Abby was our friend. Had they tortured her into talking? That was an awful thought that I didn't wish to dwell on. Or perhaps Abby had become so delusional...

"Did they do anything to Corinne?" I asked, dreading the answer. "What about Abby? That crazy old woman said she was with them."

"I don't know," Lorena said, holding her head in her hands. "I still haven't seen Abby. Corinne was still unconscious when those people burst into the house. They brought me up here before I could see what they did with her. I heard muffled screaming and crying, but I didn't know if it was you or her. Then they dragged you up here. You were unconscious when they dropped you next to me and I thought you were dead. I was so scared. What if Abby and Corinne have been killed?" Tears began spilling out of her eyes once more.

"They're not dead," I said, trying to comfort my friend, although of course I had no idea in what state they were, and there was no way I could be sure. "But I'm here, okay? I'm not dead. And neither are you." I couldn't let her get hysterical or I'd get hysterical too. We needed clear heads. We needed to feed off each others' strength instead. "We have to come up with a plan to get out of here. Let me just take a peek outside, okay?"

Crawling on my hands and knees, I approached the window, trying to be as silent as possible on the creaking floorboards. When I reached the wall, I cautiously edged myself upward until I could see out of the window. I peered through the dirty glass. It was difficult to tell because of the dense fog, but it seemed to be evening. How long had I been out? The water looked cold and uninviting, lapping at the sand as if trying to ooze its way up to us.

As I had expected, there were people down on the ground beside the house, about a dozen of them as Lorena had said. These "Somas of Light," or whatever stupid name they called themselves, all wore scarlet robes or vestments covered in golden accents. All of them had their hoods up, hiding their faces in shadow. But even when a sharp breeze lifted the edge of a hood and allowed me a glimpse underneath, I could only see faces wrapped in dirty cloth and bound tight with ropes and wires. There was no question in my mind that this some sort of damn cult.

The strangers stood side-by-side around the flat altar-like stone by a small copse of spruce trees. The area had been cleaned of weeds and overgrowth, and now a golden sheet lay neatly on top of it. Some of the figures were busy setting large red candles—about five feet tall—on the ground around the altar, all of them burning with bright red flames.

They were obviously setting up for something that I wanted no part of.

"Lorena, let's go," I whispered, crawling away from the window. "Let's get out of this room before that hag comes back."

Lorena shook her head, the rest of her body unmoving, paralyzed by fear, terror and trauma etched deeply onto her face. Her whole body shivered violently. The cuts inflicted by the old woman oozed and looked painful.

"I know you're scared," I cajoled. "I am too. But we have to move. You said so yourself." I grabbed her arm and gently tugged until she relented, getting slowly to her feet and following me out of the bedroom.

Holding Lorena's hand firmly, I peeked out of the door. There was no one around. We shuffled out of the bedroom, our shoeless feet moving as quietly as possible across the floorboards. Making sure there was nobody right below, I led Lorena down the staircase, trying to ignore the itchiness of the tunic I was wearing.

We made it all the way down the stairs without incident. We were in the living room. I could see where Lorena had put up a struggle when the bastards broke in. The dining table was flipped and broken, chairs were toppled, and a lamp had been smashed. Or had it been that freak windstorm that did this? Things were blurring together in my battered mind.

I shook my head to clear my thoughts. The couch where Corinne had lain was now empty. There was a deep crimson stain where her maimed foot had rested—the blood had soaked through the T-shirts and towel that Lorena had used as improvised bandages.

"Oh God, they took her," Lorena whimpered, not bothering to keep her voice down. "Rei, what are they doing to her? What if they're hurting her? What if they kill her? And where the hell is Abby? Oh God. They've got us trapped here. They're going to kill us all!" Her eyes were wild and her breathing ragged.

Don't do this to me, Lorena.

She had always been the strongest one in our group of four. She was our rock, our support. She had always kept us calm and out of trouble. I couldn't have her snapping now. She was the brave one. Not me!

"Lorena, calm down," I said in an urgent whisper, grabbing her by the shoulders, but she burst into loud, hysterical sobbing.

A soft rustling noise came from behind me. I saw Lorena's eyes—looking over my shoulder—fill with terror. I spun around to see two robed figures, their faces covered and bound like the others, walking out from the kitchen.

"Don't let them escape!" one of them hissed as it pointed a long finger at us.

They lunged, each one going for one of us.

Lorena leaped backward, her foot catching on a rug. She went crashing to the floor, but not before grabbing my tunic and bringing me down with her.

The pair of robed figures were instantly upon us.

Lorena and I flailed madly, trying to get them off of us. I couldn't tell whether they were men or women, but they were strong. They dragged us up and held our wrists firmly in their vice-like grips.

"Outside," the figure holding me said in a raspy voice. The stench of its breath filled my nose. It smelled like rancid meat left out in the hot sun for too long.

"Yes," the other figure responded in a voice I could only describe as slimy. "We are about to begin."

CHAPTER FIFTEEN

...and I possess the knowledge of infinite dead minds. No being, save my master, has obtained more knowledge of creation than I. Heed my dark testament, and I shall show you putrid, forbidden insights and dreadful power of such formidability that simple minds cannot even begin to fathom it, and would shatter into innumerable pieces were they to try.

Lorena had stopped crying and remained silent and seemingly compliant—though I still struggled furiously—as the two red-robed figures pushed us through the living room, down the hallway, and out of the back door to the rear of the house.

As I had seen from the window, about a dozen people gathered around the large flat stone in the rapidly growing dusk. There was no doubt now that this was an altar, with all the candles flickering around it and the golden cloth resting on top. The figures were all wearing identical crimson vestments with gold accents. The facial features of each were obscured by dirty white wrappings that encased their faces, bound tightly with dirty ropes and metal wires around their heads. It all reminded me of the mysterious figure I had glimpsed upstairs and who had later kicked me into the basement. It had to have been one of these fuckers, right?

It was an unnerving sight. Had I not been witness to so many varieties of unnatural acts and phenomena over the last few days, I would certainly have been screaming my head off and wetting my pants. If I had been wearing any pants, that is, and not this damn tunic that had me convinced I was to be part of some ritual where they sacrificed me.

The thought drained any hint of warmth from me, like water escaping a bucket perforated on the bottom.

Oh God, no. That's exactly why I'm wearing this thing.

The two figures holding us hostage guided us closer to the altar and forced us to kneel down before it in the damp grass. In unison, they retrieved crude-looking daggers from inside their robes and held them against our throats, preventing any escape or even further struggle.

A small hole had been dug in the ground near the altar in the exact spot from which I had seen the foul sludge ooze out from the dirt the other night. I glanced at Lorena, whose large eyes stared at the hole in disgust and terror. She made not a peep though, and her face settled into a defiant mask.

Lorena's initial reaction was all the confirmation I needed. That had to be the spot where she had buried the grotesque, fetus-like thing from the jar after we had pried it away from a crazed Abby.

Abby. Who knew where she was? I hoped she had found a way out of this hellish lake and had gotten herself to safety. Maybe she would even find help to send back here and rescue us.

"Ah," a now familiar voice said, approaching from behind us.

The squat old woman stepped into view, next to the altar. At her side stood another robed figure. The face of this one was obscured, not with white cloth, but with a golden mask designed to look like a woman's visage but with tall twisting horns and a fanged smile. The thing looked like it had come from straight out of an ancient artifacts exhibit in a museum.

The old woman looked at us. "I'm so glad you could join us here. This place..." She took in a deep breath, then exhaled loudly, spittle flying from her wrinkled lips. She spoke clearly in a strong, ringing voice. "This place holds such great power. Power of the world that once was. Power of the Ancients who used to rule that world. They have been gone from this reality for far too long. But they shall return! Oh yes, they shall return. And who will be the ones to usher in the return of these glorious beings? Us! It is the Somas of Light who will have this greatest honor, this most glorious gift, to bring forth the most hallowed Masters."

"What the hell are you talking about?" I shouted, rage flaring within me. "You're insane! This is all some fucking crazy cult shit! None of this stuff ever works. Everyone drinks the punch, but you all just die. Nothing grand or glorious happens. Are you going to sacrifice us to the devil or something stupid like that? Well, you can all go fuck yourselves!"

Lorena said nothing. She simply stared straight ahead, eyes unreadable.

"The devil?" the old woman croaked, then burst out laughing.

All the other robed figures began making throaty, choking noises, which I realized was the sound of them chuckling.

"Ha! There is no merit to such myths. Do not insult us with such an accusation. We serve only the *true* Ancient Ones." She threw open her arms wide and stared up into the sky.

I hadn't realized how dark it had gotten. As the old woman waved her arms toward the clouds above, they drifted apart, revealing the fading, bruise-colored sky. The thick fog around the island remained a solid barrier, however.

She couldn't have just done that. It had to be some sort of coincidence or illusion. A person could not control the weather.

"Stop all of this!" I bellowed much louder than I thought my raw throat could manage. "Please, just let us go free.

This isn't right. You know it isn't! Whatever you plan to do to us won't summon your demons or your gods or whatever. Please, stop." The last words came out as more of an entreaty than a demand.

The old woman turned her gaze away from the twilit sky to face me. "Oh, my sweet dearie. I know that. Of course, I do not have the power to summon an Ancient One to this plane from the deep abyss. Such power requires someone special. I am certainly not that person. No, no. I cannot do it."

A surge of hope rose within me.

"But," the hag continued, smirking. "I will bring forth one who can."

Whatever vestige of hope that had been momentarily kindled inside me now plummeted into the lightless pits of my stomach. What I wouldn't have given to wake up in my bed right then to discover that all this had just been a horrible dream.

"Go," the old woman ordered some of the cultists. "Bring out the nest."

I had no idea what she meant by "nest." Though I knew I very much wished to not find out. But soon enough, a diseased stench violated my nostrils with a burning, putrid stink.

Two robed figures walked into view, carrying between them a large wooden chest, about the size of a steamer trunk with eerie sigils carved deeply into it. They set the chest down before the old woman, and she gave a curt nod to the two figures. As they lifted the lid, the rank odor grew worse, assaulting me like a battering ram.

"Oh God," I muttered. "The thing from the jar?" What else could produce such a stench? But why would they need such a large box for it?

"Don't be stupid," the old woman sneered at me. "This is not the Githya! This is merely a tool."

A tool? What kind of tool?

The Soma cultists overturned the box and dumped

something just as awful as the jar-thing onto the ground. I could feel the color drain from my face. The monstrosity looked like it had once been a human, but was now a mere mockery of twisted, horrid flesh. It was curled into a fetal position with what had probably once been arms hugging its knees. All of these limbs were fused together, as if some great heat had melted the flesh. The whole thing's body was riddled with fist-sized pores, each of which was a visceral red and leaked a thick, yellowish pus.

The sickening thing was alive. It twitched and shivered every so often.

The cultists rolled it over on the ground next to the altar giving Lorena and I an unwanted better view of the thing. What the hell had these crazy people done to this wretched body? Was this a former cultist or an unwilling victim? Was this going to happen to Lorena and me? Were they going to transform us into twisted abominations?

I almost retched at the thought.

"Now bring me the girl," the old woman said after seeing that the "nest" was positioned where she wanted. My heart froze. She could only mean one of two people, Corrine or Abby.

My fears were confirmed moments later when the same two figures returned, carrying a very pale and obviously drugged or delusional Corinne, who mumbled incoherently and couldn't seem to focus her eyes on anything around her.

"Corinne!" I started to scream, but the robed figure behind me pressed the dagger harder into my throat.

"No, no, no," I heard Lorena whisper, tears flowing freely down her cheeks once more.

They lay Corinne, who was dressed in a red tunic like ours, on the golden cloth-covered altar. She tried to mutter something, but I couldn't understand her words. She lifted a weak arm, but it was forced back down and held in place by a cultist.

Oh, Corinne, was all I could think. She probably had no

idea where she was or what was happening.

No. Please no. Don't hurt her.

The old woman stepped up to the end of the altar where Corinne's head lay, brushing one wrinkled, liver-spotted finger across Corinne's cheek almost lovingly. One of the Somas that had brought Corinne then ceremoniously presented the old woman with some sort of ancient-looking crank with a sharp point on the end. The point was made of red crystal. The thing was like an old, evil-looking hand auger.

The old woman set the tip of the point onto the middle of Corinne's sweaty forehead.

"Oh shit," I gasped out as the sudden realization about what was going to happen hit me full force. "Oh shit...No! Stop! Get away from her! Don't touch her. Oh shit....Oh shit...!"

"No!" Lorena growled, despite the dagger held tightly against her throat. "No, don't do this! Leave her alone! She doesn't deserve this. What did we do to you?"

"Lorena?...Rei?" Those were the only words Corinne got out before the only sound she could make was a terrible, agonized shriek.

Lorena closed her eyes and turned away, biting her lip, her body wracked with sobs. But I could only watch in silent horror as the old hag turned the crank, piercing Corinne's forehead with the auger.

Blood, so much blood, flowed down Corinne's screaming face and into her blonde hair, coloring it crimson. The crank tore through flesh and ground against bone as the old woman used strength that she shouldn't have possessed to pierce a hole into our friend's forehead. Corinne flailed in confused agony but was roughly held down by four of the robed cultists.

So much blood everywhere.

She has no idea what's happening. Just...just pain.

I knelt on the ground, watching my friend being tortured. I was biting my bottom lip so hard, I felt warm copper flow into my mouth.

A hollow numbness grew inside me as I watched the old woman struggle momentarily to turn the hand crank as the point drilled through Corinne's skull. The low grinding noise filled my ears, punctuated by my friend's tortured howls. I knew my sanity was at risk if I had to watch and listen to this for a second longer. That was one of my best friends up on that altar, dying as her brain was being drilled into for God knows what foul purpose.

I've known her since childhood.

Scenes of our adventures over the years went through my mind. Silly games and pranks, late nights, laughing, crying, hugging, the four of us inseparable...

The crystal drill broke through Corinne's skull with a nauseating crack followed by a squelch and large spurt of blood. The old bitch paused to wipe her brow then flashed me a sinister, satisfied smile.

"Bring me a decrypter," the hag ordered, holding out her hand as she stared at her handiwork.

The Soma who had handed her the drill nodded as he stood over the body referred to as the "nest." I didn't want to see what was going to happen next, but I was paralyzed once again, and I just couldn't stop watching the horror show in front of me. Some part of me felt that if I turned away, I would be somehow abandoning Corinne.

The faceless Soma plunged a hand deep into one of the large pus pockets that covered the body of the nest. As further evidence that the thing had once been a person, the nest moaned in agony as the cultist groped around inside the pore, wrist-deep in the flesh, and its body writhed as much as its mutated form allowed.

The Soma finally extracted his hand, pulling something out of the nest's body. I wanted to squeeze my eyes shut, but I could only watch as the cultist held up a bloated spider-like creature comprised of gelatinous flesh and writhing legs with sharp barbs on each end. The thing wriggled and undulated in a stomach-churning motion.

My traumatized mind had no idea whether this creature was alien or demonic.

The cultist brought the struggling abomination over to where Corinne lay, her body slack and unmoving.

"Get that thing away from her, you monsters!" I shouted, my voice hoarse. The knife at my throat pressed more firmly against my flesh in warning.

"I hope you all burn in hell for all eternity," Lorena spat.

The cultist handed the old woman the undulating, fist-sized mass, dropping it into the hag's cupped hands. The old woman's expression was one of excitement. She whispered to the spidery mass words I couldn't make out, then let the creature plop onto Corinne's unflinching face. It wriggled around for a bit, as if feeling out its surroundings. Corrine lay completely still, her head wound oozing blood and... other matter. I saw that what was left of her mangled foot had turned a sickening purple-blackish color.

Oh Christ, was she dead? Her unfocused eyes just stared blankly up into the sky. No, she wasn't dead! I saw her breathing, and it filled me with more horror than I would have thought possible. The rising and falling of her chest was shallow and faint, and I swore I could see parts of her moving, twitching, but then they were still. Or were my eyes just playing cruel tricks on me?

God...What had they done? I began to drown in anguish. Yet, I could not tear my eyes away from Corinne's once-beautiful, but now visibly lifeless face.

With every fiber of my being, I dreaded what was going to come next as I saw the thing from the nest eventually complete its oozing exploration and discover the hole in Corinne's forehead. It squeezed and burrowed its membranous body into the wound in her skull, like a huge ravenous worm boring into spoiled meat.

Suddenly, and unexpectedly, every muscle in Corinne's body tensed. She emitted a shriek conveying not just unimaginable pain, but also an unholy horror, as if her corpse knew what was being done to defile it. No creature on earth should have been allowed to make such sound.

This was a true living nightmare, beyond anything my mind could have conceived.

As soon as the tendrilled creature had squeezed its entire body into Corinne's head, the Somas of Light gathered closer around the altar. The old woman remained by Corinne's head, then threw her wrinkled, flabby arms toward the sky, with a look of utter exultation on her face. The figure wearing the golden mask stood close behind her.

"It is time!" the old woman shouted in stentorian tones into the now cloudless and star-filled sky. She closed her eyes and chanted in a low, morbid—and yet somehow melodic—manner, each line repeated by the rest of the robed figures, like some sort of prayer:

Ancient One of times untold
Helminth, we call upon you,
Sitting upon your throne of corruption and void
Hear us, your servants of flesh and bone

We shall open up the darkest of pathways
Send your voice down to us and speak
The conduit of meat awaits its presence
Guide us and instruct us with your festering knowledge

As they ended their chant, their voices echoed off, rather than being absorbed by the endless fog. A palpable, electric energy crackled in the air. A silent breeze prickled my skin, and I felt as though lightning was about to strike us all down. I wished it would.

Corinne's torso rose into a sitting position, her bones creaking audibly.

"She's still alive?" I heard Lorena whisper to me.

"I am the Tongue of Moluc'Helminth," Corinne said. It wasn't Corinne. It sounded like her voice and certainly came from her throat and mouth. But underneath her voice, I could hear another, sounding like two voices speaking in disharmonic unison. The deeper, underlying voice seemed...distant, sinister, not-of-this-world.

Corinne's eyes had rolled up into the back of her head, leaving only the whites visible between the streaks of blood running down her pallid face. Her limbs moved awkwardly as she spoke, as if her brain...her mangled brain...were no longer familiar with how to control them.

"I speak for Moluc'Helminth, the Infestor of Worlds, the Finder of the Way, the Burrower through the Void," the double voice said. "My master slumbers in the depths. He awaits the time of awakening. Now tell me. Why have you called me here into this shell of spoiled meat?" Corinne's face remained blank, impassive, unconcerned with what her lips uttered.

The words that spilled from Corinne's mouth were not English, nor any language that I could even recognize. In fact, I wasn't even sure if what now spewed out of her mouth was even comprised of words. But somehow...I could understand each disturbing utterance.

"Tongue of Moluc'Helminth," the old woman announced, bowing formally to Corinne, whose expression changed to one of haughty disdain as she appraised the woman groveling before her. In a ringing tone, completely at odds with her cringing posture, the hag went on. "We serve your wondrous master and we serve the Ancients. We are here to bring forth the Infestor into our world. For too long have the Ancient Ones been imprisoned." Her voice rose in volume and she straightened slightly. "We are resolved to release the Great Helminth and summon His Gloriousness to this world so that He may then bore through the void and open the pathways for the rest of our masters who lie among the endless infinity." The old woman's eyes shone with zealous fervor.

"Answer me this, fleshling," the being that was now Corinne said in that unnerving, discordant dual-voice, addressing the old woman with evident contempt. "How do you plan to release my Master? I can sense your soul. I can glimpse the folds of your mind. You are no Githya Priestess." Corinne's pretty lips curled into a sneer as she spoke.

"Ah, but there is one here who is," the old woman replied with an ingratiating smile. "Although She was wrongfully struck down millennia ago and cursed with a wretched physical form. She still lives. *This* is why we have summoned you, Tongue of Moluc'Helminth. The deeper knowledge of flesh manipulation has, unfortunately, been lost to us over the countless years. We possess neither the knowledge nor the skill to rectify the Githya's condition. But you are powerful and wise. That is why we humbly called to you." There was a mad, joyous gleam in the woman's eyes.

"I see," Corinne said slowly, her gaze taking in the other robed Somas of Light as if appraising their worth before returning her attention back to the hag. "And you have a proper Descendant here for this Githya?"

"Yes, of course," the old woman answered. She waved her arm around with a flourish indicating the masked figure standing silent and unmoving behind her. "This Descendant will be perfect for Arch-Githya Kamilla."

"Arch-Githya Kamilla?" Corinne repeated, a hint of surprise in that awful dissonant voice. "Ah, a fleshling who is not unknown to me." Corinne paused, eyes closed, appearing to be deep in thought. After several minutes, she opened her eyes again, looking eagerly at the figure wearing the strange golden mask. "Very well, fleshling. I shall perform the Rite of Reshaping. Bring the Descendant here."

Corinne awkwardly got off the altar, her body looking like an inexperienced puppeteer was controlling her arms and legs. She then stood beside the stone slab and reached a hand toward the figure.

The old woman gently pulled the masked figure closer

to the altar. Moving as if in a trance, the figure removed its crimson robe, dropping it carelessly to the ground, and revealing a nude body. A woman's body. A body that was covered in terribly familiar pink scars.

"Abby?" I whispered in shock, praying I was wrong.

With languid movement, the figure removed the demonic mask, and there was no doubt. Lorena and I exchanged stupefied, horrified glances, but neither of us could speak. Meeting our eyes, Abby acknowledged us with a devious smile as she stepped forward and lay down, stretching her body atop the altar, resting her head at the end of the slab where Corinne stood.

"Bring the Arch-Githya," Corinne, or "the Tongue of Moluc'Helminth," demanded.

The spindly tendrils from the mass burrowed inside Corinne's brain protruding from the sickening wound in her forehead like an eel appraising its surroundings.

One of the watching Somas walked over to the altar and reverently presented the Tongue with a small object wrapped in a silken scarlet cloth.

Corinne received the object in her outstretched hands, carefully unwrapped the cloth, and held it up towards the night sky. I could clearly see what the object was, though by this point, there had been little doubt in my mind as to the nature of the bundle.

It was the thing from the jar. I had desperately hoped to never lay eyes on that creature again, yet here it was.

Corinne held it aloft, saying something in that unknown, hideous language. This time, I could not understand her utterances, for some reason. The flickering candlelight from around the altar reflected off the fetus-thing's slimy, raw skin. It began to twitch and writhe. Suddenly, it let out an ear-splitting screech just as Corinne finished speaking.

"We shall bring Arch-Githya Kamilla back to true form," Corinne said, triumphantly, lowering the small monstrosity and placing it before Abby's eager face.

I swallowed the bile that rose into my throat. Were they

going to drill a hole in Abby's head too?

Still lying supine on the altar, Abby opened her mouth wide, letting Corinne push the quivering, tumor-like lump into her throat. A euphoric smile spread across both of their faces. There was complete silence as every eye was trained on Abby as she slowly masticated, occasionally choking and gagging, and ate the quivering mass.

I don't believe there is a word in any language, alien or otherwise, that could accurately describe the utter revulsion I felt by this point in time, after everything I had witnessed. Again, I forced myself to swallow the burning lump in my throat.

And, with great exuberance, Abby gulped down the last bit of the foul thing from the jar.

CHAPTER SIXTEEN

Submit, and you shall share in the fearsome, hidden knowledge that my Master can provide. Yield to the dark will of my Lord, and the Corruptions shall make you a god!

My stomach had twisted itself into a hellish knot that burned like fire in my belly. As Abby swallowed that fetus-thing, I looked over at Lorena and I knew her insides were doing the same as mine.

Corinne, or rather the horrendous thing using her body like a meat puppet, placed her fingers on the supine Abby's temples and began uttering words so inhuman and abhorrent, that my ears burned and my mind refused to understand their meaning. It wasn't just the words themselves, but also the voice, the tone, the infernal, alien sound of them that assured me that a sane human being was never meant to hear them recited.

"Tentra ovu'us lasht Moluc'Helminth!" the possessed Corinne shouted, all the while keeping her fingers pressed against the sides of Abby's head.

I could no longer understand the awful, gnashing words being said. Whatever had given me the ability to understand the language at the start of this ritual was blessedly gone now. Perhaps my fracturing mind refused to acknowledge the abhorrent meaning of the alien language that slithered in and violated my ears and brain.

"Keng haptra'a ven gu'hr!" I watched as Abby's face became expressionless for a moment before distorting into a pained grimace. "He'ktha ferush mal ob'strii ma'agna Githya-Kamilla!"

The moment the last syllable left Corinne's lips, her body went limp, as if all traces of life within her had been extinguished. Her slack form toppled backward off of the altar, landing unheeded in a bloody, motionless heap on the trampled grass.

For several seconds there was nothing but a deathly silence. Not even the night insects dared make any hint of a noise. I realized I had been sweating profusely.

A new fear gripped me. Something indistinct moved around in the dense fog that surrounded the island. A painful lump formed in my throat that I couldn't swallow. There was a scent on this wind, like a strange smelling mix of vanilla and blood.

A booming crack exploded from every single direction and Abby let out a sound...a shriek? a laugh? It was an indescribably sound that could only have come from the deepest, blackest pits of horrid nightmare. The only description that came to mind was that it sounded as if Abby had been plunged into the very depths of hell itself but was happy about it.

Abby's abdomen distended from within. The bulge grew larger and larger, like some enormous tumor inflating to monstrous proportions. That thing she had swallowed, what was it doing to her? I was sure—and the thought terrified me to the core—that I would find out soon enough.

Abby thrashed around in tortured agony. As she did so, several robed Somas stepped forward, each carrying a differently-shaped piece of rusty metal. They touched the objects to their cloth-bound faces, ceremoniously kissing the metal, before they savagely plunged each sharp piece into Abby's arms and legs.

What kind of fucking twisted, sickening, horrific rituals were these?

I wouldn't have thought it was possible, but Abby both screamed and laughed even more wildly. Her abdomen was absurdly distended at this point, the skin stretched tight, unable to stretch any farther.

A thin red line appeared above Abby's bellybutton. Just as I noticed it, the red line turned into a ragged tear. With a revolting rending sound, her stomach split, sending a fountain of wet gore up into the air that splattered all over Abby and the altar as it rained down.

"Oh, Christ in heaven," Lorena whispered in absolute horror, her eyes glued to the ground, refusing to look upon the gruesome scene unfolding before us.

In contrast, I was unable to tear my eyes away. I just watched, stunned and horrified, as a slender hand rose out of the blood-soaked mess that had once been Abby's slim torso, but which now resembled just a mound of quivering entrails. An arm followed the hand. The skin was a creamy white on the few areas of smooth flesh that weren't covered in blood.

The hand grabbed hold of the edge of the altar, while a second thin arm crawled up and out to grasp Abby's thigh. Both limbs pushed upward, pulling out a head and torso of a woman. Her long, stringy hair saturated with wet scarlet gore obscured her face, leaving only her wide, grinning mouth visible. Rivulets of blood ran down her pale skin like thick tears as she pulled her hips free of Abby's belly. Last came two slim legs, uncurling in the mess. The monstrosity crawled out of Abby like a giant, smiling spider, breathing heavily from the brutal ordeal of her rebirth.

This newborn creature eased herself off of the altar and away from Abby's ruined body, setting her bare, blood-stained feet down on the grass and pulling herself up straight. She stood quite tall, well over six feet. Two Somas ran over and draped the bloody woman in scarlet robes adorned with golden patterns much more intricate than any of the others.

The old woman then reverently handed her the golden mask that Abby had been wearing. She quickly secured it to her face before I could discern any features. I could only see two large, black holes staring at me from behind the mask. Did this monster even have eyes?

"Arch-Githya Kamilla," the old woman said, breaking the silence, her voice at once both triumphant and reverent. "We are elated to have you returned to your true form. Welcome home." She bowed deeply.

This Arch-Githya Kamilla looked curiously around, gazing at the house and the small island upon which it sat.

"This place," Kamilla said, her voice low and hoarse, as if she hadn't spoken for centuries. "I know this place. I know this land. But this…all of this does not look the same. Everything appears to have changed." She knelt down in the grass, placing her hands gently on the ground. She inhaled a deep, chest-expanding breath, then let it out in a whoosh. "Ah, yes," she continued, her voice becoming clearer. "But the power is still here. I can feel it. It is faint, but I can feel the lifeblood coursing through the ground. This truly is my home." She spoke in English, but pronounced the words strangely, as if she were from some time long since passed.

"Arch-Githya," the old hag interjected. "We are beyond pleased, grateful, and honored to have your Illustriousness here with us this night. I know it has been quite some time since you were last outside of that accursed vessel within which you were trapped."

The Arch-Githya plucked a blade of grass and examined it as she stood up. "Tell me, how do you reckon this juncture of the epochs?" she asked the old woman, who still gazed up at her in awed adoration.

"The year is 2019 of the common era, according to the Gregorian calendar," the old woman replied. "But that will mean nothing to you in relation to the time when you last walked the earth. Many, many ages have passed since you were confined. Your memory may still be returning. You were struck down, Githya. You were imprisoned in ages long past by the wretched *morda'shin*." The old woman said the strange word with disgust and spat on the ground as if it had left a bad taste in her mouth. "Those damn fools locked you away long ago using their foul death magics. It has taken your descendants many attempts over many ages to restore you. The land itself has even been reformed several times since you last laid eyes upon it, as you have already noticed. But, finally, we have succeeded! For this time we procured a suitable Descendant whose body had been properly readied months in advance by preparing to bear a child." The hag gestured, and both women turned around to look at the mound of horrendous remains that had once been Abby.

"That is quite a lot to take in," the Arch-Githya Kamilla said with a hint of wistfulness. "My memories are slowly returning to me, however." She paused to chew on a blackened nail, looking deep in thought. "The Descendant's memories are also within me. It is a curious sensation."

Kamilla gazed about, surveying the other cultists who were huddled together in awe of her.

"Ah, yes. These two lovelies," she said, finally looking down at Lorena and me kneeling on the ground.

"Extra flesh for whatever purpose requires them," the old woman said, waving a hand at us. "These two and those two," she pointed at the lifeless forms of Abby and Corinne, "were companions. They thought they came to this house for a holiday. In fact, we lured them here, with a plan quite long in the making. It took generations of plotting, but we managed it so that we might have the means with which to usher in your return." Her chest rose, and she puffed out in apparent pride, her eyes shining.

She looked like a giant, wrinkly bullfrog. A stupid fucker of a bullfrog.

Did that fat bitch just say she had planned all of this? Anger began to suppress the horror that held me. *She planned for us to come here? She lured us here?*

"Let us go, you bat shit fuckheads!" I yelled at them, startling Lorena.

Kamilla's black eyes bored into me, regarding me coldly.

I bared my teeth at her. "You fucking monsters!"

The unearthly form of Kamilla glided over to me and gently caressed my cheek with a bloody, long-fingered hand before slapping me sharply across the face. "You know nothing of true monsters, pretty meatbag," she purred at me. I stared at the golden mask with its fanged mouth, twisting horns, and inhuman features and decided that I never wanted to see the face beneath.

My cheek stung like hell, and I was sure there was a hand-shaped welt rising up on it.

Kamilla moved on from me and stared down at Lorena. "And do you have anything to say, beautiful?" She placed a hand on Lorena's head.

"Yes," Lorena said, sounding calm as she stared at the masked face without so much as an eye twitching. "Go fuck yourselves in the bowels of the deepest hell." She then spit on Kamilla's metal face.

"Such meaningless words," Kamilla said in an amused tone without bothering to wipe off the spit. She chuckled, glancing up at the cultists who had the daggers pressed firmly against our throats. "Lock them up somewhere, I don't care where. I have uses for them. I will get them when I am ready."

"Yes, your Holiness," both Somas said with a bow of their heads, their voices sounding weak and frightened.

The remaining Somas then bowed in abject submission as Lorena and I were pulled roughly to our feet. My body was shaking, both from the shock of everything I had just witnessed and the consuming dread of what might happen next. What possible thing could they be saving us for? Could there be something even worse than what they had done to Corinne and Abby?

"Mother Luminescence," the Soma holding me addressed the squat old hag. "Where shall we put these two?"

The old woman's wrinkled face contorted in thought for a moment. "Lock them down in the basement," she commanded.

CHAPTER SEVENTEEN

Worship Them, praise Them, execute bloody deeds in Their most hallowed Name. For once the wretched betrayers have been utterly defeated and eviscerated, They shall ever be the true master of all existence. Give up your mind, flesh, and spirit.

"No!" I gasped, my lungs about to explode from the effort to push the words out as loudly as possible. "Please don't put us down there!"

A flame of terror coursed through my veins and spine. I thrashed in an attempt to get away, my mind shriveling as terror seeped into its folds at the thought of going back down into the basement.

My objections and struggling went unheeded. I fought with everything I had, but to no avail. I could not go back down into that dark pit! Every fiber in my being strained against going back where all those crazy people had attacked me and tortured me!

Lorena remained quiet as rough hands pushed us along. The closed, emotionless look on her face gave me no insight into what she was thinking. The two cultists shoved us savagely through the back door into the house, directing us through the kitchen, to the living room, and finally to the basement. The Soma guarding me opened the heavy wooden door with a creak, once again unveiling the yawning mouth of the abyss.

Without a word, the Somas shoved us unceremoniously through the doorway. Lorena and I stumbled down the first few steps before managing to grab onto the railing and steady ourselves. At least they hadn't bound our hands this time, otherwise we would have both tumbled down the steps. I breathed a sigh of relief that I spared a repeat of that painful experience. The aches all over my body brought back the memory of my previous fall. My broken fingers and punctured foot throbbed as an extra reminder.

The moment of relief was brief, however, as the awareness of where we now stood came rushing back to me. I stared down into the velvety pitch of the basement. Were those psychos still down there? Were they *ever* down there, or had I just imagined it? My fingers traced down my arms and the vicious cuts and wounds that covered them. No. Falling down the stairs was not the sole cause of my injuries. Many of these had obviously been inflicted with instruments of torture.

Lorena flicked on the light switch. All the bulbs hummed to life at the bottom of the stairs, illuminating the basement in yellow light. My heart skipped a beat, as I fully expected to see a horde of mutilated people with cloth covering their heads, wielding razors, knives, and other tools of torture. But there was no one there.

I cautiously followed Lorena down the steps, curious as to why the light seemed to be working perfectly now. I surveyed the dirty basement, which smelled of nothing more sinister than must and mildew. A few pieces of broken furniture lined one stone wall, and rusty, cobwebbed tools lay haphazardly on a dusty worktable. There were two large, grimy, wooden shelves filled with dozens of filthy jars—oh God, I didn't want to see any more jars—of preserves and foods. At least, I think it was food. Seeing those glass jars with unknown contents floating lazily inside them made me feel ill.

If only Abby hadn't found that stupid jar on the lake bottom! I was furious at her. This was all *her* fault. *She* had found that damn jar. *She* had released the thing inside...the thing that was this Kamilla. *She* was helping the bastards!

Had helped them.

She was dead...

An icy chill flooded my core. Abby was dead. I had watched her and Corinne die in the most unimaginably horrific ways possible. The initial shock had now started to wane, and it occurred to me that I would never talk with either of them ever again. Never hear their voices. Never go shopping with Corinne. Never have lunch with Abby and her parents ever again.

Tears streamed down my face. My anger at Abby's willingness to help this cult was quickly replaced with grief. The old woman—Mother Luminescence they had called her—had said she had planned all of this herself. We all knew that Abby hadn't been at the most stable point in her life. She was certainly depressed and not in a good or strong place mentally. This cult and their freakish leader had influenced her somehow. Abby had said something had called to her before she found the jar.

They had done this to Abby. It was all *their* fault.

Mother Luminescence said they had lured us here. But how? It had been our decision to come here. We came here because of Abby's assault and the death of her husband. We were able to come to this lake house because I owned it. It came into my possession when my parents had both passed away...

No, the cult didn't have anything to do with all those events and whatever else had led to our present situation. They couldn't have orchestrated decades of events leading to this. There was no mysterious organization pulling the strings from shadowed corners, was there? Those things didn't really exist...Did they? The old hag had said she had been working for *generations* on this plan.

No, no, no. I was certain these people didn't influence us to come here. How could they have?

The cult implied that they had needed Abby for their plans. They had called her a "Descendant." A descendant of whom? A descendant of what? Had they somehow made

Abby find the jar and open it? There was that strange symbol on the inside of the lid. And Mother Luminescence had spoken of magic.

Ridiculous. There was no such thing as magic. But could I really say for certain that something wasn't real after everything I had experienced here? Everything I had been forced to witness? Nightmares were certainly real, and now it appeared that they didn't always stay inside your head.

"Damn it!" I shouted, putting my fists to my temples. I didn't want to think of these things. It was too much. *I* was in control of my life, not them! *I* knew what was reality and what was fiction!

"You almost gave me a heart attack," Lorena said timidly from beside me.

I quickly looked around, fearing that my sudden outburst may have alerted the crazy people from wherever they were hiding.

"Sorry," I replied when I saw that we were still alone. "I'm just having a hard time understanding any of this. This is all too much. All too crazy. Too crazy..."

"I hear you," Lorena said with a sad attempt at a smile as she placed a comforting hand on my shoulder. "If you weren't standing here with me, seeing all of this too, I would think I had gone completely insane. Of course, you might just be part of my delusions." She let loose a slightly hysterical giggle that morphed into a heavy sigh. "Anyway, what should we do now?"

Before I could answer, something fluttered right above my head. Lorena and I both turned in the direction from which the noise had come. A tiny, round shape flitted around the wall farthest from the stairs. I tensed a moment, wondering what fresh hell this might be. But I soon recognized what it was and relaxed.

It was a little bird.

The bird looked the same as the one Abby and I had seen outside on our first night here. The one that had hit the window and died. This one had the same small black body with a splash of white across its tiny face resembling a miniature domino mask.

The Wagtail, or Devil's Eye, flitted and landed atop of a doorframe I hadn't noticed before. It must lead into a separate basement room. I walked over to where the bird was perched. Strangely, unlike any other bird I had ever seen, this little guy had gleaming, jade-colored eyes. Why did that particular shade arouse such a feeling of familiarity? The Devil's Eye stared at me, ruffled its feathers, pecked at the door frame, then resumed its staring.

"Strange, I don't remember that door being there," Lorena said, her voice quiet. "Corinne and I must have overlooked it somehow when we came down to search for you."

My eyes were fixed on that doorway. Did the bird want me to go in there? And why on earth was I considering what birds were trying to say to me now?

"Poor little guy," Lorena continued taking a step toward the Devil's Eye. "He must have gotten trapped down here."

I didn't respond, but took a cautious step toward the rotted, wooden door. The bird watched me, fluttering its wings in encouragement as I took more steps toward its impromptu perch.

When I was within arm's reach, I felt a presence, a sort of negative energy emanating from behind that door. But some intuition told me not to fear it. It was angry, that was true, but not hostile, at least towards us. It was more...sad.

Lorena said something as I reached for the rusty handle, but I paid no attention. I gripped the handle and pulled. The door opened with a mournful creak.

As the room was revealed, Lorena let out a shriek quickly muffled by her hands. I felt as if a giant worm squirmed and writhed around in my insides.

The room was much larger than the one in which we stood, eerily lit with dozens of dripping, smoky candles. Who had lit these candles? Both the walls and floor were comprised of weathered, ancient-looking stones. Massive tables of carved marble lined the perimeter. As we approached, the items upon them became clear: sharp, wicked-looking metal instruments which appeared to be exceedingly ancient, almost prehistoric, but somehow not primitive. There was a sadistic sophistication to them, a twisted beauty in their form. But some of their sharpened edges had evil, discolored stains on them. In fact, all the marbled tables, the floors, even the walls all displayed splotches of dark, disturbing stains. Other tables, racks, and cages, all made of a decaying metal, sat in the interior of the room. I didn't want to even imagine what all this had been used for, but nonetheless, horrid, gore-filled images came unbidden to my mind.

"What the hell is this?" Lorena whispered, peering farther into the room from over my shoulder. There was no longer any fear in her voice, only anger and sadness.

"It looks like some sort of torture dungeon," I replied nervously. I gathered up my courage and stepped farther inside. Sweat immediately beaded on my forehead. The air was much hotter and thicker in here, as if this room were somehow closer to hell. The little bird flew in after me, landing on top of a brutal-looking cage lined with sharp spikes on its interior. The Devil's Eye tilted its head as it watched me with a sort of eager curiosity. I met its gaze for a moment and then went back to examining the room. The stone walls were covered from floor to ceiling with intricate engravings and bas-reliefs. Some depicted robed people, no doubt the Somas of Light, praying and performing esoteric religious rites. Another wall depicted the cultists worshipping enormous...beings...that came down from the sky or broke upward through the earth.

What *were* these colossal monstrosities with gaping maws, hundreds of eyes, gigantic tentacles, and repulsive, writhing flesh? Were they the gods of these crazy people?

"Horrific," I muttered to myself, yet couldn't resist running a finger down an engraving.

Lorena had backed up and stood just outside the doorway. She kept glancing around as if ready to catch anyone trying to sneak up on her. We had just briefly made eye contact when she was yanked into the room by some unseen force. The door slammed shut and a great wind, whose source I couldn't fathom, blew out all the candles at once, plunging us into total, blind darkness. I could hear the bird fluttering frantically around us over the sound of rushing air.

"Lorena!" I cried out. "Where are you?" I blindly stumbled around in the complete darkness, my arms outstretched, bumping into several of the cages and racks, until Lorena and I finally managed to reach each other. We gripped each other's hands, neither of us daring to let go.

Lorena said something to me in a frantic voice, but I couldn't quite make out the words. She sounded muffled and distant. Why was it so hot down here? Was that Lorena screaming? Or was that me? My head swam, making me dizzy. No, someone else was screaming. Lots of voices cried out in pain, and the wails conveyed an infinite sadness. Then there was a thick metallic screech. A reverberation echoing from deep within the cosmos. Swimming, spinning, an energy radiating from my core. I felt close to fainting.

Everything went silent. then the voice of the child who had led me from the morgue in my dream. "Hello again, Rei," he said, his sad fluttering voice like a ruffling breeze. "She's here. She's finally here. The Metal-Faced Lady has returned to her true flesh once more."

"I'm sorry.There was nothing I could do to prevent it," I replied to the nothingness around me.

"I wish I hadn't come here," the small voice said somberly. "This house sits on land that has a close connection to the other side. Which is why the Somas like it here. I came here to help you, but I was too weak. Now I'm stuck here with all the others.I knew it was risky coming to this house."

I could hear the clear sorrow and regret.

"I am now forever trapped, tied to this corner of the earth." He sniffled and sounded as if he were holding back sobs. He continued a moment later. "There is nothing but rage, hate, and sorrow here. The other dead, those who attacked you last time in the other room, they haven't noticed you yet this time. Their attention is distracted for the time being. But still, you shouldn't stay here much longer or their hateful eyes shall land on you again." Almost as an afterthought, he added, "I'm sorry for slamming the door just now. I only wanted to speak with you before whatever the Metal-Faced Lady is planning comes to pass."

"You spoke to me before down here," I said, trying to take in everything the child had just told me. "And I think you also helped me in my dream. You're just a little boy. But you said you were dead. How did you die? Did those damn cultists kill you too? Who are you? Can't you tell me?"

"Who are you talking to?" an urgent voice blasted in my ear, then faded quickly into an indistinguishable noise. Had that been Lorena?

"Can you tell me who you are?" I asked again.

"Didn't you understand what I said last time?" the boy answered from somewhere in the darkness. "I've heard you and Lorena and Corinne talk many times before in my very brief existence. You never knew I was there, though. I was hidden in her, safe inside my mother. But I was robbed of the chance to be born."

"You m-mean..." I stuttered, the rest of the words reluctant to leave my throat. "Abby's..."

"Rei!" Lorena's voice erupted from beside me like a shrill siren. I became aware of her dragging me toward the door. Who had opened it? No, Lorena wasn't dragging me. A man's hand had gripped my arm tightly and pulled me out of the room.

He threw me roughly down onto the ground in the main basement area, the light stinging my eyes. A second Soma shoved Lorena to the floor beside me. I looked at marble-white feet and legs standing before me, stained with splotches of wet crimson, from beneath an ornate crimson robe. I looked up at the hooded head and metal face of Kamilla. Her features, as always, were hidden behind the golden mask, but I could feel her grinning at me. Chills ran down my spine.

"Hello, pretty girls," she said in a deceptively soothing voice. Even at this proximity, I couldn't see her eyes through the mask's eye holes. "I hope you've been enjoying my home."

"This isn't your home," I said through gritted teeth, glaring up at that horned mask, surprising myself with my own lack of fear. "I own this house. It's mine. None of this belongs to you."

"Oh, but it does," Kamilla contradicted, caressing my head with her pale, slender fingers. "Of course, the land has changed greatly. It's much smaller now. This realm is not as it used to be. But this is my home. I can feel it." She breathed in deeply. "So much energy here, left untapped for too long."

I heard a wet sound that I realized must be her licking her lips.

"I was trapped in that accursed form for so many ages. It feels exquisite to stretch my limbs again, to breathe in the fresh air of the wilds, to feel the grass and blood beneath my feet. Ah, you think you know suffering, but you truly don't. Your friend, Abby, she gifted me her memories and her knowledge when I was reborn through her. She has known much pain, but not true pain. None of you have yet experienced such." She paced around on the dirt floor, reaching out and examining various objects around the basement before turning back to me, continuing. "The world has changed so much since my time. So much has been lost to the ages." A sigh. "The influence of the Ancients has been reduced to almost nothing. Nothing! The kingdoms of this world, of this time, are ruled by ignorant fools who desire real power but know nothing of it. Fat swine who enjoy wallowing in their own wretched filth. They are worthless except as servants and extra flesh to manipulate."

She raised her arms ceremoniously toward the basement ceiling, her fingertips almost touching the support beams. She stared upward without saying a word.

"The Ancients are angry," she went on after a long moment of silence, keeping her arms raised and her face tilted up. "Their bodies writhe with the fury of a million suns. They have been forgotten by all but a few, and even to those, they are but vague and fleeting memories. They seldom receive they worship as They used to. Their connection to this world has been severed, save for a few tenuous threads." She lowered her arms and stared back at Lorena and me with those black eye holes. "We will repair this connection. We will open the pathways once more for Them." Her voice became low with a sinister edge to it. "To do so, we must awaken Moluc'Helminth, the Infestor, the Burrower." She licked her lips again as she said the name.

She nodded at the two Somas. The one to my left grabbed Lorena by the arm and pulled her to her feet like a rag doll, proceeding to drag her up the basement stairs.

"Where are you taking me?" Lorena roared, desperately trying to pull away. "I'll beat the fuck out of you crazy fuckers until you're nothing but a shit stain on the ground!"

Lorena must have been beyond feeling fear at this point. Fury dripped from her voice.

"We must make a sacrifice to the Infestor!" Kamilla announced in a ringing, zealous voice. "Your essence shall be that which attracts His gaze."

"No!" Lorena spat as she was dragged out of the basement. "No, no! I won't be anything for your false fucking god!"

I struggled furiously, trying to go after her, but the second cultist held me in place with a foot on my back.

"Lorena!" I yelled.

CHAPTER EIGHTEEN

It is worse than hate, than loathing, that which They feel toward you. For it is indifference. They feel nothing for your soul. They care not!

Screaming. Endless screaming. I couldn't shut it out, no matter how hard I tried. Agonizing shrieking and howling. Nonstop. It made me feel sick. Not just physically, but sick in my mind, as if each horrible, tortured screech ate away at my brain. At my soul.

What were they doing to Lorena out there?

It had been hours since that bitch, Kamilla, had come and taken the last of my friends away. Yet still I heard screaming. Ceaseless, eternal screaming. I would have thought a person's vocal cords would have given out by now, shredded, swollen, raw. But the suffering was too great, too infinite, too hellish to be restricted by the simple limitations of human physiology.

I desperately didn't want to think about it. I didn't want to think of yet another of my friends being tormented for the sick rituals of these crazy, deluded assholes. But no matter how hard I tried, I was unable to block any of it out.

Two of my best friends were already dead, and the third was about to be murdered as well. It sickened me to admit it, but I hoped Lorena would die soon. End both our suffering. Save us both.

Oh God, Lorena... You didn't deserve this.

"Stop it!" I screamed at the basement ceiling.

The only response I received was the continued

miserable, anguished din of Lorena's agony too clearly audible from outside. Horrific images of her lying terrified on that bloody stone altar flashed through my tormented mind. Images of her being slowly vivisected, having her limbs disarticulated and torn off, her skin removed, her head drilled into, her eyeballs gouged out...all while she was awake, aware, and in torment.

I fell to my knees, clasping my hands over my ears as tightly as I could. My body shook uncontrollably, and I felt like vomiting. Breathe. I couldn't breathe. Had to breathe.

A cold numbness flooded through my limbs. My hand clutched at my chest as my heart raced so ferociously, I was sure it would burst from its own effort. Every artery in my body throbbed in time with the pounding. I could taste tangy copper in my mouth.

Was I having a heart attack?

Just breathe.

Time ticked slowly by as I used whatever willpower I still retained to calm myself, but nothing worked.

No doubt my mind was fractured by everything I had seen here in this awful place. Even if I managed to get away from here, there was no guarantee that I could escape from all of this. I knew that, should I somehow leave here alive, I would never be the woman I had been before coming here. Could I even live a life after experiencing something like this? Or would I be too deeply scarred to function normally in society?

It might be better to just end it all right now. Did I really want to carry all these memories around with me for the rest of my life? There would be an endless parade of therapy, anti-depressants, and paranoia awaiting me should I ever find a way to flee these accursed grounds.

Lying down on the dirt floor of the basement, I closed my eyes. Nightmares flashed behind my eyelids, and shadows danced in my mind. I could feel a presence in the other room, that sick torture room. I had made sure the little Devil's Eye bird was not in there before I shut the door and moved several heavy chairs in front of it. I wanted to prevent anything evil from unexpectedly bursting out of that den of horror. If only I could somehow move some furniture up the basement stairs to barricade that door as well.

Depression and hopelessness had taken firm hold of my spirit. An eternity could have passed while I lay there in the musty, filthy basement.

It was then that I realized that the sounds of Lorena's suffering had finally ceased. Most likely that meant that she had finally passed beyond the ability to feel whatever those sadistic people had been doing to her.

She was dead. I was alone now. Only I remained.

What were they going to do to me?

What a fucking stupid question, I berated myself. They were going to do to me what they had done to my three best friends. Or maybe they had wanted to save the worst torment for last? In that case, it really *would* be better for me to just to end it all right here and now. Then I could be with Abby, Corinne, and now Lorena, with my parents, with everyone else I had ever lost in my life. If there was an afterlife, that is. Otherwise I'd be nothing except an empty husk, lying and rotting in this basement. Still, that would be better than being at the mercy of Arch-Githya Kamilla, Mother Luminescence, and the rest of the insane Somas of Light.

I clambered to my feet and made my way over to the decrepit workbench. There were tools scattered across it like metal carcasses, long-dead and cobwebbed. I grabbed a large, rusty clawhammer, gripping it tightly with my grimy, bruised hand. I didn't want my fate to be the same as what had befallen my friends. If I could lodge this far enough into my head...

Would that even work? I examined the flat face of the hammer, then turned it over to examine the claw. It wasn't terribly sharp. I didn't know if I possessed the conviction or even the pure strength to ram this deep enough into my skull to end my life, even if it hadn't been dull. The whole thing sounded quite painful. But I knew it had to be better than whatever hellish thing Kamilla and the Somas of Light had in store for me.

A creak on the basement stairs behind me caught my attention. I spun around, gripping the hammer. The Arch-Githya Kamilla and a tall heavy-set male Soma slowly descended the stairs, Kamilla's golden mask sneering at me.

"What are you going to do with that, child?" Kamilla chuckled, gesturing at the hammer in my hand as the pair of them came to a stop at the bottom of the staircase.

"What did you do to Lorena?" I spat angrily, gripping the hammer in a white-knuckled fist. "Tell me, bitch."

Kamilla laughed. "Ah, the girl made for an extraordinary sacrifice to the Glorious Helminth." I noticed all the fresh blood on her hands.

I tried to swallow the baseball that had formed in my throat. "No..." I had known Lorena must be dead, but my mind hadn't really accepted it. Now, the full weight of the fact that all three of my best friends were dead hit me like a crushing, unforgiving sledgehammer.

"Yes," Kamilla replied, circling me, her crimson robes flowing behind her like a dark river. "Did you hear her transcendent screaming? Such delicious, wondrous music we made together." She sighed, as if momentarily lost in the memory. "The manipulation of the flesh is such a beautiful art. What is more, Moluc'Helminth has whispered to me. His attention has been gained. What a blessing!" Her voice was low, husky, and tinged with an unholy excitement, like she anticipated the arrival of a lover. "My Master shall—"

My body reacted before I was even fully aware of what I intended to do. I swung the hammer with all of my might, connecting with the Arch-Githya's head. There rang a resounding *thunk* as rusted metal met shiny, golden metal. The mask flew off of her face, a large dent now visible on its left cheek. It landed on the floor beside us, the tip of one of its twisting horns snapping off as a result of the impact with the ground.

The force of the bludgeon had spun Kamilla's body around. She hunched, cradling her face in pain, unmasked. All I could see at the moment was a rat's nest of filthy, tangled hair trailing down her back. Before I could do any more harm, though, the large cultist had knocked the hammer from my hand and sent me spiraling to the floor with a vicious, back-handed smack. I spit a mouthful of blood onto the dirt while getting to my hands and knees. I hoped that I had at least done some permanent, painful damage to the witch's face.

But then I heard a soft, raspy, mocking laugh. "Stupid girl," Kamilla said, straightening up. "Foolish, brainless girl. You can do nothing to truly hurt me. I have experienced things within the many realities that your tiny mind could not even begin to comprehend." She turned around to face me and I gasped, shrinking away from her in horror. "The pain you just gave me was delectable," she purred.

She smiled at me then with a crimson-lipped mouth that was much too wide, full of too-long teeth which she licked hungrily with her thick black tongue studded with metal rings. She had no nose to speak of, just two disturbing slits for nostrils. Even without the mask, her eyes were not visible. All over the top half of her face, metal plates had been grafted to her skin, covering her forehead and eyes. I could not fathom at all how she could see. The top of her face resembled some sort of metallic quilt, with the plates flaring outward near her temples. The metal was etched with strange, unearthly symbols that reminded me of the symbol I had seen on the altar.

She licked her long teeth again with that horrendous, studded tongue and smiled at me. The smile reached all the way back to her ears, which were also pierced with numerous metal spikes.

"What the hell are you?" I whispered, unable to yield to the desperate desire to crawl away because of the large Soma holding me in place, my knees pushed into the hard-packed dirt floor.

"I am *that* which all aspire to be," she said.

I could smell her hot, foul breath as she leaned in close to my face.

"Even if they do not know it or refuse to believe it. I used to be nothing more than a simple girl like you."

Her smile stretched farther across her face. "But now I am blessed. I am powerful. I am...more...thanks to the might of my gracious Masters. I am *krugga'shin*." She placed her slender hand gently on my cheek. "If you had lived during the golden age of our power, I would have gladly had you join us, for you have potential. I can feel a spark within you. Alas, the human race has become pathetic and weak over the millennia."

With a flick of her wrist, her dirty nails clawed into my face.

I glared up at her as the witch stood to her full height and chuckled. Hot blood dripped down my cheek.

"We shall find a part for you to play in the coming of my Masters," Kamilla said with an obscene grin. "You have a flame in you that I haven't seen in a long time. You may be worth something to me after all."

Her black, studded tongue oozed out of her mouth like a giant leech, licking my blood out from under her long, filthy fingernails. She savored it greedily, then froze. Even though she had no eyes, I recognize an expression of surprise and repulsion dawn on her face.

She spat out my blood furiously. "It cannot be!" she howled. She kept spitting globs of bloody spittle onto the ground as if the inside of her mouth burned.

"Mistress?" the Soma asked in a deep, worried tone. "What is wrong?"

"This girl!" Kamilla growled, her voice rising in fury. "Her blood is bitter and hateful in my mouth. She is descended from the *morda'shin*! How is this possible? The Abby girl, I gained all of her knowledge. There has been no mention of the morda'shin in her lifetime. No mention in all the history she knew. These modern people do not even believe in powers beyond the mundane. Yet here is a morda'shin before us!"

Through his cloth wrapped face, the Soma looked at me in confusion. "But, it cannot be," he said, doubt clear in his gravelly voice. "We didn't know, Mistress. I swear to the highest, we had no idea. Mother Luminescence told us they were all gone. Perhaps she was in error. Perhaps the morda'shin have lain hidden in secret, as we have." He cowered back as the witch straightened.

"A filthy necromancer," Kamilla said furiously to herself, letting another glob of saliva land on the floor. She then turned to me. "Been speaking to the dead, have we? If you have contacted any of those from beyond, you'll wish you had not. I will find out." She made a disapproving noise in her throat. She licked her bloodied nails once more before spitting and turning back to face me. "No, I see now. She is no morda'shin. She is but a descendant far down the line. The blood has been diluted to almost nothing. It is far from pure, mixed with generations upon generation of weaker lines. She knows not of the power that barely runs through her weak veins." With a swish, she spun away and stomped up the basement steps. "But just to be safe, kill her," she ordered the Soma before disappearing upstairs. "Lest she speak any more to the dead, and they tell her secrets she ought not to know."

As the last bit of Kamilla's robe flapped out of the basement door and around the corner, the large Soma looked down at where I still knelt on the floor. He kicked me in the stomach, causing me to double over.

"This is going to be fun," he said, and unwrapped the wires and cloth that covered his head.

It took me a moment to recognize who was standing before me, my eyes trying to focus through the pain on the familiar face that sneered at me.

"Mr. Neilson?" I choked out incredulously. It was my father's friend, Mr. Neilson. The man who had been taking care of this house after my dad had passed away. The man who had given me the keys to this place once I had turned old enough. This couldn't be!

"Hello, Rei," he said, with a smile I had seen many times in the past, but which now looked evil and sinister. "It was so good of you and your friends to help us with our plans." He grabbed my hair and pulled me up.

I shrieked from the pain.

"I haven't taken a life in some time. Not since your dear mom and dad."

"No…" I whispered, my entire body trembling with a maelstrom of emotions.

"Your parents were fun to take care of," Mr. Neilson said in a hungry voice. "I'm going to savor you." He winked at me.

I grabbed the hammer and swung it with all of my strength. It connected with his face.

He staggered backward, holding his jaw.

In a strange, perverse way, I found it funny that Mr. Neilson didn't scream. Only a hacking, spluttering sound emanated from his mouth as if he choked on something. Probably his own broken teeth.

I rose to my feet and clobbered him again. The front of his dirty robes became soaked with a wet redness.

Oh God, it felt so good to hit him. It scared me how much I had enjoyed hurting this man. I couldn't hold myself back. Not that I tried to. It just felt so right.

Mr. Neilson stumbled backward and fell heavily onto his back, knocking the wind out of him.

I stood over his body, both hands gripping the hammer—I couldn't care less about the pain in my broken fingers—my knuckles becoming as white as bone.

Rage flared up inside me. I raised the hammer to administer the justice he deserved. A voice shrieked inside my head at me.

Hit him! Hurt him! Kill him!

I brought the hammer down, smashing it once more into his face.

Anger at the death of my friend Lorena flowed through my heart. I struck Mr. Neilson's face again, hearing and feeling things crunch beneath my weapon. God, it felt good to feel his skull bones break beneath my force.

Anger at the death of my friend Corinne also fueled my movements. I lifted the hammer as a beacon for the insane gods of the cult to see. I brought it down again, nose, brow, and lips breaking and tearing. I could see his bloodied, wide-eyed face, full of terror and pain. The same terror and pain my friends had felt.

The hammer found its target once more, twice more, again and again and again. Loud, squelching smacks resounded as the hammer's head sank deeper into the man's face. His body spasmed with each blow. His cries of surrender were nothing but pathetic gurgling, suffocating on his own arterial fluids.

Anger for the manipulation and death of Abby blazed within the very essence of my being.

A wrath like I had never in my life known before filled me to the brim. Hatred seethed out of every pore. My jaw clenched, and a fire filled my chest. I couldn't contain it. This man deserved this. He had butchered my friends. All the Somas had. They should all be here, receiving what they had wrought.

I brought the hammer down over and over. Mr. Neilson had been a family friend. And he had just admitted to causing the death of my parents! He lay unmoving now, but I didn't care. I kept bringing that instrument of vengeance down upon him. I wept and roared as I pummeled his head. His skull had split open like an overripe melon perhaps minutes ago, but I couldn't stop. His blood and pieces of flesh and bone flew everywhere. I showered and bathed in this deceiver's scarlet life force, painting every inch of my skin with hot crimson.

I smashed his head in until it was nothing but a red pulpy mess. A stain on the floor.

CHAPTER NINETEEN

You are one. You are none. But you can be all. The ichor of eternity slowly seeps into your brain like a deadly poison that will wither the body into nothingness. Consume the waste like the maggots you are. No need for penitence, no need to cry out. Your agony shall fall on deaf ears.

All the Somas of Light carried knives. Fortunately, the one whose head I just turned into bloody mashed potatoes was no different.

I removed the dagger from the belt inside of Mr. Neilson's robes, exchanging it for the gore-covered hammer. I thought for a second about taking his robes, but eventually decided against it. Mr. Neilson was at least a foot taller than I was. I would be fooling no one by wearing them. Besides, if I had to make a run for it, my feet would certainly become tangled in the fabric.

I took one last look at the motionless bastard and his Jackson Pollock head before creeping stealthily up the basement steps. One hand gripped the dagger—awkward with the pain returning to my broken fingers—the other slid lightly along the wooden railing. I tried to make the least noise possible, pausing and holding my breath each time one of the stairs groaned in protest.

I could hear a faint commotion outside. Kamilla and the Somas of Light were probably performing another one of their disgusting rituals to appease their mockery of a god.

Chills ran through me like icy electricity as I allowed

myself to actually contemplate the malignant cosmic entity training its sights on our world. The things I had seen here over the last few days were unnatural, unbelievable. Totally beyond the realm of the natural or the sane. I had seen a full-grown woman crawl out of the belly of my best friend, for Chrissakes.

Chanting floated in from outside, growing louder and louder as I made it to the top of the stairs and cautiously exited the basement. I was in the short hallway between the basement door and the living room. There was a window to the left. None of the lights were on inside the house, so I felt it safe enough to take a peek outside. I moved up to the window in a crouch and peered out.

The Somas of Light were gathered around the stone altar, vocalizing one of their ugly, guttural chants. One particularly tall cultist stood atop of the altar performing a slow, eerie, ballet-like dance with unnerving, disjointed movements. The dancing figure wore a brown robe I hadn't seen any of the others wearing before. It was ragged and flapping and seemed to be glistening as if some parts of it were wet.

The red candlelight illuminating the ghastly scene grew stronger as the chanting grew louder. The eerie scarlet light flickered across the face of the dancing figure as she turned.

All battered and bruised, purple and swollen—it was Lorena. Why the hell were they making her dance?

But no, it wasn't Lorena. Dear Lord, as I stood, transfixed with fresh horror at the horrendous performance, the face of the dancing figure...slipped off. Underneath Lorena's once beautiful countenance was the twisted, inhuman visage of Kamilla, smiling her too-wide grin with those crimson lips.

She wore Lorena's skin like a suit! Like a fucking human skin costume.

I forced myself to tear my eyes away from the dancing monstrosity and her morbid display, turning away from the window and sliding down, my back pressed against the wall. Pain stabbed at my heart like hot knives as I crumpled to the floor, using all of my remaining strength to stifle the sobs fighting to erupt from my mouth.

Managing to swallow my grief for the moment, I wiped the tears from my eyes. The sorrow vanished. The anger, the fury, that had risen inside of me in the basement as I killed Mr. Neilson flared again. It burned like a blazing fire in some deep black pit of my soul, burning away all other emotions. I was hurt. I was tired. But any thoughts of ending my own life here were gone. I had every intention of leaving this damned house and the godforsaken little island it sat upon in this wicked, fog-enshrouded lake.

I examined the blade in my hands. It seemed home-made, somewhat crude, but extremely sharp. I had never seen anything like this sold in a store. The blade had some illegible writing etched onto it. Probably more of the cult's weird glyphs and symbols. The handle had been forged into the shape of a bone with an evil-looking eye on the end. Perhaps it was some sacred thing in this cult to craft your own dagger? All the cultists most likely carried daggers to torture and kill their victims in whatever unholy rituals they had to perform.

Well, every person whose blood this blade had drunk would be avenged with it. Instead of stealing the lives of unwilling victims, this dagger would now liberate the soul of any cultist who was foolish enough to get in my way.

Hoping that all of the Somas of Light were outside, focused on watching their Arch-Githya perform *Swan Lake* in her wretched Lorena-outfit, I made my way through the house. I reached the front door and slipped outside. The door clicked softly as I pulled it shut behind me. It was extraordinarily dark with no city lights anywhere within a hundred miles of this place. But the light of the moon, penetrating the heavy clouds, shone down on the sandy shore past where our car was parked. My heart leapt. Jutting out from the lake fog and waiting lazily in the calmly lapping water were about half a dozen small rowboats.

So that was how the Somas of Light had gotten to the island after the bridge disappeared. They obviously had something to do with the bridge not being there anymore. And they must have brought with them the animals in the water that had attacked Corinne. It was all that made sense to me. But did the cult have full control over those lake monsters? Or were they instead like wild animals dumped into a moat to prevent prisoners from escaping?

There was a sudden loud barking yell from inside the house. A second later I heard it again, this time more clearly.

"The bitch killed Michael Neilson!" a scratchy female voice that I didn't recognize bellowed. "She's killed him and escaped!"

"She murdered Mike!" a different male voice echoed. "Look what she did to his head!"

"Find her this instant!" I heard the distinctive voice of Kamilla shout with rage.

A dozen of pairs of feet ran into the house and around its perimeter. They thundered through the night. If I didn't move now, they would catch me.

I ran toward the rowboats, grabbing the closest one and using all of my strength to push it into the water. I jumped inside, not wanting to touch the water for even a second. I was on my way, heading into the nebulous fog that blanketed the lake.

"It's only a hundred feet to shore," I told myself, fumbling with the oars.

"You!" a screeching voice bellowed, causing my head to snap up.

It was Mother Luminescence. Her squat, toad-like outline approached at a run.

I could never have imagined that such a fat old hag could run so swiftly. Nor had I thought she could jump such a distance. She leapt from the shore and landed in my boat. She landed with a loud *thunk*, causing the whole thing to bob up and down violently in the water, almost capsizing us. She was definitely no ordinary grandma. I wished I *had* run her over on the road, leaving nothing but a stain.

There was a hatred in her eyes as her wrinkled hands shot out for my neck.

My initial shock had me stunned for a second too long, and I now gasped for air as she squeezed the breath out of me. My vision blurred. It felt like a snake had wrapped its muscled form around me.

"Screw you," I croaked before plunging Mr. Neilson's dagger into Mother Luminescence's eyeball. A spout of blood and eye juice hit me in the face.

She shrieked in pain, letting go of me instantly, her hands retreating to cradle her wound.

I had not withdrawn the knife. The blade scraped against bone as I forced it deeper into the old woman's skull.

Luminescence staggered in the boat, the whole thing rocking dangerously from side to side. Her hands feebly grasped at the dagger protruding from her ugly face. Her features had lost all of their anger and were now beginning to droop as blood continued to pour from her eye.

"You..." the old woman mumbled, swaying like a drunkard. "She's here!" she managed to shout with the last of her strength before she toppled over the edge of the boat, her plop throwing a wave of ice cold water over me, emphasizing the fact I wore nothing but this damn itchy tunic.

As I wiped my face with my hand, smearing water and blood everywhere, Mother Luminescence choked and cried out in agony.

Unable to restrain myself, I leaned to look over the side of the boat in time to see her being attacked by some indistinct and incomprehensible shapes—the monsters the cult had brought into the water to guard the island.

I felt a perverse joy as she met my gaze.

"See you in hell," I snarled and spat on her already half-eaten body.

She could only stare at me with her one remaining eye, her flabby mouth opening and closing wordlessly until the things under the water pulled her body entirely beneath the obsidian surface.

"The boats!" I heard a deep voice call out from the shadows near the house. "She's taken one of the boats!"

The sound of running footsteps grew too loud for comfort. I grabbed the oars, plopped myself onto the unpadded center thwart and hauled them over the gunwale. As soon as the wooden blades hit the water, I rowed away from the island, into the seemingly impenetrable fog. It didn't matter how much my battered body protested. I had to get away.

I didn't even care which direction I was going. The lake was big, but no matter which way I went, I would eventually reach the shore. I vaguely hoped I was crossing where the bridge used to span since I knew it led to a road.

I had only ever rowed once before, and I had forgotten how quickly and utterly exhausting it was. Gritting my teeth, I rowed furiously, ignoring the burning sensation that grew in my arms—my broken fingers didn't help the situation whatsoever. Soon the house and the island were swallowed up in the dense fog behind me, and I could make out nothing around but calm, black water and an endless sea of heavy mist as thick as wool. From beyond the gray wall, I could hear muffled splashing and distant voices from somewhere. The Somas of Light had no doubt reached the rest of the rowboats and were out on the water, looking for me, but the fog made it impossible to discern which direction the sounds came, as the voices were absorbed by the gray. I hoped that they were finding it at least as difficult and tiring as I was.

Rowing as quickly and as silently as possible, I pushed my boat farther out into the lake, trying to keep the oars from banging in the oarlocks or splashing too loudly. The clouds had gradually become a lighter shade of gray, and I realized that it must be close to morning. I was spent, exhausted, but as much as my body craved a rest, I couldn't give out now.

My boat glided across the calm, inky water. The voices of the cultists grew fainter and fainter. I wasn't sure how long I had been rowing, but I felt pretty sure that if I had headed in a straight line, I would have touched the shore by now. That meant I must have gotten turned around and had been moving deeper into the lake.

No matter, I knew I would reach land eventually, and steeled myself to continue rowing. Looking back over my shoulders at the swirling mists, I tried in vain to see if I could make out any shapes that might indicate exactly where I was. Like a mantra, I kept telling myself that I would be okay. I had managed to escape from the insane cult. And the lake was not an infinite expanse of water. I had to reach firm ground at some point.

At least, I hoped so.

CHAPTER TWENTY

I weep tears of putrescent blackness for those who do not comprehend, for those who shall never come to know, and for those who refuse to accept what is truth.

Something tapped me on my head. I reached up to swat whatever it was away so I could focus on rowing. Probably a bug. Rapid fluttering noises filled the air, and then something poked me again.

"Rei," came a soft voice from everywhere around me.

"What?" I mumbled, my lips dried and cracked. How long had I been out here on the water? Time felt as if it had slipped away from me. I was so tired. My brain felt like it was malfunctioning.

Taking a deep shuddering breath and rubbing my eyes, I cautiously peered around. I was still surrounded by the ever-present gray, opaque fog and enveloped in a bubble of eerie silence. I was beyond exhausted.

You have to keep going, Rei!

Looking about, there was nothing to help me determine what time it was. The dawn had obviously come, seeing as the clouded sky was a light gray instead of the black of night. When had that happened?

"Rei..."

That voice again. I thought it had been the remnants of some hallucination I'd been having from being so out of it. But I had definitely heard it that second time, and it hadn't been in my head. Was somebody out here with me? Had Kamilla and her Somas of Light finally found me? "Ow!" I exclaimed as something sharp and pointy poked me hard on the top of my head. "What the...?" That couldn't have been part of a hallucination either.

Whatever it was that had poked me jumped off my head and flitted down onto the bow of the little boat. It was that small Wagtail bird. One of them, anyway. Although, as it stared at me, I sensed a strange familiarity and couldn't help but notice its jade-colored eyes.

"Well, if it isn't the Devil's Eye from the basement," I said. "Are you following me, little guy? Here to take my soul to up to heaven or whatever it is you things are supposed to do?"

Great, now I'm talking to birds like my crazy upstairs neighbor talks to her horde of cats.

The little black bird chirped a sharp note at me as if trying to get me to focus.

"Rei, please," the bodiless voice said again.

No, wait. This was a different voice.

I surveyed my surroundings but could see nothing.

The bird chirped at me a second time. He turned his tiny white-feathered face to me, blinking his little jade eyes, tilted his head to the side, then turned his gaze back out to the expanse of grayness.

"Rei, go," the voice drifted toward me again. This time I could discern the direction from which it came. The same direction in which the small bird still gazed. It was a female voice. Comfortingly familiar. "You have to get out of here."

"Abby?" I called out, then immediately regretted it. What if this was a trick? What if the cultists knew my exact position?

"Please, Rei," the first voice wailed softly like a faint breeze passing through a tunnel. This one was familiar too. Young, boyish. Did the voice...did it come from the bird? "You mustn't stay here. Go now. Don't linger. She is coming. Go!"

Dread colder than the arctic chilled every nerve in my body as I suddenly heard something moving through the water behind me. I didn't need to be told twice who was coming. I was completely alert now.

Grabbing both oars—and trying to ignore the fierce agony of my broken fingers—I began to row as quickly as I could. I had no idea where I was going, but any direction except back toward the island or my pursuers, wherever they were, was fine with me. I had to get away. I couldn't let those freaks catch up to me.

Again, I chanted inside my head, *Get to shore. Find help.*

Without warning, my oar was pulled viciously downward, deeper into the water, causing my hand to crash into the oarlock. I let out a yelp of pain. Whatever lurked just out of sight was strong.

"Screw you!" I yelled at the unseen pursuers, instantly regretting the loud outburst. My fingers turning white as I held onto the jerking oar. "Leave me alone! Why can't you just leave me the hell alone?" I gritted my teeth as I struggled to keep the boat moving.

Water splashing on the other side of my rowboat caught my attention. A second creature grabbed the other oar.

I pushed the grip down and pulled the paddle fully inside the boat. And not a moment too soon. Where the oar had just been, an elongated webbed hand with rubbery-looking gray skin grasped but found nothing to grab.

"Fuck off!" I screamed as I struggled to hold on to the oars. I felt like my arms were going to be ripped out of their sockets.

With a sudden, incredibly strong yank the oar flew from my cramping hands and disappeared beneath the surface of the evil lake.

Without much hope, I glanced down into the rippling water, but the oar was nowhere to be seen. Instead, two shadowy figures lurked just below the surface. I couldn't begin to imagine what they might be, but I was certain I could see the outlines of long, thin arms with webbed hands, eel-like bodies, and a flash of yellow eyes.

"What are you?" I whispered. It was like staring through a window into a hellish pit that no one was ever supposed to see. The vague, shadowy shapes that swam down there caused talons of fear to dig their malicious points deep into my heart and brain, squeezing without mercy.

"They are servants of mine," a silky voice said.

Before I could even react, a hand gripped my hair and tossed me forward. My face smacked into the bench, and the whole vessel rocked precariously from side to side.

Recovering quickly and spinning around, I was met with a dreadful image. Balanced effortlessly on the row-boat's transom in her long flowing, scarlet robes was the tall, spindly form of Arch-Githya Kamilla. She ripped off her broken golden mask and let it drop to the bottom of the rowboat. Her inhuman features were revealed once more. I shuddered at that wide-mouthed face with its slitted nostrils and metal-plate-covered eyes.

My stupid shouting had led her to me. But how she had gotten to me? I didn't see any other boats around. Or, for that matter, how had she gotten into my boat without me realizing it? I hadn't heard or felt a thing.

But none of that mattered. I knew she was here to kill me.

Or worse.

"Why can't you just leave me the hell alone?" I screamed at the grinning witch, my throat feeling raw. "I want nothing to do with you. You're not going to take me back for your sick ritual. I won't let you!" I don't know how or from where I had summoned so much courage.

"Stupid girl," Kamilla derided, and then smiled even wider, showing off rows of too-long teeth literally from ear to ear. Her studded, wormy tongue licked her lips as if she were drooling before a sumptuous meal. Namely me. "We have finished the ritual." She barked a laugh of triumph. "Even now, Moluc'Helminth travels through the cosmic ether toward this world. He is preparing the way."

These people may be truly insane, but I no longer

doubted that the things the Somas worshipped were real, no matter how much I wished with every fiber of my being that the opposite was true.

Perhaps Moluc'Helminth existed, but I refused to accept that a handful of lunatics could summon a world-infesting, cosmic entity to open up a passageway from here to some other hell-wrought plane in which even more horrific world-ending beings dwelled in wait.

"I swear you'll rot in whatever shithole you came from," I spat as another unexpected wave of rage-filled bravery washed over me.

Before the Arch-Githya could respond to my taunt, I pushed myself upward of the bottom of the rowboat and kicked her in the shin as hard as I could. Unbalanced, the witch fell forward, toward me. I scrambled to get out of the way, which was not very easy in such a small boat.

As Kamilla struggled to right herself, I managed to get on top of the ugly bitch, hitting her in the back of the head. But she soon succeeded in worming around to face me and shoved me off of her. She leapt up with unnatural speed and grabbed my throat with a powerful, long-fingered hand, still smiling at me. I struggled, focusing all of my strength on trying to break out of her grasp, but she was too strong.

"I must say, I have not met someone as feisty or as dreadfully irritating as you in a long, long time," Kamilla said to me, her foul, coppery breath wafting over my face in a miasmic cloud. "I suppose I shouldn't be surprise, as you are descended from the accursed morda'shin." She spat out the strange word as if it tainted her mouth. "They likewise used to bother me to no end. Insignificant insects trying to interfere with the plans of gods they could not possibly comprehend!" Kamilla forced me against the edge of the boat. I tried to resist her, but to no avail. My bones would snap long before I could ever hope to overpower her. My hair hit the water as she pushed my head over the lip of the boat, the wooden edge digging painfully into my back.

My hair weaved back and forth in the inky water. The sudden thought of the two creatures swimming around just below me entered my mind. My breath caught in my throat and my heart hammered wildly at my ribs like a savage animal trying to break out of a cage. My hands thrashed at the arm holding my neck.

"Just die," Kamilla growled, pushing the crown of my head down to touch the water. "Feed my pets with your flesh. Nourish them with your lifeblood. The quicker you let it happen, the quicker your suffering will end."

Two pairs of grotesque webbed hands rose up on either side of my head like they were gratefully accepting an offering. They wrapped their slimy, rubbery arms around my face. I could taste their bitter, mucus-covered skin as fingers groped into my mouth, and they began to pull me into their watery realm.

I screamed with more volume and fury than I would have thought possible. Adrenaline coursed through my body. I thrashed about wildly trying to shake off both Kamilla and the water creatures. I used every ounce of strength to keep my head from going below the surface. I couldn't allow them to pull me under or it would be all over.

What remained of the rational part of my brain told me to give up. It was no use. I couldn't keep going. There was no chance of me overpowering all three of these monsters. My neck was about to tear in half, and I pictured my head separating from my body like a fruit being ripped from a branch by a hungry passerby who was eager to get at the sweet inner meat.

Without warning or reason, the webbed hands let go and retreated back beneath the water with haste.

Kamilla seemed surprised, and in her brief confusion, her grip slackened.

Seizing the chance, I managed to kick her off of me. I bolted upright, gasping for air, my hand shooting up to my throat to make sure my head was still attached to my shoulders.

"Come back here this instant!" Kamilla snarled at the creatures, her mouth still too wide but no longer smiling. "Ungrateful piles of filth!"

I caught a glimpse of two shapes swimming away beneath the surface of the water. They gained speed and disappeared beyond the distant wall of fog as if they had been spooked by something.

Kamilla let out a howl of fury into the air, titling her head back and screaming like a rabid wolf, before training her eyeless face back on me.

"No matter," she said, the wide grin returning to her face. "I do not need them for the task at hand. I shall kill you myself. And I shall happily bathe in your blood tonight. I shall wear your skin as clothing."

She made to move forward, but stopped abruptly. A blank expression briefly appearing on her face. She gazed around as if she had heard something, her metal-covered eyes glancing from the water to the surrounding fog to the cloud-covered sky.

The witch sucked in a deep breath, her body swelling with some unholy emotion.

"Yes," she exhaled, bowing her head. "Oh yes, I feel it. I feel it! Do you?"

"W-What?" I stammered, her reverential tone dousing me in chills. "What are you—"

"Silence!" she bellowed, her smile as wide as ever, her wet tongue wagging about on her chin like a fat worm as she bowed her head. "Witness what you could have never imagined before!"

Just then, an inconceivably large bell tolled all around me from nowhere and from everywhere at once. But no, it wasn't a bell, but something else. The sound coming from deep in the water blared as if heralding something monumental.

Enormous air bubbles rose to the surface all around

us, as if the lake were filled with giant scuba divers. Each time a bubble popped with a wet *bloop*, a noxious stench, resembling the odor from the jar, was released into the air. The water, once placid, now roiled. A sound that I could only describe as a guttural moan resonated around us. Or was it thousands of voices chanting in unison? Or perhaps it was the reverberation of the very earth tearing itself apart?

I didn't think it was possible, but the fog and clouds grew thicker and more ominous. Cold, heavy raindrops hit my face as the lake churned angrily around me. The rowboat rocked even more wildly, and I was terrified that it would capsize at any moment. An intense heat rose from the water, almost as if a strange energy coursed through it.

"What's happening?" I whispered with a horrified dread, my hands gripping onto the side of the boat for dear life.

"Moluc'Helminth," Kamilla said reverently, raising her head a bit to look at me with those metal-covered eyes. "Has come."

CHAPTER TWENTY-ONE

Unworthy, we all are, to stand before the Truth!

A primal fear gripped my heart.

An enormous surge of bubbles rose to the inky surface and broke, like a bomb had exploded on the lake floor, releasing blood-curdling shrieks of beings in immense pain. In seconds, the sky grew ever grimmer, and the raindrops transformed into a deluge. Mother Nature herself seemed to be protesting the approach of whatever horror was attempting to tear its way into our world. Thunder rumbled from somewhere up above.

Kamilla was still focused on her obeisance, her head bowed as she stood with her arms crossed in an X across her chest.

Without thinking, I seized the opportunity offered by her inattention to pull the oar from the oarlock and swung it with all my might, sending the flat end crashing into her ugly skull.

Screeching out in pain and alarm, Kamilla tumbled over the side of the boat and into the lake.

Dropping myself onto the center thwart, I plunged the oar into the water and paddled with a furious madness. It was much more difficult to move the boat with just the one oar, having to paddle alternately on each side, but it would have to do. I didn't care how tired I was. I didn't care how much my injuries hurt. I didn't care that my muscles burned fiercely from the unfamiliar exertion of rowing and paddling. I did not want to be here when whatever was coming arrived.

Kamilla sputtered in the water, shouting curses at me in a guttural, harsh language. From the sound of it, she was struggling to keep her head above the water, and soon her wretched voice receded into the distance. At least I was moving now.

I had to keep moving.

Can't stop. Must get out of the water. Must reach land. Must return to a sane world where things make sense! My new mantra seemed to flow in time with the exhausting paddling motion.

I had just settled into a rhythm, when something smashed into the side of the boat, causing it to nearly capsize. Throwing my weight to the opposite side, I kept the boat right-side up.

Peering over the side, I looked to see what it was I had hit. There was nothing in the dark water, however, except for the ominous gloom of its depths.

Just then that gloom shifted.

It was not the effect of the rain rippling the surface, but of some movement deep below. What I first thought was the monolithic shadow of the abyss now moved. It shifted beneath the water like a gigantic black fish. But something that big couldn't possibly live inside a body of water the size of this lake.

"This can't be happening," I said to myself, and found that I was beginning to laugh in a frenzied and hysterical way. "I've made it this far! I'm so close!"

Something shiny flashed deeper in the water. It rose, displacing water and rocked my boat. As it neared the surface, I could just begin to make out its shape. It was a great, white, bulbous orb, far larger in diameter than the length of my puny rowboat. In fact, it had to be far larger than half a dozen of my rowboats. Was it some kind of vessel? In the center of the orb was an enormous indentation, some sort of pit. An opening of some kind? An entrance to the vessel?

Staring at it, I felt that I was peering into endless, starless space. I was momentarily entranced by the sight. My mind wanted—no, needed—to figure out exactly what it was. I wanted to touch it, to stare into it forever. That's when the first face appeared from within the void. It was not human, but there was no denying it was a face, distorted as it was from the incredible agony it now suffered.

More and more faces appeared within that pit. They couldn't get out; couldn't call for help. They dissolved and reformed, as if dying over and over again.

A fleshy lid swept across the white surface of the thing, obscuring the pit in the middle, before retracting. It was then that I realized the entire orb had just *blinked*.

"Oh God," was all I could articulate as I backed away from the edge of the boat. My mind roiled more furiously than the lake.

This couldn't be real, my mind cried, despite all the impossible things I had seen since arriving at the house on the island. *Things like this didn't happen. I live in a logical world. Things like this don't happen. Couldn't happen.*

Everything I had seen *had* to be some fever-induced hallucination brought on by illness or extreme stress. Something like that. There had to be some logical explanation.

Just row, Rei. Fucking row!

I couldn't let myself think of anything else. Picking up the one remaining oar, now cracked from its recent contact with Kamilla's face, I pushed my body to the limit. My broken fingers and the muscles in my abs, shoulders, and arms burned with exertion as I paddled, first on one side, and then the other. Dream or actuality, hallucination or reality, I did not want to be face-to-face with that thing. Every so often, I caught flashes of other white orbs—*eyes*—all of varying sizes, opening and rising to the surface, all of their pupils filled with horrible faces.

Eyes. So many eyes everywhere in the water...

I shuddered at the thought of what it might mean and

from exhaustion. My breathing was labored and ragged. Blood pounded in my ears like rapid cannon-fire. My tongue lay like sandpaper in my mouth.

The rain had become a torrential downpour of liquid bullets, and visibility was reduced even further. As before, I didn't know in which direction lay the closest shore, and now an inner voice bombarded me with the worry that I hadn't been moving toward any shore, but instead had been rowing in circles. This thought threatened to overwhelm me and lock my brain in a hopeless despair.

No!

I refused to let doubt and fear paralyze me. There would be time to rest when I had reached the safety of land.

You're getting out of this alive, Rei, I kept telling myself, trying desperately to make myself believe it.

But my cherished hope deserted me a moment later when I felt a drastic shift in the water, like something pushed the entire lake upward. The monster who saw with those massive eyes rose out of the water from under me, and I cowered in terror. Its form was so impossibly big that it caused the entire lake to heave and surge like the continents themselves were moving. The water churned and boiled as never before.

Suddenly, the boat flew several dozen feet into the air, as if a bomb had detonated right underneath. It came crashing down with me inside it, splintering into a dozen pieces as it hit the roiling water. My boat was shattered, and the last remnants of safety were lost along with it.

I grabbed on to a floating plank, watching the arrival with a terror that grew in the deepest part of my soul. Water exploded into the air all around me, in opposition to the torrential rain. Spouts like gigantic geysers violently surged upward from all around.

Colossal monoliths—covered in slimy, mucus-coated flesh—the height and width of redwoods and the color of blood and rust—erupted out of the water near the center of the lake. What the hell was this? I counted twelve of the things rising up before—

Oh my God.

Joints...They were attached to...It looked like...fingers.

They were followed by two massive palms connected to gargantuan arms, covered in the same wormy skin.

"No, no, no," I uttered, watching the monstrous hands flex as they reached high into the sky to disappear into the rain and clouds. "Fuck no!"

I squeezed my eyes shut, lest the sight before me drive me quicker into insanity. But I couldn't shut out the sounds. I could still hear that blaring, tolling, screaming din. I abandoned my plank and swam away from...it. The swelling waves formed from the monster's upsurge helped push me away, but not fast enough.

Swim, fucking swim!

I had to open my eyes to be sure that no new horror had appeared in my path. As I briefly glanced back at the chaos, I saw a mound rising out of the water in between the arms, fog swirling around it like a maelstrom of smoke.

No, not some mound. A mountain. The colossal head of a giant, malformed eel with no lower jaw was the only comparison my fracturing mind could manage, as I was granted brief glimpses of it through the obscuring weather. In reality, it was unlike anything on earth, or anything that should ever exist on earth. The silhouette of an elongated, pyramidal skull, and as patches of fog swirled away, rusty skin covered in pulsing, ropey veins, dripping with fetid corruption rose before me. The thing shrieked toward the sky, and I glimpsed its cavernous, lamprey-like maw filled with rows of black teeth and giant, writhing worms, along with the flash of sickly white eyes dotting the thing's foul head, even more impossibly humongous than the other eyes still lurking everywhere under the water.

Thank the holy mother of Christ for the concealing fog and rain that protected my sanity by hiding most of it.

I wasn't scared, afraid, or terrified. Words are wholly inadequate to convey the true horror of what I felt as I watched this monstrosity rise out of the water. A profound terror boiled inside me and infected my brain, born of the primal fear that reached back to the early days of humanity's infancy. Days before history had been recorded. Days when darkness ruled over the earth and our ancestors huddled together in caves for fear of what lurked unseen out in the ebon nights of eons past. I endured absolute, incomparable terror in every atom of my being. My spirit shriveled. My heart withered. If this thing was the sort of nightmare that truly existed in our reality, that festered in the shadows behind the comforting veil of our perceived world, then life was truly a hopeless, meaningless delusion.

But did I really want to believe that? Could I accept it and go on living?

No.

Despite the violent waves tossing me about, I never swam faster in all my life as I did while racing away from that abomination. I began to forward crawl as quickly as I could, my arms alternately sweeping through the water, my feet kicking behind me, and all the while my body was freezing to its core. If the downpour hadn't obscured most of my view of the unholy creature as it rose, towering out of the lake, my mind would have likely crumbled to dust right then and there. But I had torn my eyes away from the abomination. I didn't dare look toward it again. I kept my eyes focused straight ahead of me. I told myself I could do this as long as necessary. If something else burst forth from the water in front of me, I could turn and swim in another direction.

Don't look at anything else.
Must keep going
Just get away from it.

I desperately hoped that this abhorrent leviathan would take no notice of me. I was less than an insignificant speck compared to its detestable, unspeakable majesty as it burst forth from the void and into our realm. The Infestor of Worlds had come to corrupt our entire reality. Surely it wouldn't concern itself with me.

Something touched my calf as I kicked. All my mind could discern was something slimy and rubbery. A reflexive kick punted it away from me.

Don't stop.

Keep going.

My arms, my legs, they're so tired, so exhausted.

I tried to push these unhelpful thoughts from my mind before they could take hold. The water currents were too strong. My cuts and bruises stung, ached. The large gash on the bottom of my foot throbbed fiercely, and sharp jolts of pain were a constant agony in my broken fingers. My lungs were on fire and I couldn't get enough air. Every cell in my body screamed for respite, and I felt my mind screaming for surrender.

But there it was—the shore mere yards ahead of me.

I had made it. Overwhelming relief pushed me beyond the physical limits of my body. With the very last of my energy, I propelled myself toward the gloriously welcoming land. Another sudden surge swelled the water around me, propelling me forward like a bullet. I crashed onto the sandy shore, my entire body cringing from the impact.

But I was on land. Blessed land. I crawled on my belly, my rubbery legs pushing me forward up the shore, my uninjured hand clutching at the wet sand, feeling its rough, muddy grains slipping through my fingers.

I was barely conscious at this point, but instinct rallied the dregs of my resolve, and I crawled as far as I could away from the hazardous water toward the trees of the sheltering forest that surrounded the lake.

Propping my bruised, slashed, and battered body against the rough trunk of a large oak tree, out of direct line-of-sight from the shore, exhaustion finally overtook me and my body gave out. I couldn't move, perhaps not even if my life depended on it now. My body, my soul, yearned to sleep, perhaps forever, never to wake up.

Rain fell heavily around me, large drops pelting the

ground like blunt icicles. The full leafy branches of the tree provided some shelter from the storm and I was grateful.

As my body settled into the lassitude of total fatigue, I reflected on the fact that I was cold and ached all over. I couldn't think straight. So tired. Beyond exhausted. My eyelids felt like lead weights, but my brain tried in vain to prevent me from sleeping. What if the Somas of Light found me?

And what if I really never woke up again? That might not be so bad, considering what I had just experienced, and what had just arrived from the darkest abyss.

My eyelids drooped, and all thought seeped from my mind. My vision doubled and blurred. My brain began to shut down. A fraction of a moment before I lost consciousness, my brain registered a darting movement at the edge of my vision. Something with green eyes flitted about.

But nothing could stop the unconsciousness from overtaking me.

CHAPTER TWENTY-TWO

Stinging! Wailing! A dead call that flies through the evernight, the necrogorge. Turn from the untrustworthy life of the betrayer. Skulk in the light. Lurk in the dark. Intertwine in the skin of your neighbor, become an amalgam of putrid bodies and squalid flesh.

I lay on the floor in the basement of the lake house, that horrid dungeon with its implements of torture. My arms flailed about as I was dragged toward—

I opened my eyes.

I still sat under the oak tree. It had only been a dream. Against all odds and obstacles, I had made it out. I had escaped.

The rain had finally ceased. Everything around me was wet and gray. But the fog, that ever-present opaque wall of endless mist was gone. With a grunt of pain, I repositioned myself on the damp ground and peered around the tree's wide trunk toward the lake. From where I sat, I could see the lake and all of its surrounding shore. The bucolic beauty of the landscape belied the sinister events that I knew had occurred here. Blinking sand out of my eyes, I could just make out a vague shape off in the distance across the water. It had to be the house, although it looked to be several miles away. I must have rowed, paddled, and swam a very long distance—perhaps to the farthest shore.

There was no sign of that heinous monstrosity. The water was as calm and smooth as a mirror reflecting the overcast sky. Where could it have gone? A braver, or perhaps crazier, person than I might go to the edge of the lake and peer into the water. But not me. I was done with water. No more bathtubs or hot tubs for me. I was done with swimming in pools or lakes or even in the ocean. Oh God, the ocean. What could come out of those lightless, oceanic depths that humanity had yet to explore?

No, I wouldn't think about it. *Couldn't* think about it. My brain was still completely fried from everything it had faced this past weekend.

Weekend? I didn't really have any idea what day it was. It didn't matter, though. All that mattered now was that I was—somehow—alive. I needed to find my way out of this forest. I had no idea which direction I should go, but I found that I didn't really care. Just getting as far away from this lake as I could would be good enough.

Using the rough tree trunk for support, I managed to stand up. My muscles screamed and my joints felt like rusted hinges being forced to move. I was covered in mud, sand, and blood, and some of my injuries had reopened. My broken fingers seemed frozen, and my left foot throbbed dully. I was unable to put my full weight on it. My feet were so covered in grime and muck, I couldn't tell if the gash on my sole had begun to bleed again.

My stiff back ached and spasmed with pain after only a few steps, but I had to ignore it. I had to put as much distance between me and the lake as possible. I had to get through the woods, find a road, find help, find someone—anyone.

I briefly wondered how insane I must look. A filthy, bloodied woman staggering out of the woods, barefoot and wearing an ugly red tunic. Who in their right mind would pick up such a hitchhiker?

Using the trees as supports along the way, I limped through the thick, dank forest. Remnants of the downpour dripped onto my face every so often from the sodden leaves. It was rough going, even without my bruised and battered body and torn foot. The ground was covered in a carpet of fallen leaves, rotted logs, and hidden roots that slowed my progress to a snail's pace.

But I was determined.

CHAPTER TWENTY-THREE

Know the Truth, and the Truth shall know you.

"Can you hear me?" a sweet voice asked from far away. "That's it. Easy now. You've been out for a while."

The darkness around me began to dissipate. My vision returned, unblurring like a camera lens coming into focus. I blinked my eyes several times. Bright white light glared at me, causing me to squint. Indistinct figures loomed above me.

Everything came rushing back, and I tried to sit bolt upright.

"It's here!" I screamed, the words erupting like vomit from my mouth. "Oh Christ, it's here! Moluc'Helminth!"

Such pain. I felt such pain all over, but I had to warn people.

Someone, gently but firmly, pinned my thrashing arms down and forced me to lie still. Where was I? Had the Somas captured me again? I had to get away!

"Miss, please calm down!" an unfamiliar voice demanded in an authoritative tone.

"Get the fuck off of me!" I shrieked in panic and fear.

"All right, sedate her."

I felt a pinch in my arm, and everything faded away into nothingness.

\- ⋰ -

"...you hear me? Can you speak?"

"Where... Where am I?" I coughed out as I opened my heavy lids. I ran my tongue over dried and cracked lips. It hurt a lot to speak those few words. But I realized that I was warm, comfy.

"You're in Sacred Light Memorial Hospital in the town of Black Ashes," the gentle voice answered. An even brighter light flicked on and shone into my right eye, then my left. "Do you remember how you got here?"

I tried to organize my thoughts, but the voice went on.

"Can you tell me your name?"

"R-Rei Hashimoto," I rasped out. "No...I mean, no, I don't...remember how I got here."

My vision gradually sharpened, and everything came into focus. I lay in a metal-framed bed, covered in a white sheet in a white room. Monitoring machines, attached by wires and sticky pads to various parts of my body, beeped softly behind me. An older, smiling woman with frizzy hair, wearing a long white coat over scrubs, with a stethoscope around her neck bent over me.

"Well, Rei," she said in that same gentle voice, "my name is Dr. Mason. And you, missy, are very lucky to be alive. You were found collapsed by the side of the road near Devil's Eyes Lake, wearing ragged clothes and splattered with dirt and blood. You were extremely dehydrated and covered with injuries. Can you tell me how you got them?" She smiled reassuringly with delicate coral lips.

"I..." A whirl of memories flashed through my mind. I found myself desperately wanting to tell this doctor about all of it. I wanted her to call the police and have them to go find those cult freaks and arrest them all. Or shoot them all. Actually, I wanted the police to bring in the military to bomb that damn lake.

"Yes?" Dr. Mason pressed.

"I don't remember," I lied. How could I even tell this person what had really happened? She wouldn't believe a single outrageous word of it. Would *I* believe me? *Did* I believe me? Yes, I knew it had happened. All the hellish events had been real. But for now, they had to stay put in my head.

"Well, that's okay," Dr. Mason said, her smile faltering just a bit. I was unsure whether she knew I wasn't being truthful with her or not. But she was obviously curious to learn how I had ended up in such a state. If only she could realize how lucky she was that she still remained ignorant. "We'll get you back on your feet in no time, Miss Hashimoto. Some—a lot—of your injuries required stitches, especially the one on your foot. You're going to have to rest for a few days. We have an IV in you for fluids, and for the time being, you'll be hooked up to several monitors. If you need to go to the restroom, just press the call button on the side of your bed. A nurse will come help you. Okay?"

I nodded wordlessly.

"A hospital case manager is going to stop by," Dr. Mason continued. "He should be here in a few minutes. He's going to take some personal info from you. If you want the hospital to notify someone that you're here, be sure to give him that information as well." She glanced at her watch. "When your lunch arrives, I want you to eat all of it, all right?"

"Okay," I said, staring down at my arms which were stitched up in imitation of Frankenstein's monster.

The doctor straightened up, took a clipboard from the foot of my bed, and left the room as she read it. I watched her go, feeling as if my body floated pleasantly on air while I lay on the soft bed.

I think I slept for the rest of the day. I dreamed about waiting tables and making pizzas at Valentina's, watering my houseplants, going shopping; very mundane things. Perhaps my mind was trying its hardest to block out all the recent events. I was grateful for that. But every time I awoke, all the memories came flooding back. I wept profusely, recalling that I would never see Abby, Corinne, or Lorena again.

What would I tell their families? I could not even imagine telling their parents. It would break them. Especially Mr. and Mrs. Brennan. They had already experienced unbearable heartbreak when they lost their son-in-law and grandchild in a brutal mugging. But now Abby was gone. Could they go on? Would they blame me?

I could never ever tell them what had really happened. Not unless I wanted to be guaranteed a room in some mental institution for the rest of my life. The head shrinkers would think that only a broken, demented mind could fabricate such stories. Or maybe they would conclude that I had made up these gruesome tales to hide the fact that I had killed all of my friends myself.

Either way, I couldn't possibly tell my friends' families the horrific ways their daughters had suffered and died. Maybe it'd be more merciful to let them think that Abby, Corinne, and Lorena had simply vanished without a trace. I felt sick at the memories and the horror they must never know.

Then my thoughts began to focus on that last, ultimate horror. That...thing from the lake. Someone had to have seen it. It had been so horrendously immense. Those sounds that it had produced. I was positive that they must have been audible for miles. Didn't anyone wonder what had made them? I couldn't have been the only person who witnessed this thing. And what had happened to the Somas of Light? Had they all just crawled back into the woodwork? But if their damn ritual had been successful, why would they bother? And Arch-Githya Kamilla must still be out there...somewhere...

Grabbing the television remote, I powered on the TV and flipped through the channels to find local and national news reports. There was no mention of the horror that had been summoned to our world.

Perhaps it would be better to let the rational part of my mind dismiss everything as a grand hallucination. But if it were a dream or delusion, Abby, Corinne, and Lorena would still be alive. They would be here with me.

But they weren't.

～✲～

I was in my hospital bed the third evening of my hospital stay, finishing my dinner of dry chicken breast and bland mashed potatoes. I had the television on but wasn't really paying attention to the game show rerun that was playing. I had just put a spoonful of green gelatin into my mouth when three people walked into my room.

The spoon fell from my hand, clattering on the little plastic dinner tray. My eyes grew wide. My mouth hung open, and my hands began to shake.

Standing there were three familiar figures smiling at me. They walked farther into my room, their sneakers squeaking on the linoleum floor.

"Corinne..." I choked. "Lorena...Abby! What? I don't understand." My head spun like a top as I looked back and forth from one to the other. Was I dreaming? Had the nurses slipped sedatives into my food?

"Hey, Rei," Corinne chuckled musically. Her familiar grin lessened a bit as she glanced at all the monitors surrounding me. "How are you doing? Are you feeling better?"

I gawked stupidly at the three of them as they stood beside my bed. They were all bundled up as if they had just come out of the snow, and I figured it must be cold outside. Their faces were covered in cuts and bruises, that, like mine, were cleaned and dressed. Corinne had a large bandage wrapped around her head.

"I'm...But..." My eyes began to tear up as a storm of emotions overwhelmed me. "You're all alive!"

"Well of course we are," Abby said, puzzled, yet with cheerful encouragement. "Why wouldn't we be?"

"Remember what the doctor warned us about," Lorena said to the other two in a whisper, though I heard her words clearly. "She was lost in the woods for days without food or water. They think she might have hallucinated things."

"Oh God, Rei," Corinne said, her grin fading completely. She sat on the chair beside my bed, her eyes taking in my injuries. "What happened to you out there?"

"I...I don't know," I whispered, then cleared my throat. "What's going on? Where have you guys been? What happened?" I was torn between a feeling of wild joy that they were all alive and rejecting the whole scene as a dream.

"You don't remember?" Abby asked, her gloved hand gripping mine. "We had a car accident on our way up to the lake. You had gotten distracted and then tried to avoid hitting some old woman who was walking on the side of the road. We smashed into a tree. It was pretty bad. Your car was a total wreck. But thank Christ for seatbelts! When the rest of us woke up, you were gone. We've been looking for you for days. Then we found out this morning that you were here! I'm sorry it took us so long to figure out where you were."

I shook my head. "No, that didn't happen," I said. "Did it? But the things we experienced..."

"It's okay," Abby said soothingly, gently pushing the hair off my brow as she sat on the edge of my bed. "We're here for you now. You don't have to worry anymore. Just rest, get better. We'll talk with the doctor and see if she'll release you tonight so we can take you home." They all seemed to brighten at the thought.

My friends made sure I didn't need anything, then headed to the door. Before leaving, they all turned back to smile at me—the old familiar smiles on those beloved faces.

I smiled back. My brain was still attempting to make sense of everything, but I felt truly happy for the moment. I couldn't wait to get home.

"Wait," I said, a thought nudging me. "How did you know I was here? Who called you? I didn't give the hospital any numbers to call. I want to thank them."

They stared at me.

My elation faltered. My throat seized up and my heart

dropped into the pit of my stomach. Why did Abby suddenly look so tall?

Abby's eye twitched, then her face began to...droop... To peel away. To slough off.

She caught it before it could fall to the floor. She smoothed it back into place, but not before I caught a glimpse of rusted metal plates underneath her skin.

My three friends smiled at me. Smiles that were no longer friendly, not reassuring. Smiles that did not belong to my friends.

I stared at Abby, my eyes unable to tear themselves away from her face. The face that didn't truly belong to the person standing there. That smile...The smile that was far too wide. The smile that revealed teeth that were too long. The smile that was parted by a black, wormy tongue reaching out to lick its false lips.

"Time to go with your friends, Rei," Abby said in a voice that was not hers.

Before I realized what was happening, I had leapt from the hospital bed and lunged for the creature posing as Abby, bringing the IV and monitors crashing down.

"Get the fuck out of her skin, you disgusting, sadistic bitch!" I shrieked as our bodies tangled. Abby and I fell to the floor in a heap.

I pummeled her face, my knuckles smacking against rubbery, cold skin. Abby didn't even try to defend herself. She just laughed. But that laugh did not belong to my lifelong friend. I wrapped my bloodied hands around her throat.

"I'll fucking kill you!" I screeched as Abby just continued to laugh, not even struggling.

Several pairs of firm hands grabbed me and pulled me off of her. Three large nurses hauled me away. I thrashed and flailed in their grasp, and another nurse had to come help.

"She attacked me!" I heard Abby yell hysterically. "Why would she do that?"

"No!" I screamed, struggling to get away. "It's not

them! They're wearing my friends' skin! Take the skin off of them!"

"Miss Hashimoto, please calm down," an unfamiliar doctor said to me in a loud, authoritative voice.

I paid no heed.

"She tried to kill me!" Abby sobbed as she got to her feet.

How could they not hear how fake she sounded?

"It's not them!" I continued to yell at the doctors and nurses. "They killed my real friends. There are monsters under their skin! They're not my real friends!"

I was dragged back to bed, restrained, and sedated.

Abby, Lorena, and Corinne smiled at me as consciousness faded.

Was I the only one who could see the malevolent smirks on their false faces?

EPILOGUE

The harsher the light, the darker the shadow.

Two months later...

I sat on my white bed in my white room, staring down at the white linoleum floor beneath my feet. My toes felt cold, but I didn't care. There wasn't much that I cared about anymore.

My friends were dead. That, at least, I knew. Wherever they were now, whether in heaven, or simply gone from existence, at least they suffered no longer.

But how could anyone think that I could have hurt them? How could they think that I would want to cause harm to the people I loved most in the world? They didn't understand.

No one understood.

I stood up, the bed creaking. Walking over to the narrow rectangle of a window, I gazed out across the dreary sky. Gray clouds crawled slowly overhead, ready to let loose the rain they held. Down in the large driveway, a few orderlies chatted and smoked as they stood next to a sign that read *Pacific State Psychiatric Hospital*.

If only these bars across the window weren't there, perhaps I could get out. But no, the glass itself was probably also reinforced.

Get out. I had to get out. I couldn't stay here. I had to escape this place. I couldn't let those...imposters get to Abby, Lorena, and Corinne's families.

As the day turned darker outside, I caught sight of my own reflection in the window. A pale, gaunt face stared back at me with unbrushed hair and dark-circled eyes. The months in here had not been kind. But I could handle it. I had bided my time. I could take anything they put me through in here. I had already experienced true hell.

The jangle of keys sounded from outside my room. The hefty lock slide open and the door swung inward. I already knew who had opened it.

"Hello, Rei," said a voice behind me. I turned around to see a burly orderly standing just inside the doorway, arms crossed. "Will we be cooperating today? You've been doing well this week. I'd hate for you to cause another incident and lose your television privileges."

I nodded at him. "I'll behave," I said.

"Good," the orderly replied in a soothing voice. "Well, let's go get in line at the nurses' station for medication, then it's time for dinner. Alright?"

"Okay," I answered.

I walked out of my room, the orderly right behind me. As we made our way down the hall, I turned around and gave him a timid smile. His face softened, and he gave me a brief smile of his own.

As I faced forward again, I slid something out of my sleeve. My hand gripped the spoon that I had managed to hide. The spoon that I had managed to sneak past the staff one day after dinner.

The spoon that I had managed to sharpen.

We passed by a barred window. I paused to stare out. Drops of rain thrummed against the glass as the clouds finally let loose their cargo. A flash of lightning lit up the sky, bringing with it the rumble of thunder seconds later.

"Keep moving, Rei," the orderly said, grabbing my shoulder. "No dawdling."

Another flash illuminated the gray celestial ceiling. For the briefest of moments, in those mountainous clouds, I saw shapes. Silhouettes of gigantic hands, an inhuman skull. They were gone in an instant, but the image was burned onto my retinas.

"Holy shit!" the orderly exclaimed. "Did you see that in the sky? Looked like a face and hands or something."

I gripped the sharpened spoon tighter and looked back at the orderly. I don't know what sort of expression he saw on my face, but he took a step backward.

Words slithered out of my mouth.

"Moluc'Helminth is here."

ACKNOWLEDGMENTS

First, I'd like to thank Kate Jonez of Omnium Gatherum for taking a chance on my very first published novel. I can't express my gratitude enough. My younger self would never have believed that I could ever have a book written and published in the genre I love so much. Thanks Kate!

I want to give much appreciation to John Palisano for giving me so much help and advice over the years. He truly is a great guy. Thanks to Cherry Weiner for helping me improve this novel since the first draft. Definitely a big thank you to Sharron Lee Finch for being an awesome beta reader and giving me a ton of help.

And of course, the biggest thank you to my wife. This book would never exist without her enormous help and support.

ABOUT THE AUTHOR

S. Alessandro Martinez is a horror and fantasy writer living in Southern California. His writings have appeared in several magazines and anthologies. He was first published in *Deadman's Tome* with the story "The Corruption in the Deep." He enjoys writing about all sorts of horror, especially about unspeakable creatures, body-horror and supernatural terror. He also enjoys writing high fantasy. He has a fantastical world of his own creation filled with stories of mystical and terrible creatures, fantastic races and powerful magic.

Made in the USA
Monee, IL
27 January 2022

90027737R00154